RUNAWAY MILLIONAIRE

A novel

RUNAWAY MILLIONAIRE

DAVE SCHOOLS

Kick a Dent Publishing

Copyright © 2017 by Dave Schools

All rights reserved. This book or any portion thereof may not be reproduced or used in any manner whatsoever without the express written permission of the publisher except for the use of brief quotations in a book review.

Printed in the United States of America

ISBN-13: 978-0-692-87769-2
ISBN-1076: 0-692-87769-X

Kick a Dent Publishing
413 Fox Catcher Road
Bel Air, MD 21015

www.daveschools.com

First Edition

14 13 12 11 10 / 10 9 8 7 6 5 4 3 2 1

To Mom

CONTENTS

PART 1
TURMOIL AT HOME 1

PART 2
THE CITY OF DELORRE 65

PART 3
A LONG WAY DOWN 203

PART 4
THE STREETS OF SOUTH BENNINGTON 281

PART 5
BACK FROM THE DEAD 345

A NOTE FROM THE AUTHOR 371

PART 1

TURMOIL AT HOME

1

"Let's go," said Thomas Degland in his low voice. In the living room, his youngest son Nathan sat below a recent picture of the Degland family. The photograph showed them standing in front of a wheat field next to a tractor, as though the tractor were a part of the family. He put his book down and followed his father obediently. Thomas called up the stairs, "Paul!"

"Yeah?"

"Let's go see your mother."

Footsteps thumped upstairs, and Paul's lumbering frame came pounding down the wooden steps.

"We'll be back," Thomas said to Mary, the cook, as the three men walked through the kitchen.

The smell of roasted curry chicken and onions filled the huge room. The three walked with hunched shoulders through the back screen door. Nathan hated this part of the week. Every Friday Thomas made them do this, and Nathan withered inside every time.

The sun was setting as they trudged along the grass pathway through brown-dirt gardens. They passed by a white equipment shed, then a red hay barn, and walked along dry fields of wheat until they reached the edge of the property. They turned right and followed the forest line like a wall. Nobody spoke.

In the distance, Nathan could see the legendary burned lands. Thomas looked up and saw the cursed earth. He shuddered.

They turned from the field into a small clearing in the woods. Long green grass grew between stones and boulders. The sun set behind them and lit up a small meadow. The men stopped and stood next to one another, casting equal shadows on five gravestones lodged in the ground.

"You boys don't remember him, do you?"

Paul and Nathan didn't speak.

"He was the greatest farmer in Virginia."

Nathan and Paul glanced at each other.

"I remember being around the dinner table," Thomas went on, "with your three aunts and Grandma. Grandpa Walker would come in from the fields, wash his hands and face, sit down, and not say a single word. He insisted on silence but your aunts were not the quietest hens in the coop."

"He'd scold them if they asked a question. He'd say, 'I've worked all day to provide the food on the table and now you want to antagonize me with words?'"

Paul and Nathan shifted their feet.

"The only thing he loved was his dog Pepper."

"Didn't Grandma always say he snored real bad?" asked Paul. Nathan rolled his eyes.

Thomas nodded, keeping his eyes on the grave. "Mom called it the lawn mower that would never start."

Nathan fidgeted. He had heard these memories countless times and he dreaded what was coming.

"How old were you when he died?" Paul asked ignorantly. Nathan exhaled loudly, crossed his arms, and leaned in the direction of the house. He pictured his book on the living room table.

"Sixteen," said Thomas solemnly.

The sight of the burning hay barn flashed in Thomas's mind. He had arrived too late, and stood helplessly as he watched his father thrash fiercely at the blocked door before the barn collapsed on top of him.

"Grandpa Walker was an example to the Degland family," said Thomas respectfully. "'You can talk all you want,' he would say, 'but in the end, if you ain't got land, you ain't got nothin'.'"

They stood there, still and quiet, their shadows stretching over the gravestones. Thomas's frame was the tallest and the broadest. Paul's was short, thick, and wide. Nathan was thin, lean, and tall like his father. They moved to the stone with name Marcy Degland.

"Miss you, Mom," said Thomas, he rubbed the scar on the side of his head.

One day following Walker's death in 1962, when Thomas was delivering a calf, it kicked him in the side of the head. He fell to the ground, knocked out cold. His mother found him an hour later and summoned a doctor, who said he was severely concussed. Thomas slipped into a coma for the next three months, and the farm's production fell behind.

Eventually, Grandma Marcy sold everything for two million dollars and moved the family to the City of Delorre, the large metropolis five hours east.

"Best cook there ever was," said Thomas.

In Delorre, the Deglands invested in Mr. Martin's Grocery Store. While Thomas and his business partner, Mr. Martin, managed the store, Marcy and his sisters cooked breakfast and lunch sandwiches for the store's patrons. Eventually they expanded into the adjacent space and opened a restaurant called Degland's Deli. Over the next ten years, the grocery store and deli grew and prospered. It became a favorite café of the neighborhood, known for its fair prices and Marcy's ambrosial desserts. Within a year, they opened a second shop in a former nightclub six miles away on the fringes of the city.

The trio shuffled to the last gravestone with fresh edges and a lighter hue. The words "Abigail Degland" were carved into the stone.

"Any words?" said Thomas.

Neither Paul nor Nathan said anything.

"Alright."

He turned to leave and Paul followed. Nathan stood alone in front of his mother's gravestone. *He did it again.*

Furious, he turned and yelled to his father's back. "That's it? That's all you're going to say?"

Thomas stopped and both boys watched as he turned around slowly.

"Words change nothing," he said bitterly. "Especially yours."

"Just say something."

Thomas paused. He pictured the first time he met her. It was in an Irish pub over a round of Arliss—her favorite stout. She always said he smelled like a cow, and he thought she was as friendly as a tack. But she was the most beautiful person he had ever seen.

"Anything," repeated Nathan.

Thomas turned his back and left the clearing. Paul gave Nathan a stern look before catching up to his father. Nathan waited for them to turn the corner before he knelt at his mother's grave, hot tears forming in his eyes.

2

"Look, Thomas!"

Abby's blonde hair flowed behind her smiling face as she ran towards him. Thomas looked up from the pothole he was repairing in the driveway and put the shovel on his shoulder. She took fast steps in her white and black dress as she ran down to him from their house's porch on the farm.

She held a letter in both hands. Her white teeth never disappeared behind her lips as she spoke excitedly.

"It's from Kitch."

Thomas's elevated eyebrows sunk to a frown on his forehead.

"Not again. I don't want to hear anything else from that stubborn miser."

"No, no," said his wife. "It's different this time. Read it."

Begrudgingly, Thomas pinched the folded paper with his grubby fingers.

"Different? He always says n...."

Slowly, the expression on his face changed from disappointment to absorption. He gripped the letter tighter.

"Abby?" His voice was higher. He pulled it closer to his squinting eyes.

"Abby?" He repeated, incredulous now.

"Yes, Thomas, it's true," his wife began jumping up and down on his arm.

Thomas read the last line of the letter, "I've accepted your offer and agree to sell you the 400-acre plot of land on the western border of your farm."

Thomas dropped the shovel and turned to his happy spouse. She nodded briskly. Bending his knees, he swept his arms around her and hoisted her in the air. She laughed and put her arms around the back of his head. They spun around in a dance.

"He agreed," Thomas shouted happily. "After four years, he finally agreed. Do you know what this means?"

"It's your dream, my love," answered Abby, her white dress now covered in dirt. "We're growing our land."

3

Nathan's bare feet scuffed through the soft earth as he hurried to keep up with the others. Paul was only a year older but his thirteen-year-old legs outpaced Nathan's smaller limbs. They were adventuring in the woods with two other boys from the farm, Ryan and Jacob, while Thomas and Abby were out walking. Paul dared Nathan to follow Jacob up a tree. Jacob was at least a foot taller and much stronger. Yet intrepid Nathan followed Jacob up the tree as he climbed out onto a branch and hung from it with his arms.

Ryan yelled, "Nathan, betcha can't hang as long as Jacob can!"

He thought about it, assessing that his lighter weight may be manageable to his smaller arms. He climbed out onto the tree branch next to Jacob and instantly felt exhaustion in his hands and shoulders. He looked down at Ryan who was covering his smirk and then at Jacob whose eyes were wide as he breathed heavily. Paul had disappeared. Suddenly, Nathan felt something violently wrench his shorts down, burning the skin of his legs as they reached his ankles. He screamed in pain and in embarrassment. Paul ran out from underneath him and pointed up at Nathan hanging from the tree branch. He broke into laughter, and Ryan and Jacob joined. Jacob let go of the branch and landed on his feet easily, bending over to catch his breath between wheezes. Nathan wanted to let go but the ground was more than twice his height below. If he let go he would surely break a foot. He was stuck. His arms burned, he could hardly breath. His heart pounded, and his face flushed hot with shame. He was completely exposed. A spectacle. The three boys continued to laugh and point. Confused, betrayed, hurting, and stuck, he began to cry. At least he tried to cry. He couldn't breath and his hands were slipping. "Mom!" He screamed for help. He kicked his legs up, trying to give his hands a little break.

"He looks like a worm!" Paul shouted.

The other boys roared. Tears rolled down Nathan's face but he couldn't wipe them away.

Abby and Thomas came running from behind the boys.

They shouted to hold on, and yelled at the other boys. Thomas snickered when he saw his naked son but quickly put his hand over his mouth. Meanwhile, Abby was already at his feet and said, "Nathan, oh, my Nathan," as she supported them with her hands. He pushed off of her and relief flooded into his shoulders and hands. Thomas put his hands on Nathan's ankles and said, "I've got you. You can let go now. We've got you." Nathan let go and fell into their arms. Abby quickly pulled his pants up and hugged him. He shook from physical exhaustion and anger-induced adrenaline. She held him as he buried his wet face into her neck.

Abby turned to the other boys and yelled, "You should be ashamed of yourselves." She glared at Paul.

"Ryan, Jacob, go home," she commanded.

Thomas knelt down and put his arms around Nathan but he wriggled away from his father. Nathan shouted at him.

"You're just like them. I saw you laugh."

Thomas glanced at Abby. She scolded him with her eyes.

"Son."

"No!" Nathan wrapped his arms around his mother and together they walked towards the house.

4

Nathan stood up from his knees at the graveyard and walked along the grass path back to the house.

Despite his displeasure towards his father, Nathan readily admitted he knew how to build a farm.

Thirty years since his parents founded the Degland Farm in 1977, it now stretched for thousands of acres. They had apple orchards, wheat, corn, cows, chickens, pigs, grape vineyards, vegetable gardens, a lumber yard, potatoes, berries, and horses. Often, Nathan would hear visitors say how impressed they were, lauding the farm's unparalleled management and production in the state. Forty-four employees lived on the farm in custom-built homes, each on their own plots of land.

Turning the corner, Paul stood in the path, eyeing a boulder.

"Pop said to move it to the woods."

Nathan saw the opportunity to take a jab at his older brother. "What's the matter? Need help?"

"No."

Paul crouched, gripped the boulder with both hands, and thrust his full weight into it. No amount of torque rolled it over.

Nathan amplified the grin on his face.

Paul shouted, "Don't just stand there. Give me a hand, will you?"

Somewhat satisfied, Nathan aided him and the two wrestled the boulder into the woods.

"Remember that time when we were younger with Ryan and Jacob? When I dared you to follow Jacob up a tree?"

Nathan knew what Paul was doing.

"You climbed out onto that branch and couldn't get down. And then I yanked your shorts down."

He laughed. He was trying to regain his superiority.

Nathan remembered his skin burning down to his ankles.

"You looked like a wriggling maggot," mocked Paul.

Nathan relived the shame of being stuck and completely exposed.

"'Nathan, oh, my Nathan,'" Paul's high-pitched voice mimicked their mother's voice from the incident.

"Stop, Paul."

"Grandma was right about you," snarled Paul. "You're no Degland man."

It was true. Now, in his twenties, the farm repulsed him. The repetitive tasks of the farm bored him to death and he became restless quickly. He yearned for change, for the big city.

"That's what graduating from Flaggert College *summa cum laude* will do to you," Nathan responded airily. "There's more to life than dirt and animals."

"There's more to life than sitting on your ass all day pushing paper."

"Just wait," said Nathan smugly. "You'll see."

"You think you're so smart," defended Paul. "It's like Pop always says, 'The Deglands are farmers and always will be. It's in our blood.'"

Paul walked towards the house and delivered a final gibe over his shoulder. "You're not like us."

5

It was the Degland Farm's 30th anniversary and Thomas wanted the whole farm to gather together around a bonfire to eat, drink, and share stories from the year. It was the largest annual event on the farm.

In the kitchen, Nathan found the kitchen manager frantically chopping apples with a large knife, barely missing her fingers. She had the tough job of feeding the hungry stomachs of the farm three times a day.

He said, "Not sure about you, Mary, but I actually like a finger or two in my pie."

She looked up from the cutting board and snorted like an angry horse. She rolled her big brown eyes. Mary was a strong, mature, spiritual woman with dark skin and thin shoulders. While religion softened her, it didn't soften her enough to love a man. "Men were pigs that no amount of soap and scrubbin' could cleanse," she'd say. "Religion still has more of its work to do on me." Her wardrobe never changed, a well seasoned apron over a black dress. Though one could hardly make out the original color of the apron, she always managed to keep her dress beneath spotless. She was careful to never show her ankles, "lest a man be tempted beyond what he could bear." She had the biggest, whitest smile and the loudest voice on the farm.

"Mr. Nathan," she said. "Are you here to comment or to contribute?"

"Here," he said. "Let me." He took the knife from her hands and continued chopping.

She sighed, "Good Lord, I'm glad you're here, deary. I'd about lose my mind had another hour gone by. With the party and all, I don't know what I would have done without another set of helpin' hands."

"Mary, I can't stay long," he said. "I have to check on the vineyard in a couple minutes."

"You can't stay?"

"I'll stay for a little. Let's get these apple pies ready for the oven, then I'll go. How's that?"

Mary lowered her chin at him and gave him a stern look. "You boys. Always busy. Always got something going on."

"Busy hands, bigger lands. Still feet, lost sheep," he replied. "It's the Degland way."

After a moment of listening to the sound of knives chopping apples, she said solemnly, "Your mother would be proud, you know."

Nathan didn't respond and kept chopping. He remembered the countless times he stood right there, helping Mother cook dinner. A wave of nostalgia crashed over him.

Now that she had had two ears to talk to, Mary's motivation returned.

"You know, Nathan, your mother and I knew something was different about you."

He looked up from the cutting board and drilled into the wall with his eyes. *Please don't talk about Mother...*

"I'm serious," she said, noticing his displeasure. "You know what she said once?"

"I can't possibly imagine..." Nathan mumbled.

"It was the time when I made smoked chicken, cheesy potato scallions, and green bean casserole. Then that corn pudding to top it off."

"I actually remember that meal." Nathan was home from his first year at Flaggert College, a small, prestigious private business school three hours West of Sanctilly. The family was sitting down to the dinner table. Thomas was quiet and only grunted acknowledgments as he ate. Abby talked with the boys about the newest family to the farm, the Turners. The house they were building was enormous to fit their eleven children.

Mary recalled, "Y'all were talking about the Turners and you had a book at the table."

Nathan could see the cover. *The Implications of Free Market Capitalism, Vol. II.*

"Miss Abby said you got straight A's. It's too bad your father didn't say more."

Nathan could see Thomas hunched over his food. He grumbled. He wanted Nathan working on the farm. But Abby always defended his interest in learning.

"What your father means to say is that he is very proud of you, Nathan. You're doing an excellent job in schoo–"

"He doesn't need to be spoon fed everything," Thomas cut in. "He's a man now. I can tell him myself and he can handle it, Abby."

She said, quietly, "He isn't an animal, Thomas…"

Paul spoke up, "Damn school don't even matter for a hard day's work, right, Pops?"

Abby shushed him. "Gentlemen use gentle speech. You both know better than that. Don't be brutes, especially not at the table."

"I agree, Ma," Nathan said. He couldn't let Thomas and Paul outnumber her.

"Suit yourselves." Thomas scraped his chair away from the

table and stood up, mumbling under his breath, and took his plate to the kitchen sink. He washed the dishes while the others finished eating.

"She said she was puzzled," said Mary. "She said she didn't know what to do with you. You got this big head on your shoulders... one too big for the farm."

"Right," he said, trying not to think about it.

"No, no," Mary said as she poured the apple filling into the pie crusts. "She was truly bothered. She asked me once, 'Mary, what would you do with Nathan?'"

Nathan laughed. *Oh god.* "What did you say?"

"I told her my mind," Mary said. "I said, 'They ain't never too old to get spanked, Miss Abby. If he ain't gettin' his work done on the farm, then he ought to be chastised. Scripture says, 'Poor is the man with a negligent hand, but the hand of the diligent makes him rich.' Your father didn't get rich just sittin' around and readin' a book!"

"Okay, Mary," he said, chuckling off-handedly. *This is what I'm tired of. There's more to life than spreading manure. Am I the only one?*

The clock chimed on the hour, and he said goodbye to Mary and ran out the back screen door.

6

As the sun sank into the mountains, Nathan ran down the grass and turned left onto the dirt road to the vineyard storehouse. On either side of him, rows of grapevine extended for acres. In a few minutes he arrived at a wide red wooden building with an angled roof.

A man sat outside the winepress storehouse smoking a pipe. He was a burly fellow with a dense beard and long dark gray hair. Leaves stuck to his clothing, and mud stained his dark green pants. He looked as if he had just rolled out of the woods in the fall after a rain and sat down in the rocking chair with a book.

"Hello, Tim." Nathan said. Tim nodded a greeting.

Nathan inquired, "I just want to double-check on the wine for tonight."

Tim said in his deep voice, "Take a look inside the storehouse, my boy."

He grew up with Thomas and was one of the first to move out to the Degland Farm. He knew grapes like Thomas knew how to manage a farm. Tim could tell the difference between hundreds of types of grapes. His wine was renowned in the Sanctilly region and coveted in the cities.

He followed Nathan through the large open doorway of the

storehouse. Lining the walls were shelves stocked with ironclad barrels full of wine. Nathan's nostrils filled with the aroma of straw and dried wine-stained wood.

"Tim."

"Lad?"

"What about..." Nathan's voice trailed off and he lowered his eyes looking over his shoulder. "... for me?"

"Keep walking about halfway down and look on the bottom shelf."

Nathan took ten steps and looked down by his feet. There was a smaller corked barrel on the bottom shelf. He brought it out and jammed his palm into the side of the cork. It gave a small *pop* and came out. He lifted the barrel up to his nose and sniffed the hole. The strong scent of fermented grapes, bitter tannins, and mulled spices enveloped his senses and his head felt light for a quick second.

Tim came up behind him and pat him on the back. "That's the good stuff," he said gruffly.

It's sherry wine. Tim made a small batch of it just for Nathan per his special request. His father didn't know—he forbade the wine to be too strong because it might lead to "unwanted behavior" among the community. But Nathan liked it strong. It helped alleviate his restlessness.

Nathan turned to him. "Not bad."

Tim replied, "This one is rewarding and sensational and leads to a calm relaxation afterward. It strikes the balance between invigorating and unknotting."

Nathan put the barrel under his arm, satisfied. "Smells a little weak. Maybe a little stronger next time, okay?" he winked.

Tim frowned. "Grapes can only yield so much. You know this. If you want something stronger, we'll have to find another base. And you know we don't make anything like that around here."

"You know I'm playing, Tim," Nathan said.

He grunted. Nathan liked Tim.

He said thanks and walked out of the backdoor of the storehouse with the barrel of sherry under his arm. The sky shone with crystal dark blue as the moon chased the sun over the trees. He walked across the wheat field listening to the crunch of the dried kernels under his feet. He arrived at the barn on the edge of the property where the field met the forest. The old red barn was built to hold machinery, surplus hay, retired tractors, and tools. It didn't see much use. This was his barn.

The door creaked as he pushed it open. Inside the barn, bare light bulbs swung from the ceiling. On the second floor, a large loft overlooked the open ground floor. He and his friend, Chester, went out there often to get away from the farm and think. They drank the sherry, let their imaginations flee the farm, and talked openly. He told Chester the previous day to meet him at the barn that night after the anniversary gathering. He climbed up to the loft, opened up a floor chest, and stashed the small barrel underneath some wool blankets.

"I'll see you later tonight."

7

THE FOUR HUNDRED acres of Kitch's land turned out to be a desert with no streams running through it. In the summer of 1980, Thomas hired well-diggers to drill water wells for an irrigation system. Four men came out to set up a rig and Thomas stood next to the foreman. The foreman was a lanky man with a thick moustache, jeans, and cowboy boots.

The foreman said, "Mr. Degland, did you ever think about why there's no vegetation on this land? I don't see a lick of green anywhere."

Both men looked up and scanned the plateau. The grass was dry, yellowed, and brown. The scant trees were dwarfed and thin. Dust and sand covered the ground.

"That's why we're digging wells," said Thomas. "For an irrigation system. I know the land is dry as a bone."

"I'm not sure you want to do that. Waste of time if you ask me."

"What do you mean, a waste of time?"

"The water might be bad. I've got a feeling you could be sitting on an oilfield."

Oil. Thomas's lower lip popped out. He took a deep breath through his nose.

"Can you test for it?"

"I can't," said the foreman. "You'll want to get a geologist out here to check. I know a seismologist back in town if you're interested…"

Thomas shrugged. "Sure. Couldn't hurt."

"Wait." The foreman paused. "You know," he looked at his yellow drill rig. "I *could* just keep drilling and see what happens."

"You mean drill for water but keep going down?"

"Yassir. Oil tends to be deeper down, around three times deeper, beyond three thousand feet. You start to hit groundwater around a thousand. My drill ain't quite cut out for it but I'm willing to keep her going as far as she'll go."

Thomas scratched his chin. "Could I interest you and your men in some lunch and a cold beverage? I'd like to talk with you a bit more about it."

8

All the farmhands and their families gathered around the huge bonfire in the backyard of the Degland home. The flames licked the stars. There were parents, young children, and men and women standing and sitting on wooden log benches around the fire. Dogs ran everywhere. The guitars, woodwinds, and drums were out and everyone was enjoying Tim's wine and Mary's curry chicken kabobs with onions, peppers, and cherry tomatoes. Nathan sat on the bench to the right of his father, who was busy scarfing a slice of apple pie. Juices from the kabobs glimmered in the glow of the fire on everyone's cheeks. Mouths were full of food and talk.

"Mary!" Thomas called to her across the fire, wiping the juices off his beard. "You have outdone yourself. The apple pie is fantastic. How did you do it?"

She called back. "Oh no, sir! It was your son," Mary looked over at Nathan. So did Thomas.

"I did nothing," Nathan said. "Mary did it all."

Thomas stood up and bellowed, "Fathers and mothers, brothers and sisters, sons and daughters! Listen!"

The music lowered in volume and the chattering dissolved, with all eyes turning to the founder of the farm. He looked around at each person, knowing each one of them by name.

Everyone waited for his next words but he let the seconds pass in silence, just grinning. He raised his mug of frothy wine in the air above his head.

"Thirty-two years ago when I started this farm, it was nothing but acres and acres of dirt. Now, we have wheat, corn, grapes, potatoes, cattle, pigs, orchards, gardens, and—my favorite crop of all—families."

Obligatory chuckles sounded from around the gathering.

He spoke, "I was telling Jacob earlier today, hard work can be rewarding, yes, and it is good, sure, but my greatest satisfaction is knowing each and every one of you and seeing your families grow and prosper."

His eyes met each pair of pupils around the fire. "Thank you for the work you have put in this week. I know it was difficult. But it's paying off—we've never done better. Thank you for your diligence and strength. You make me and... "

He stumbled. Everyone knew what he wanted to say.

He recovered, "If it were just me and my boys, we'd still be surrounded by acres and acres of dirt!"

Laughter broke out among the crowd. Nathan looked at Paul. Paul shook his head. Thomas raised his mug high. Other mugs met his in the air around the circle. He said, "To family!"

"To family!" The gathering resounded together and wooden mugs began clunking.

"My boys," Thomas turned to Nathan and Paul and clunked mugs. They drank deeply and thankfully. Many exhaled after gulping as the bonfire let out a large pop.

Thomas clapped his big hands together. He clapped them again. And again. Others joined in, following his rhythm. It got faster and faster. *Clap. Clap. Clap.* Louder and louder as more people joined in. The night pulsated with the united cadence like repeating thunderclaps. It got so fast that some started to lose the beat until it became an absolute free for all. Hoots and hollers accented the roar of applause. Finally, at the loudest moment, the musicians burst in with strings, pipes, tambourines for a lively jig.

Thomas broke into dance, along with other men in the crowd. They swung their arms and pounded the stress of the week into the ground with the heels of their boots. They followed Thomas as he pranced and spun and clapped his hands.

Nathan watched his father. As embarrassing as it was, Nathan loved to see his father dance. Such expression rarely happened anymore. *It's good for him to let go like this. Even if he does dance like a cow.* Nathan rolled his eyes. *Where's Chester?* Just as he was looking around the circle he felt a tug on his elbow. He whipped around and it was Chester.

"Let's go," Nathan said and they slipped away from the fire and crossed the field in the darkness towards the barn.

9

Thwap!

A knife sunk into the wooden stump slab hanging on the wall of the loft in the barn.

"I just want to get out of here," Nathan blurted. "Nothing ever changes. We just do the same thing over and over again."

He took a swig of the sherry. He clenched his teeth to soak in the burn as it ran down his throat. "I'm sick of it." He threw another knife and it struck the poster of a girl to the right of the wood stump.

"Why am I here?" said Nathan.

"Maybe you should go to the city," Chester said. Chester was the red-haired, freckle-faced, fair-skinned son of the accounts manager. He was five years younger than Nathan, who tolerated Chester but still enjoyed connecting about things beyond the farm.

"I don't have the money saved up," Nathan said to Chester back in the barn. "Besides, and you know this best, we get paid in 'food, fun, and freedom,'" he said, mocking his father's tone of voice. "There's no cash in that and no way to save money."

"True," Chester said, taking a drink.

"Wretched farm," Nathan said under his breath. He took another gulp.

"I guess you'll just have to wait for your half of the farm," Chester said. "Good luck with that," he snorted. "Mr. Degland will never die."

Nathan shot him a menacing glare. It sure seemed that way. Thomas was as strong and as driven as he was twenty years ago.

"I'm stuck." Nathan drank more wine, pulled the knives out of the wall, and reset his stance.

"I feel like I could be doing so much more than just sitting on a tractor all day and pushing manure around."

He threw the knife hard into the target. *Thwap!*

"But," Chester said. "Don't you wanna be just like your dad?"

The second knife struck next to the first knife. *Thwap!*

He drank more of the sherry. His stomach warmed. He said, "I'd be really disappointed if I turned out just like my father."

"Why do you say that?"

Nathan jerked the knives from the wall.

"Do you see him? He does the same thing every day. He doesn't do anything new. He doesn't care about anything beyond the farm. He hides in his work. He has no ambitions or dreams. I can't respect that. He just does the same thing every day. I want to do something new. Something big. Something with lots of people watching."

He threw the knife again, it sunk deep into the wall. He poured himself another glass from the half empty sherry barrel. The wine sloshed around as he threw it down his mouth.

"But no, every day is the same out here. Over and over again. And Father loves it. He'll probably die with a pitchfork in his hands."

Chester said, "He's done a pretty good job of building this farm from nothing. Isn't that something?"

Nathan threw the second knife, it bounced off the wall and landed on the floor. He could feel the alcohol toss in his head as he bent down to pick it up.

"I know the farm is good," he said. "But isn't there more? Isn't there more to life than seeing the same people, in the same place, doing the same thing? Don't you realize what I could do in the city if I was allowed to go?"

Chester said, "I bet you could do a lot."

Nathan pulled the knife out of the wall with a satisfied grin. The comment felt good, even from Chester.

Thwap! Pain tore into his finger. He had cut himself from throwing it so hard. Chester sipped from his wine glass.

"You see, Chess, my life is like this couch," he motioned to the old brown fabric couch across from Chester. He had both knives in his hands.

"It's just sitting here. Not moving. Not doing anything but getting sat on. It's what it's supposed to be doing, right? Good, right? Well, every day is like a little knife..." He punctured a knife into the couch.

"Each day passes..." He stabbed the other knife into the couch.

"...Day... after day after..." He kept thrusting the knives in and out of the couch. Chester inhaled sharply. Nathan held his bleeding palm up to Chester who looked alarmed, and said, as if defending himself, "No, it's okay. See? The couch is fine. But when enough days go by..." He grit his teeth together and started thrashing the couch. "It starts to lose its mind and won't let anyone sit on it anymore," He was shouting as he stabbed the couch frenetically.

Flaps were hanging off of the couch, cushion material was everywhere, the frame was broken. The couch was destroyed.

"See, Chester?" Nathan smiled at him wryly. "This is why I need to get out of here."

Chester was sitting straight up, eyes wide, and alert. Nathan breathed heavily, knives in his hands.

"I-I-I'm ready to go," Chester stammered, nervously.

"I'm sorry," Nathan said, realizing he just tore apart a perfectly fine couch. His words slurred.

"It's okay," he said. "You're going through a lot right? It's okay to be upset." He got up, grabbed his coat, and climbed down the ladder.

Idiot, Nathan said to himself as he watched his only friend walk out of the barn below.

He poured another glass and took a couple more swigs of the sherry before sitting down on the shredded couch. He eased into it, testing to make sure it would still hold his weight. It felt like it would. He relaxed, leaned back, and brought the mug up to his mouth again to take a drink.

Snap!

The wood cracked and the back dropped out. The mug of wine emptied onto his face as he fell. A jagged edge of the couch frame cut his arm but he didn't feel any pain. When the couch finished collapsing, he lay there, splayed out with wine in his face, blood seeping out of his arm and finger, and his feet above his head. He started to laugh. And he laughed until he slept.

10

Abby and Mary placed trays of fresh sandwiches and vegetables on the large oak table. Thomas spoke with the foreman and his men about business.

Josh, the drill operator, said, "They finished the airport last year, and it's been a land grab since then. Retail stores, strip malls, and office buildings are popping up everywhere."

"In Delorre?"

"That's right," said the foreman, guzzling iced lemonade. "Mayor McDowell is investing heavily in commercial development, jobs are exploding. Tons of new businesses are starting up."

"Sounds like a lot of opportunities," said Thomas.

"You're not interested in the city much, are you, Mr. Degland?" asked Josh, his hands on a ham sandwich.

"We used to be," added Abby, putting a bowl of watermelon slices on the table.

"We sure were," agreed Thomas. "Don't care for it anymore."

"I don't blame you," said Josh. "You have a beautiful farm."

"If you're interested in getting out of Delorre, I'm looking for a new manager of all that land," Thomas nodded his head in the direction of the dry acres.

"Now wait a minute," the foreman said putting his coffee

mug down. "Don't even try to poach one of my boys. I pay 'em way too much."

He did his best to maintain a stern face but his moustache flickered and then he couldn't hold it any longer. Laughter burst from the full bellies around the table.

Thomas was the first to gather himself. "Tell me more about this drilling for oil idea."

The foreman grunted and for the next half hour explained the process, including the risks considering it was a water well rig.

To the surprise of the room, Thomas cut the man off.

"I'll quadruple everyone's pay, if we hit oil."

"Thomas, don't." There was disapproval in Abby's voice.

The foreman's mustache stretched across his face in a grin. Josh and the others exchanged hesitant glances.

Thomas crossed his arms and said, "I'm serious. If there's oil, it's worth the money."

"But what if something breaks? You're not going to let them leave with a broken drill," Abby insisted.

"Of course not. Whatever damages are incurred, I will cover. If we strike oil, we all benefit."

The foreman rapped his knuckles on the table. "We all saw the land. If I know anything after all these years, I'd bet my hat there's an ocean under that ground."

Thomas stood to his feet. "It's time to find out."

As the men geared up, Thomas avoided the concerned eyes of his wife. He followed the men to the door and right before he touched the doorknob he heard Abby's cold warning.

"You don't know what you're doing, Thomas."

He didn't look at her as he pushed through the door.

11

Nathan woke up to hammers pounding on an anvil inside his head. Sitting up, he felt aches everywhere in his body from sleeping in the broken couch. *Oh no*, he remembered what Thomas had said about that day. They were receiving a large shipment of cattle tomorrow afternoon and he was supposed to be in charge. This was his new "responsibility." *Great.*

Thomas told Nathan he was ready for a big task now that he was back on the farm for good. Now that school is over, he gave Nathan more cattle to take care of. *Is the farm not a business? Why can't he give me something I actually enjoy doing?*

Morning quietness filled the barn and sunlight shone through the cracks, illuminating the dust specks in the air. He wrestled his body up to its feet and stretched. He heard pops up and down his joints. *Better get going, Father will want to know where I am.*

He stumbled into the kitchen where Mary was cleaning up after breakfast. She was wiping the table when she saw him walk in the back screen door. She paused.

"Where in God's creation have you been?" She said with play shock in her voice. "You missed breakfast. Your father's looking for you. I was all by myself for breakfast. It's not easy feeding thirty people all by yourself. Many hands make—"

"Apologies, Mary," he interrupted her. "Had a late night. I could really use some coffee right now."

"Well, you're a lucky one," she said. "I was just about to dump it."

He sat down in one of the twenty wooden chairs around the large oak kitchen table. Mary brought a steaming cup of black coffee over to him. He perked up at the smell. His head still felt like a sledgehammer was lodged in it. He asked Mary about the morning's happenings to see if he missed anything important. She said a call came in to confirm the huge cattle order. She plopped a plate of biscuits and sausage gravy in front of him. He leaned over it and took a big sniff. The hunger quaked within him.

"Can I tell you something, Mary? You have to promise not to tell Father."

"What is it?" she said.

"Honestly, I don't want to take care of any more cattle," he confessed. "I'm sick of cattle."

"Don't tell your father that," she said.

"I know, but I feel stuck," he said. "I don't know what to do." His head hurt. He took a sip of coffee. He heard the front door open and close. Thomas walked by the kitchen and noticed them. He stopped and said, "Sleep in, did you?"

Nathan stuffed a gravy-soaked biscuit into his mouth. Thomas walked towards him. "You know Borby's called. Everything's all set for tomorrow's shipment. Are you ready?"

Nathan never knew if he should be honest with his father. Something in him said to tell the truth. *Just be honest.* But he didn't know how his father would take it. *He's sensitive about farmwork, and he gets angry if you challenge him on it.*

"You don't seem too excited about the job," Thomas said sitting down next to him. Nathan hated disappointing him but maybe it was worth it this time.

Encouraged by the coffee and food, Nathan looked his father in the eye and said, "I'm not sure if I'm the best fit to look after the cattle."

Thomas gave him a look that said, *go on.*

"Paul can do it," said Nathan. "Or someone who actually enjoys the work can do it." He shouldn't have said that, but it was too late.

"Every day, I wake up, do my chores, get on the tractor, spread manure on the field, feed the cattle, cook, clean, and do everything you tell me to do. But my heart's not in it."

His hands began to sweat. Thomas didn't flinch. He said, "What do you mean, your heart's not in it?"

"I have dreams, Father. I have goals and passions that are not here on the farm. I want to use my college degree. I think there are great opportunities in the city."

That last comment stung, he knew it did. Thomas shunned the city. He waited for him to respond.

Thomas said slowly, "You… don't like it here?" He said it as if the thought was unimaginable.

"I'm sorry, Father, it's nothing personal. The farm is great. And I really respect what you've been able to do. But I think I'm supposed to do something else with my life."

"You… want to go to the city?"

"Yes, I do."

"…But you have no money."

"No, I don't." *What is he trying to say,* Nathan thought. *He knows I don't have any money.* Thomas scratched his chin and nodded as he thought.

"What do you think you'll do in the city?"

"Something with business, investing most likely. I've studied business finance for four years. All my professors said I would have a bright career at a number of companies in Delorre. Plus, I've read books about the stock market, real estate, and–"

"Wait a minute, where did you get the books?"

"Mother ordered them for me. She called up the bookstore in the city and had them shipped to me."

Thomas wrinkled his nose.

"Yes," said Nathan. "I have *dozens* of business books, and I've read them all."

Mother supported me unlike you, he thought, but he didn't dare say it out loud.

Finally, Thomas sighed. "Son, there's some things you don't understand."

Of course, here it comes, Nathan thought. *The same old you're-too-young-and-don't-know-anything lecture.*

"You don't want to go to the city," said Thomas. "I've lived there. There's nothing there for you, trust me. You belong on the farm. It's a safe, stable place, and look around: you have everything you need."

"Not everything," Nathan said. "What about stores, markets, shops, industry, commerce? Where's the technology, networks, people, shopping—"

"Stop," Thomas said, holding up his hand. "You don't know what you want."

"You don't know that. All I want to do is see the city and live a little. Is that too much to ask?"

Nathan stood up from his chair and looked down at him. He raised his voice. "If Mother were still alive, she would let me go to the city," he said. "She would have let me go a long time ago."

"No," Thomas said. "She would have kept you around here because she knows what's best for you."

"Mother actually knew who I am." He was speaking too much.

"Whatever," Thomas said coldly, parrying Nathan's accusation. "Work is work. You're not going anywhere."

"You're just saying that because you're bitter." He was almost shouting. "Look. I'm sorry about Mother. But you could have done more to save her."

Thomas's head shot up. He flared his eyes. "Are you saying *I* let her die?"

"You just let her lay there dying when you should have kept her at the hospital." Nathan's cheeks flushed red. He knew he was babbling, but he'd been wanting to say that for a long time.

Crash!

Mary dropped a coffee mug and it shattered on the floor. She bent down to clean it up.

"Mary, would you leave us for a few minutes," Thomas said as more of a command than a request. She scrambled out of the room. He turned back to his son and lowered his eyes.

"You listen to me. Your mother never asked to be taken to the hospital. I asked her plenty of times to stay, but she always said no because she didn't want to worry you or your brother. She thought it would frighten you too much if she stayed away. She didn't think you could handle it. So when you tell me that it was my fault, you better check yourself before you go pinning Abby's death on me."

Hearing her first name felt like a dagger come from his mouth. Nathan sat down back down in his chair. He didn't know what to say.

Thomas got up from his chair and turned to leave.

Nathan yelled to him, "I'm leaving and you can't stop me. I'm going to Delorre."

Thomas looked up at the ceiling with his back to him. He sighed and put his hands on his hips. He shook his head and continued to walk away.

Nathan stood up and shouted, "Walk away and you'll regret it!"

He walked out of the door and slammed it.

"Mother would be ashamed of you," he called after him, half

hoping he would hear it. *He is a stone of a man. Unfeeling and bitter.* As much as he hated him right then, he couldn't help feeling sorry for him. He lost his Abby. But why did he blame it on him? He didn't do anything but love her. *Father let go of her a her a long time ago.*

Nathan put his dishes in the sink, grabbed a broom and dustpan, and swept up the broken shards. His thoughts raced. His secret was out. He had broken the news. It was time to start planning.

As he swept, Mary returned with a maid, who rushed to Nathan and took the broom from him.

"No, I've got it," he said, holding onto it. At that very moment, an idea popped into his head. *The safe.*

12

Thomas walked with Paul along the dirt path around the farm. This was Thomas's nightly walk, the time he could clear his head and think. This time, Paul joined him, and he had a lot more to think about because of Nathan's news.

It was getting dark and thick blankets of clouds darkened the sky. The wind blew dust and leaves in the air, and small droplets of rain touched their skin. The path wound around the wheat fields, past the vineyard, through the orchard, and along the fence of the grazing fields.

Neither man was a big talker. They left talking to the women—and to Nathan. Most of the walk was silent. Thomas thought as he walked, *Nathan... He's so young. So naive. He doesn't know what he wants to do with his life. He certainly was a curious boy. Not really one to be outdoors like his brother. He loved books. Books! Where on earth did that come from? His mother was much better with him than I was. She listened to his endless questions. I don't know what I should do...*

"Paul?" Thomas said.

"Yes, Father."

"Nathan told me today that he wants to leave the farm."

"Leave the farm?"

"He said there's more to life than working on the farm. He said he's meant for the city."

Paul grunted and thought. *What else could Nathan want? He has food, he has work, he has family and friends. How could he want to leave this for the city? The city is a terrible place, Pop always said it was. Nathan's just ungrateful and immature.*

Finally, Paul said, "Did he say why?"

"Yes." Thomas bent down and threw a rock into the woods. "He said he wants to get into business, something with investing. What that means exactly I don't know. He has no money."

"Ha," Paul laughed coldly. Paul laughed because he didn't know the first thing about business.

More minutes passed as they walked. The misty rain thickened slightly, but both men plodded along unaffected.

Paul said, "So what are you going to do?"

"He's not going," said Thomas.

"You always did tell us the city was full of greed and evil."

"That's true, and it's still true. I wouldn't want either of you to go."

"What are you going to tell him?"

"Well, let me ask you that question. What would you tell him if you were me?"

Paul inwardly beamed. It was a rare occurance for his father to be interested in his opinion.

"I'd tell him to grow up. Get serious. And stop taking everything he has for granted. You've given us the farm, with plenty of work, and a bright future. I already have plans to build another house on the north bend of our land."

Paul was in the middle of courting a girl named Marissa, Chester's older sister. She had orange frizzy hair, freckles, and big teeth. She wore glasses, cotton t-shirts, and baggy light blue jeans. To Nathan, she was a fright. But to Paul, she was beautiful. The house he mentioned to Thomas was the house he wanted to build for Marissa—and their future family.

Thomas thought quietly. Paul... A true Degland man.

He saw great potential with Paul and the future of the farm. But this didn't comfort him. Nathan's discontentment would only grow with time. *He'd become more and more impatient and angry the longer he stayed at the farm. But he doesn't know what he wants. It's my responsibility to instruct him and teach him to be a mature adult. A life in the city will only harm him and he will backslide. Who will do his work when he's not here? What if he runs into trouble? I can't be there to help him if he is in the city.*

13

Thomas kept Grandpa Walker's old safe in his bedroom on the second floor of the house, down the hall from Nathan's room and Paul's room. Nathan knew his father kept all the family's important documents in the safe. It wasn't a large safe–maybe the size of a small microwave–big enough to fit folders, documents, cash, and other small items.

Nathan sat at the desk in his room, in front of a green and white chess board. He sniffled and advanced a white pawn. *If I steal the safe, Father will never forgive me.* He jumped the black knight from behind the wall of pawns. *But the safe probably contains everything I need.* The white pawn diagonally attacked, removing a black pawn. *How could you steal? From your own family?* He slid a black rook forward. *What choice do I have?* He slammed the white bishop on the board, forking the rook and knight. *It's stealing.* He threatened the white queen with a black knight. *It's coming to me anyways.* He retreated the white queen back into the safety of a nest of pawns encircling the king. *I'll only steal what I need and then mail everything back to him.* The black knight claimed the dangling rook. *The second he discovers you and the safe gone, he's going to shut everything down. A phone call the next morning will take it all away.* The white queen zoomed diagonally and stuck a base pond, trapping the rook. *What if he can't make the call?* Ignoring the trapped rook, the black knight bounded into an exposed green square. Check. *Wait.* The white king moved one space to the right. *What if no one can make a call from Degland Farm because the phone lines are cut?* The black queen shook in his hand, then he flanked the exposed king. *The nearest phone is in Gladesville an hour away... That's not a lot of time.* The white queen emerged and threatened the black queen, offering piece-for-piece sacrifice. Nathan shook his head. He bumped a black pawn forward, threatening the white queen. *Sacrifices must be made.* The white queen pounced on the black queen. *There will be consequences.* He could hear his father's voice. A black pawn avenged his queen. *Not if you plan correctly.* He developed a white bishop. *So many unknowns.* A black rook lunged forward, positioned for attack. *It's now or never.* The white bishop pivoted to prevent the attack. Nathan cleared his throat.

In a gruffer, more baritone voice, he said, "Thomas Degland." He looked over his shoulder at the mirror hanging on the door. "Thomas Degland," he said again. *Hmm.*

Turning back to the game, he pierced into the cluster of pawns with the other black knight, protected by a rook. Check. *Get a pair of scissors.* He backed the white king into the corner. *Cut the phone line.* He hurtled the black rook down the board into the back row. *One week. Checkmate.*

He looked at the board, forehead sweating, imagining his plan. It could work.

His heart hammered on his sternum thinking about it. *I won't take it all. Just enough. I'll leave him plenty. The farm and everyone will be fine.* He could take only what he needs to get started, actually use his education to make more money in the city, come back, and repay his father. *This is the way it should be. Mother would have let me do this. I wouldn't have needed to steal.*

He got up, walked downstairs, and ran around the side of the house. He looked right and left and then climbed behind a bush to the steel electric box. He opened it up. In colorful braids, wires were plugged into labeled jacks stacked in columns. He identified the phone lines. *This will be easy.*

14

THE NEXT DAY, Nathan scheduled a charter van to pick him up in six days at midnight. Secretly, he began packing his belongings.

Helping Mary bake bread in the kitchen, he asked Mary if she ever lived in the city.

"I did, as a matter of fact," she said. "I cleaned a house for a rich young movie producer. His house was a three story condo in downtown Delorre. He lived alone. That man..."

She stopped mid-sentence, lost in thought.

"...had more shoes than we have corn."

She spread the dough out on the slab countertop. "He treated me well. Kind words. Good pay. But he lived a dark and secret life. He threw big parties late at night. I always cleaned the next day. My goodness, it was a mess."

She flattened the dough with a rolling pin.

"I never knew what to expect—or who to expect—when I walked in the door to clean in the mornings." She snorted. "One time he had a woman and a man come out of his bedroom."

Nathan laughed. *Oh, dear.*

Thomas poked his head in from the living room.

"Nathan, may I speak with you?"

He dropped the dough in his hands, washed, and ran to him.

Thomas was sitting in the biggest chair in the family room, his chair, as if on a throne.

"Nathan, tell me, very specifically, what you plan to do in the city."

Surprised by his father's curiosity, Nathan thought for moment. In one of the books he read, *How to Win the Money Game*, he studied Alan Grothwell's plan for investing success. He recounted it to Thomas as his answer.

Thomas's face didn't move.

"What job will you take to begin saving, because, as of right now, you don't have any money—or am I mistaken?"

Nathan thought about his plan with the safe. *Not yet.* He fidgeted with his hands.

"Uh, retail, or a grocery store, I'm very skilled with produce and—"

Thomas interrupted. "Grocery store? Did you say grocery store?"

He stood up.

"You won't make any money in a grocery store. Trust me, I know. I *owned* one for more than a decade."

Nathan asked, "But weren't you able to save enough to buy the land out here to start the farm?"

Thomas shook his finger at him.

"I owned the grocery store, Nathan. There's a difference. I paid my employees $3.50 an hour. That's nothing for living in the city."

"Well, okay then, I won't work at a grocery store."

"That's not the point. I'm saying the city is no place to save money. If you're new to the city it will drink you dry of any cash you have. It's expensive and if you're not careful, you'll lose everything. I've seen it happen."

"I'm sure there are many things to waste money on, but I'll be responsible, Father. I swear. I'm not a big spender. I know what I need to do."

"Did I ever tell you about the time I arrived at my store just as I was about to open for the day and I caught a stream of black spraypaint spidering across the front windows?"

"A thousand times," Nathan groaned.

"Vandalized," continued Thomas. "Ragged black scrawlings everywhere. I scrubbed for hours but it didn't go away. Had to close the sto–"

"Alright, I won't work at a store!"

Thomas crossed his arms and in a stern voice said, "Nathan..."

Nathan hated when he said his name that way.

"You're not going."

The words felt like a steel shovel slapped against his stomach, but it didn't sting as much as he thought it would. *You can't stop me.*

Still, it angered him that Thomas would be so close-minded and clearly mistrusting towards him, even after he was vulnerable with him about wanting to leave.

"What do you mean I'm not going? You can't say that."

"Yes, I can. I'm your father and I forbid you to leave."

"I can make my own decisions, Father."

"I know what's best for you, and I know you might not understand right now, but I'm putting my foot down."

"You *think* you know what's best for me. Well, I'm sorry I'm not a bone-headed, dumb animal like Paul who blindly obeys whatever you say."

"Alright, that's enough." Thomas shouted, "Go to your room."

He pointed up the stairs in the direction of his room.

Enraged, Nathan kicked the end table on his way to the stairs. *Crack!* One of the wooden legs split and he knew he broke it. He didn't stop to look at it, or at Thomas, but he could feel the entire room heat up with anger behind his back.

He clomped up the stairs, walked into his room, and slammed the door. *Father doesn't get it.* It reminded him of the time when he was home from college sitting at the kitchen table with a book and Abby was teaching him how to appreciate wine, how the clay soil they had at the farm produced bold and muscular wines with high extract and color but in Delorre, where the soil is sandy, she said, you'll find more elegant wines with high aromatics, pale color, and low tannin.

Thomas had entered the room and overheard them. His next words were a branding iron into Nathan's memory. "Don't tell him anything more than he needs to know," he said crossly. "He should be out plowing the corn field right now."

Abby defended Nathan's intellectual interests as much as she could but Thomas wouldn't have it. Hard work trumped knowledge work on the Degland Farm.

Nathan couldn't wait for the van to arrive. *Three more days.*

Paul came into his room just before bedtime and stood with his arms lazily bracing in the doorway. Reading in bed, Nathan looked up.

"Did you really ask Father if you could leave?" Paul asked with a scoffing tone.

"What are you talking about?"

"Didn't you ask Father if you could go to Delorre?"

Nathan rested his head on his pillow. "Maybe. Why do you care?"

"I don't care," said Paul. "I just couldn't believe anyone would ever want to leave."

Nathan sighed. "You don't know anything."

"I know how to be grateful," snapped Paul.

"It's easy to be grateful when you have half a brain," Nathan mumbled.

"What did you say?"

"Nothing."

"Suit yourself. So what did Father say?"

"What do you think he said," Nathan shot at him. "He said no, of course."

"Thought so," said Paul. "Good for him."

"Whatever," Nathan said. Paul snorted and shut the door with a smile on his face.

15

Thomas and Tim sat in the rocking chairs outside the wine storehouse. Fireflies, starlight, and the flood lamp in the back of the house lit the faces of both men rocking back and forth as the night went on. Tim smoked black cavendish tobacco in his knobby pipe while Thomas held a mug of wine.

"He has no idea what he's doing."

"So you're putting a stop to it, just like that, Tom?"

"I told Nathan he's not allowed to go to the city."

Tim stopped puffing from his pipe and paused his rocking.

"What did you say to him?"

"I told him it's not a good place to be. It's expensive. It's crowded. He'll lose all of his money if he's not careful. There's no reason to go to the city when you have everything you need right here."

He stomped his foot on the earth.

"He's probably not cut out for the city," said Tim.

Thomas agreed, taking a drink of the red wine from his mug; he swallowed and wiped his face.

"I know. He asked me if he could go to the city," Thomas said. "I said no, because he's young and he doesn't know what he wants. I told him the farm is good for him; it's safe. He'll be fine."

"Mmhm," said Tim, the pipe buried in his mouth.

"Well, he didn't like it, and he's not speaking to me. It's been days. Not a word."

"What are you going to do?"

"I..." Thomas crinkled his brow. "I don't want my son to feel like he's imprisoned here. But there's not a whole lot I can do. It's up to him to change his attitude. He's old enough now."

"That he is, " said Tim, releasing the smoke. "I wonder if you could give him something to do more along the lines of his interests and education. I mean, you did pay for his schooling, Tom. Perhaps something with the finances. Or the supplier accounts. I could see him doing pretty well at that."

Thomas mulled it over in his mind. *I suppose. If that would make him happier, I don't mind showing him how to run the books. I don't know if I trust him with the finances.*

"I suppose you're right," said Thomas. "There's probably some work I could give him that involves a calculator and sitting on his duff inside."

Both men raised an eyebrow at the other and held in a chuckle.

"I'm sure he could bring some insight and efficiencies to the operations of the farm as a whole," said Tim. "Perhaps you could offer to buy him a computer and give him the accounts information of the farm. He likes the numbers more than the cattle."

Thomas rocked back and forth. "It's true. He's not like Paul at all. He's too heady for his own good... let me think about it. There may be a good compromise."

16

As they dug, the men were abuzz with chatter, shouting above the pounding of the drill. They knew they were drilling for more than water, and the unknown electrified the air. The back of the drill rig churned and bucked as the cable drill went deeper and deeper. The drill operator, in a yellow hard hat, work gloves, and full blue Carhartt suit shouted the depth measurement from the back of the truck:

"Three hundred!"

The front tires of the drill rig were suspended in the air, held up by steel braces. The diesel engine aboard the truck vibrated the ground.

"Six hundred!"

"Keep 'er goin', Josh!" shouted the foreman, proudly.

As the drill bore into the earth behind the truck, water mixed with crushed sediment. The mud-pump sucked the slurry up through the flow line and poured it out of the dart valve into a mud pool twelve feet away. One of the men made notes on a clipboard as the mud sputtered out.

"A thousand!"

The operator raised his eyebrows at the foreman; the foreman nodded and motioned to proceed. The striking of the drill sharpened as the drill pulverized through bedrock. Water leaked everywhere from the drill, soaking the ground.

The men pointed to the drain pipe; the opaque slurry flowed with rock cuttings.

"A thousand three-fifty!"

The foreman listened to the drill carefully. Up and down, the drill pounded away at the rock like a mallet on an anvil. The cadence slowed down. One of the men shook his head. The operator flicked levers and bent over to clear grime from the glass gauges.

"A thousand eight hundred. We've only got a few hundred feet of cable left!"

Thomas scratched his head, unnerved by the loud noise and the men's glances. He tapped the foreman on the shoulder.

"Wait," the foreman warned. He sniffed the air. Slowly, he walked towards the drill and put his hands on his knees. Making circles in the air with his pointer finger, he indicated to the operator to proceed.

The drill bored further into the Earth's crust. The rig truck shook erratically.

"Two-thousand, thr—"

Slam! The drill kicked. The operator jerked back, catching himself on a cable. The truck seized. The viscous silt from the drain pipe darkened, and for a brief moment Thomas thought it was blood. He looked up to see the two men join the operator by the borehole. They raised their hands and shouted excitedly. In that instant, Thomas heard a cry as the operator grabbed one of the men and violently ducked his head down. The hole screamed as the pieces of the drill and cable shot out of the casing like a torpedo. Fiery gas erupted from the casing, and a heavy liquid black mist blew into the air.

The exploding geyser startled the standing man and he fell backwards into the mud. The foreman scrambled towards Thomas, his feet slipping beneath him. He shouted with the ends of his lips curled up, "It's a blowout!"

Thomas crouched and ran from the noise.

"Get away! Get away!" yelled the foreman.

The hot mist soaked through Thomas's shirt and burned his back. He smelled smoke. The foreman pushed him behind Thomas's black truck.

"She's gunna blow!"

Thomas turned back to the rig. Bright yellow flames burst from the borehole, lapping at the control platform of the truck. Above the fire, a thick stack of acrid smoke plumed into the air. The operator pushed the other man away towards Thomas and the foreman. The operator ran around to the side of the truck and snatched the fire extinguisher. With his gloves on he wrestled with it clumsily.

"No!" The foreman cupped his hands. "No!"

The operator couldn't hear him. The hole coughed infernal gusts and the flames splashed up the back of the truck. Black smoke filled the sky.

"Run!" The foreman screamed, "Run, Josh, it's too late! Come on!"

Thomas, the foreman, and the other man watched in horror as the operator charged around the corner of the truck with the extinguisher in his hands. Just as the white cloud streamed from the fire extinguisher in his hands, the flames reached the diesel tank of the truck.

A flash of light cut through the air and a deafening boom shook the ground. The roar of the explosion felt like a sword sliding through Thomas's stomach. His ears rang. The truck launched forward and the drill rig split away from the engulfed truck, which flipped and landed with a loud crash in a fiery heap.

Hands to his ears, Thomas opened his eyes. The foreman was already up and sprinting towards the smoldering remains of the truck. One man lay nearly submerged, surrounded by small fires burning everywhere. The foreman pulled the heaving and coughing man out by his arm, but his eyes were searching the wet, black ground. The operator was nowhere to be seen.

"Josh?" The foreman yelled, leaving the man and beginning to search. The borehole spit up fiery gas between bubbling black crude oil. "Josh!"

The foreman ran around the other side of the burning truck. "*Jesus Christ!*" He knelt, out of sight.

Thomas ran to the foreman. A hot gust of gas reached his nostrils and he swallowed his palpitating heart. He saw the foreman kneeling by the body of the operator, feeling his neck for a pulse. The operator's feet were missing, leaving only the glistening, bloody shreds of his burned suit and legs.

"*Ohhhhhh,*" he groaned.

Thomas ran up to them. *Oh my God. He's alive.* The foreman's oil-stained face twisted.

"You're gunna make it, Josh. You're okay, son."

The man writhed. His burnt face was raw and blistered. Thomas doubled over and wretched.

The foreman held Josh's head and shouted at Thomas. "Call an ambulance!"

Thomas wiped his mouth and took off running for his truck. A growing pond of crude oil covered the ground.

17

ON THE MORNING of Nathan's secret departure, he took an extra long time "cleaning" his room. *Today is the day.* He waited for Thomas, Paul, and the others to be out in the corn field. At 11:00 a.m., when Mary took her nap, he tiptoed up to Thomas's room. The wooden steps creaked and the second floor grumbled its complaints as he walked on it. Down the hall, Thomas's door loomed in the darkness. *Closed.* He couldn't remember the last time he was in parents room.

He stepped up to it. Wrapping his hand around the doorknob, he turned it slowly. The door swung open and his head spun. His eyes engorged themselves on things he knew he wasn't supposed see, and it made him dizzy. Thomas's clothes were spread across the floor. Keys, cash, old pictures, tools, and papers cluttered the tops of his cabinets. His bed was poorly made. He had three tissue boxes on his bedstand. The unkemptness surprised Nathan. *I thought Father was a tidier man. His room is not like his farm.* His eyes eagerly scanned the room for the safe.

In the corner of the room was a pile of dusty boxed up picture frames. He picked one up and wiped off the film of dust. They were family pictures. He thumbed through them—Christmas, birthdays, random photos of Abby. She was in every one of them. *Wait a minute. Is he getting rid of all the photos with Mother?*

He remembered his mission and replaced the picture frames and turned to look for the safe. He opened the closet and found Abby's clothes still hanging on the wooden beam. The mint green dress she wore to church caught his eye and a memory jutted into his head of driving to an Easter service as a family in the truck. He blinked rapidly, exiting the daze, and scrambled around the room desperately looking for the safe. *Where is it?* He checked for clues under the bed, in the drawers, and in the bathroom, careful to put everything back in place. It was nowhere to be found.

The front door closed downstairs. Nathan heard his father's work boots clop around the kitchen and into the family room.

His heart jumped out of his chest. He stood up and tiptoed to the door. *Get to your room, the worst would be getting yelled at for reading when you should be working.*

Nathan put his sweaty hand on the doorknob to turn it when he heard Thomas's footsteps on the stairs. *Clomp, clomp.* It was too late. He wouldn't make it to his room. *What if I dashed? No. You won't make it.* Shaking, he realized he was pinned. He ran to Abby's closet, cringed, and stuffed himself behind the clothes. The musty smell was suffocating. Crusty leather and dry stale perfume filled his nostrils. He closed his eyes and waited. *Clomp, clomp, clomp.* He heard Thomas's footsteps approach the bedroom door. The door creaked open.

Nathan held his breath. *Do not sneeze.* Thomas walked up to the bureau and Nathan heard small objects shuffling and papers crinkling. Thomas muttered softly. He breathed heavily and took another step closer. Nathan's heart pounded so hard he thought his father would hear it. *If he found me in here...* Thomas took another step closer, still mumbling to himself.

Thomas picked up a photo of Abby. She was pictured at the

counter of the store helping a customer. He ran his dirt-stained finger along her thin strong arms. His business partner. His partner in everything. How long had it been since her bright smile filled his chest with hope? There was nothing they did apart.

Nathan couldn't see what his father was doing. Suddenly, a mid-heeled woman's shoe landed at Nathan's feet in the closet, and he jumped. It took everything in him not to scream. Adrenaline stabbed into his legs. He froze, hoping his father didn't see the dresses shuffle when he jumped.

Thomas had found the shoe behind the stack of photo frames and threw it into the open closet.

It was quiet and Nathan nearly asphyxiated himself not breathing. Finally, Thomas put the picture in his pocket turned to go.

Nathan waited until he heard the front door close and boots pound down the front porch and away into the distance. He gasped for air and stumbled out of the closet, coughing dust out of his lungs. Under the bed, his eyes caught the corner of an old black metal box. *Is that it? It's right here.* He lunged to his knees and pulled it out from under the bed. The thing was heavy but he could still handle it with one arm. He picked it up by the handle and shook it next to his ear. *Clunk!* It was full of documents and something solid.

He darted out of the room, down the hall and into his own room. He threw the safe into a large duffel bag and zipped it up. His chest heaved and his breath was short. *That was close.* Only a few more hours stood between him and the freedom of the city.

18

At supper that evening, Nathan was a nervous wreck. Around the dinner table, beef stew filled bowls and plates were full of fresh baked bread and butter. Mary, Tim and Tabitha, the Fields, the Latinskys, the Kutchaws, Thomas, Paul, Marissa, Chester, and Nathan sat, and conversation proceeded as normal. Nathan was quieter than usual. He feared the more he talked the greater the risk of having some sort of detail about the stolen safe or his intended departure that night slip out.

Thomas sat at the head of the table and slurped and chewed aggressively. This was typical after a long day of work in the sun. Nathan couldn't stay focused. At any moment, Thomas could say, "Nathan, were you in my room?" or "Nathan, I'll be taking that safe back now." His mind jumped around, thinking about how he'd escape. But dinner went on and neither man said a word. Thomas's silence tormented Nathan, worrying him even more. It was as if he were waiting for the right time to expose him. Or maybe he just didn't care. Either way, he could feel the blood pumping in his neck. Thomas just stared at his food.

Finally, Nathan had to speak.

"Mary, this stew is wonderful." The others around the table chimed in. Thomas looked up at Nathan and he could see the whites in his eyes. "Wait, you mean you didn't make this, Nathan?"

Nathan replied, "No, sir, Mary did. And she did well." He gave her a small smile. She blushed and then looked down.

"Then where were you this afternoon?" asked Thomas. "I thought you were preparing dinner."

Nathan swallowed a gulp of stew. His knees started to shake. "No," he said, "I was cleaning my room."

"Cleaning your room?" Thomas said. "I didn't see you in your room today."

Nathan trembled. *Oh God, no. He knows. Not when I'm so close! He can't be saying this now.*

"Yes, Father, it had been a while since I had... prepped my room for painting," he lied.

"Oh?" he said. His face darkened as he returned to his bowl. He put a spoonful of stew in his mouth.

"He's painting it pink," Paul quipped.

"Why are you painting your room?" asked Thomas.

Nathan stuttered. "I-I, uh, I—" He wanted to melt under the table, anything to escape his father's eyes.

"Is something the matter?"

"No," Nathan said hurriedly. "Nothing's wrong." *Please, no more questions.*

"I'd like to sit down with you tomorrow, Nathan, there's something we should talk about."

Nathan nodded. "Okay." *What is this about? Is it about the safe? Is it bad? Maybe it's good?* He didn't dare ask.

Thomas took his last bite and stood up. "Let's plan to meet before dinner at 4:00 p.m."

"Alright."

Paul's mouth hung open with a large chunk of bread in it. He was silently repeating, "Wha? Wha?" to himself.

Nathan checked the time. It said 8:00 p.m. He had four

hours to be out by the road.

"I'm off to bed, all," said Thomas. "Good job today, even with Nathan missing. Shows we can still get a good day's work done, even without him."

He didn't look at anyone as he walked up the creaky wooden stairs. "Goodnight."

"Goodnight," Nathan murmured in unison with everyone else. *That might be the last time I see him in a long time.*

"What's that all about?" Paul asked, putting his dishes in the kitchen sink.

"Not sure," Nathan said, washing his drinking glass with the washcloth.

"You don't know?" he asked.

"Nope," Nathan said.

Paul stepped closer to him. "What are you not telling? There's something going on with you, isn't there?"

Nathan chuckled nervously and said, "What are you talking about, Paul?"

Paul gave him a light punch on the shoulder, almost knocking the glass out of his hand. "Come on," he prodded. "Tell me."

"Ask him yourself," Nathan said, "I don't know."

Paul's voice hardened. "I hope you're not planning on doing anything stupid like you normally do."

"Get out of here," said Nathan, splashing Paul with the soapy dishwater. He didn't want their last conversation to be a nasty one. But some things never change. Paul dried his face and threw the towel at Nathan.

"That's what I thought," Paul said, turning to leave.

Have fun on the farm for the rest of your life, Nathan thought, sneering.

Paul followed Thomas upstairs. Nathan finished up the dishes and said goodnight to everyone, and went up to his room. He waited until the house was still, quiet, and dark.

19

When the clock struck 11:00 p.m., Nathan unzipped the duffel bag to double-check to make sure the safe was still there. It was, along with his clothes and toiletries. He zipped it up and grabbed his other bag of shoes and books. With the light off, he cracked his bedroom door. The dim house slept. Moonlight shone through the window blinds. Nathan listened and didn't move. All was quiet, except for Paul's snoring.

With both bags in his hands, he passed Paul's room and then Thomas's room and slipped downstairs. In the back of his mind, he wished he could say goodbye because he knew he wasn't coming back. He took his final steps in his home as he descended down the front porch steps.

The driveway was a long walk out to the main road. The cool night breeze blew gently and the stars shone with brilliance. He barely needed a flashlight. The gravel driveway extended into a wooded area, curved back and forth inside a green forest, and then broke out into a clearing where it met the main road. The driveway was so long, the mail only came once a week. The mailman refused to bring it everyday, conceding to deliver all mail to the front porch on Wednesdays only.

Nathan trudged along, thinking. As excited as he was for the city, his heart felt like a brick. He pictured Mary's tears in the morning when he didn't help her with breakfast. Tim's frown when he realized he left without saying goodbye. He heard Paul's indignant, "Hmph, I knew it." And he saw his father on his knees beside his bed, searching for the safe with his hands under the bed, when the thought hits him that he stole it. He could see his father's tight lips, angry eyes, and balled fists. He shivered and quickened his pace. It wasn't impossible to be discovered right then. Hungry farmers eat at all hours, even in the middle of the night. Someone could have seen him. He looked over his shoulder. No flashlights. He grit his teeth and walked faster.

Entering the forested part of the driveway, he flicked on his flashlight. The jet blackness surrounded him and the hairs rose on his moist skin. His ears were alert and the adrenaline pounding through his veins made the bags feel weightless, despite his aching shoulders.

The forest broke open and the moonlight flooded onto the driveway. The main road lay ahead and a parked black van idled at the end of the driveway. A light was on inside the van. Nathan looked behind him. Complete darkness. No pursuing lights. *Good.* He walked up to the van. Dropping his bags in the rear, he circled to the driver's window.

A small, skinny, bald and fluorescently white man in a dark suit was scrolling through photos on his phone. Nathan hated to startle him, but didn't know what else to do. He rapped on the window. The man jumped. His phone flew out of his hands and he sat straight up. Nathan waved. The man didn't look pleased. He picked up his phone and opened the door.

"Hello," Nathan greeted the man.

"Hey," he growled. "'Bout shit my pants."

"Oh, sorry about that," Nathan said, trying to mask his snickering.

"Are you Nathan Degland?"

"Yes, I am."

The man got out of the driver's seat and walked around to the back of the van. He was even shorter than Nathan expected. Maybe five feet tall. He loaded his bags and Nathan took one last look down the driveway to the woods. No pursuing lights. This was goodbye.

PART 2

THE CITY OF DELORRE

20

They drove for over five hours. The driver had an Italian accent and the van smelled like smoke. A woman kept calling him and they talked heatedly about cats fishing in the goldfish tank.

Nathan tried to start a conversation. He needed to know where to get the safe open. "Sir," Nathan said.

"Hm?" The man said with a fresh cigarette in his mouth.

"Do you know where I could find a locksmith?"

"A locksmith? You need keys?"

"No, I need to crack a safe."

The driver thought for a moment. "Sure, yeah, there's one a couple blocks from The Charles on 40th street. I forget the name."

Nathan looked at the clock in the dashboard. 5:16 a.m. *That's my first stop.* His stomach was in knots.

"Can you take me there?" he asked. The man tapped the screen of the device stuck to his windshield.

"Lockpoppers," he said. "That's the place. You want me to drop you off there?"

"Yes," said Nathan. His head ached. *What have I done? What am I doing? Am I a thief? I'm running away from home. This is unbelievable.* The guilt was thrilling. Every mile was lengthening his distance from his father. He was free.

The van bumped along the highway. *I'll need a place to sleep.*

"What's The Charles?" Nathan asked.

"Ah, best dirty martini in Delorre, my friend," the man said fondly from experience. Nathan had never had one.

The driver continued, "It's a hotel, a giant one, right in the epicenter of the city. Goddamn expensive, too. Sheesh."

Nathan nodded. "What's it like?"

"The nicest place in town," the driver said into the rearview mirror. "Celebrities, politicians, and other important people always stay there. The rooms are supposed to be outta-this-world."

He kissed his fingers. The way he pronounced "world" rhymed with "boiled."

"I'd like to see it. I've never been to the city before."

The man's fraying dark gray eyebrows wrinkled his forehead, taking up the whole rear-view mirror.

"Never been to Delorre?"

"No sir. What do I need to know?"

"Don Chino's. Best pizza in the world."

Woild. Nathan liked the man.

"I'm sure there're a lot of restaurants and places," said Nathan.

"More than you can imagine, kid."

The driver glanced at him. He muttered something about needing another cigarette.

The driver, whose name was Franco, told Nathan the story of the City of Delorre. It began as a refueling station between two larger cities along the Stein River. Over the years the small town grew in accommodations, markets, and entertainment for travelers and traders spending the night in between cities. Eventually, it developed into such an eclectic place that it became a destination itself. Powerful families, corporations, religious groups, small businesses, and colleges found it and settled in, naming it the City of Delorre. And it was booming now that the airport was finished.

They crossed the bridge over the Stein River. A gorgeous deep orange sunrise backlit a dark city skyline. Nathan recognized it from photos and postcards. *Delorre.* Nathan saw the high-rises. He had never seen man-made things so enormous. *Such feats of engineering.* He pressed his face against the van window. The sunshine reflected off the dark water around the buildings. On the five lane highway, a dark car with pure blue lights shot by the van, startling Nathan.

"How do you keep track of where to go?" Nathan shouted to the driver. He didn't know why he was shouting. He was already beginning to feel small.

Franco naturally shouted back, "When you've lived here for fifteen years you don't even need the signs anymore."

The bridge ended and they headed straight into the epicenter of the city. People and cars were everywhere on the sidewalks, walking quickly in the early morning shadows. They passed rows and rows of shops, green parks with bronze statues, restaurants and bars with closed parasols above sidewalk tables, and window-covered office buildings. Everybody had a lidded coffee cup in their hand. *The city,* Nathan thought, amazed. *I'm here.*

"Ten minutes," the driver said. The clock said 6:48.

Nathan felt lost in the cascades of skyscrapers. Gladesville, the hamlet where he went to high school, was a speck of dirt. He had lived in the City of Sanctilly, the town after which the region was named, where he attended Flaggert College, but even it was a fraction of what he saw then. Rolling down his window, he leaned out and filled his lungs with the cool industrial air of the city. It smelled like fresh dry grass baked on rubber with a twinge of fish. *The smell of opportunity.*

Franco said five boroughs formed the whole of the city, each with their own ways of living. Each borough met in the center of the city, intersecting at one location, *The Charles Hotel.*

In a busy downtown square they stopped at a traffic light. On the right loomed a titanic of a building. The muted gold plates outlined the large window exterior that stretched up into the maroon clouds. The ornate portico above the enormous revolving doors read in elegant lettering, "The Charles Hotel."

"That's her," said Franco.

They drove seven blocks down to 40th street where Franco dropped Nathan off on the sidewalk. In front of him was an old steel door with a sign over it that said *Lockpoppers*. The windowless entrance was sandwiched between Earl's Hall of Music and a convenience store. It made a hole in the wall look grand. Below the sign the opening time for a Monday was 8:00 a.m. It was 7:45 a.m.

Exhausted, Nathan put his bags down and stood in front of the door to rest.

"See you around, kid." Franco sped off.

Despite the sun's generosity with its rays, Nathan immediately felt cold and alone, similar to his first moments at Flaggert College, but this place made a college campus seem microscopic. People walked hurriedly everywhere.

He remembered the safe. *Father would be finishing up breakfast right about now and probably already yelled up the stairs at me. No time to waste.*

Nathan pounded on the steel door. He hit the door again, but it was more like a punch. His heart tripled its pace. *Father and I are supposed to have that meeting at four. He would probably go through most of the day before wondering where I went. No doubt the dead phone line would be discovered tonight.*

Nathan pounded on the steel door. He put his ear to it. A woman jogging with her little dog glowered at him. At exactly 8:00, the lock in the door unbolted. *Zzchrkt.* It sounded electronic. Nathan turned the handle and pushed the door in.

"Hello?"

His voice sailed down a narrow hallway with almost nothing on the white walls and met a man wearing a gray t-shirt and a red bandanna sitting behind a desk at the end of the hallway. The man looked like he'd never worked a day in his life. He carried the typical weight of a man who didn't care about his physique, but he wasn't fat. The man was unshaven and his puffy eyes were encased behind thick framed black eyeglasses. Nathan walked down the hallway, his shuffling echoed loudly down the hall. The man didn't look up. Nathan placed his bags on the floor and cleared his throat.

"Is this Lockpoppers?" he asked, out of breath.

The man snapped the magazine shut and the volume of his voice startled Nathan.

"What do we have here?"

Nathan unzipped the bag and put the safe on the pine wood desk next to a full coffee pot and a name card that read Dwayne Cobb, Locksmith. "I need this opened immediately," Nathan instructed. "Can you do it?"

The man's voice sounded as if his voice box was in his nose. "Where'd you get it from?"

"Nevermind about that."

"Yep, that's what I thought." He shook his head and clucked his tongue. "Everyone says that."

"My father gave it to me. He said he's had it for ages but never got around to cracking it... Are you up for it?"

"Yeah, right," he smiled with his teeth but his eyes didn't move. He picked the safe up with a groan and rotated it up and down, side to side. His lower lip stuck out as he examined the metal box. He grunted. Paying special attention to the combination wheel, he asked Nathan, "So no ideas, huh?"

"I don't have a clue. That's why I'm here."

Dwayne didn't say anything. Finally, he got up and opened the door to the back of the shop, disappearing. Nathan looked over his shoulder towards the entrance and noticed that only two lights lit the whole place. One above the door entrance and one above the desk. The desk had two flexible lamps on it. The shop smelled like metal shavings.

The man reentered. His melon-like head was coated with three days worth of scruff and his "Mobocracy" t-shirt hugged his shallow chest and hung off his round belly like a curtain. He placed the safe on the desk with a *thud*.

"This is a Sargent and Greenleaf lock. It's a tricky bastard, for sure."

"Can you do it?" Nathan asked.

"Probably. Liquid nitrogen would take me no time at all. The lock is old. With a good spray in, out, and all around and then a hammer, I bet she'd fall off faster than a buttered bullet."

"Alright," Nathan said. "As long as the documents aren't damaged..."

The locksmith suddenly held up his pointer finger, opened to the door behind him, and said, "Be right back."

Nathan stopped him.

"Wait. How do I know you won't steal any of the contents?"

"If I stole from my customers I wouldn't have a business. And I've been open for fourteen years." He let out a short *ha*. "Hell, if I wanted to do that, I'd just sell insurance."

Dwayne pretended to curtsy and excused himself.

The safe could be a complete dud. It may be full of junk and worthless trinkets Father deemed meaningful. It didn't matter at this point. All I can do is hope for the best.

Twenty minutes later, the door opened and Nathan gulped

down the third cup of coffee in his hand, scalding his throat. Dwayne emerged with the safe, a hole where the lock dial had been.

"Captain, we've done it again," his voice sounded like a radio commercial.

"Came right off after a few good smacks," he said as he laid it on the desk. The front opened slightly and closed. Nathan nearly jumped at the sight of it.

"I think you'll be pleased," Dwayne grinned.

He must have looked through all the contents already. Not alright. Not at all. How do I know he didn't take something from it?

"Here you are," he said, opening the door of the safe.

The small door swung open easily. Half a dozen folders were stacked on the bottom shelf. Nathan saw a handle on the second shelf. He pulled it out. It was an old, flintlock pistol. The wooden handle and dark rusted steel pieces were aged and worn. He had no idea if it was operational, and even more puzzling, he had no idea why his father had it. Along the barrel, the letters R.W.D. were imprinted on the metal plate. *Grandpa Walker?* He recalled his grandfather's full name: Robert Walker Degland. He raised his eyebrows. *Must have been his gun.* It sure was old enough.

He placed the pistol down on the desk and noticed a glass object in the safe. He grabbed it. His fingers felt something hard and round. He pulled it out, he heard a sloshing sound. It was an unopened bottle of single malt scotch. The frosted, scripted letters on the smooth crystal decanter read *Constantinople*. He didn't recognize the brand.

"It's rare stuff," Dwayne said, snapping Nathan out of his trance. Annoyed, Nathan placed the bottle next to the pistol. *I don't need any commentary, thank you. Why is this stuff in Father's safe?*

Before getting to the folders, Nathan reached into the safe again and this time felt a soft material, possibly felt cloth, perhaps a bag. He slid it out and held it under the desk lamp. It was a brown, leathery bag no bigger than his hand with a pull-string tie. It felt heavy with little things.

"Mmm," Dwayne groaned with pleasure.

Ignoring him, Nathan undid the string and opened the bag. His head reared back. Brilliant, clear diamonds filled the small bag. *The bag was full of diamonds.* Sparkling, wintery cold crystals with sharp points and shimmering faces lay spread on the dark leather in his hand. *There must be a hundred or so.*

"There's more," said Dwayne, noticing his excitement. Carefully, Nathan pulled the string of the diamond bag closed. *How much were they worth*, he couldn't help thinking. *How did Father have these? Where did they come from?*

Resting the bag next to the scotch and pistol, he guided his twitching hand into the safe again. No objects. But he felt a tight stack of small papers wadded together. He grabbed one and pulled it out.

Cash. All hundreds.

Dwayne squealed with delight. There was more. Nathan grabbed five more and pulled them out.

"Looks like $50 grand to me if those are stacks of pure bennies."

Fifty-thousand dollars. Nathan inhaled sharply through his nose. He'd never seen, nor held, *let alone owned*, this much money.

He turned his attention to the folders. There were seven manila folders stacked on top of each other. The bottom one was more than an inch thick.

Each of the tabs had names. The top one had *Nathan* on it. The next one said *Paul*. The next said *Abby*. Below that, it said *Thomas*. The next said *Store*. The next said *Farm*. And the last said *Oil*.

Nathan's hands shook. *What were these?*

He said, "I'm going to go. Thanks for the help, Dwayne. Here."

Nathan took two hundred dollar bills and handed them to Dwayne who was clearly disappointed he didn't get to see the rest of the show.

"You don't want to open the folders here?" He complained.

"No, I'm going to get to a place with a phone."

"But I have a phone."

Nathan packed the cash, folders, pistol, scotch bottle, and bag of diamonds into his bag.

"Want the safe?" he asked Dwayne. "I don't need it anymore."

Dwayne hugged the broken metal box.

Strange man. Nathan said goodbye and marched down the hallway and out of the door.

21

"N<small>ATHAN</small>!" *T<small>HAT LAZY</small> boy*. Thomas stood at the bottom of the stairs in his house with one leg perched on the stairs and a hand on the railing.

"Nathan, get down here!"

His old black digital watch read 11:47 a.m. *What is wrong with him?*

He sighed and with his heavy boots he barreled up the wooden steps. The hallway creaked. He turned the doorknob to Nathan's room.

"You sick, boy?"

The room was empty. The bed was made. Everything was neat. An untouched game of chess sat on top of the desk.

"Nathan?" Thomas said.

He wasn't there. Thomas wheeled around and ran down the stairs.

"Mary!" he exhaled.

She was preparing macaroni salad for lunch. "Yes?"

"Have you seen Nathan today?"

"No, I haven't. Is he in his room?"

"No."

Mary chuckled. "Probably got himself stuck in a book somewhere."

"I don't know," said Thomas. "I haven't seen him all morning."

Paul came bulldozing in the front door. "What's going on? Did you find Nathan?"

Thomas didn't hear him. He was too busy thinking, frowning.

"We're supposed to meet at four this afternoon but I want to make sure he gets his work done before we sit down. Did he say he was going somewhere today?"

Mary and Paul looked at each other, hoping the other would have the answer.

"I haven't seen him."

"Can't say I have either," said Mary. She returned to a boiling pot of peas in the kitchen.

"Did he run to Gladesville for an errand?"

Paul shrugged.

Thomas walked to the small corner room next to the family room and picked up the phone handset. He put it to his ear and waited for the dial tone. He bobbed the hook up and down but it never came.

22

Nathan stepped out of the cab at the grand entrance of The Charles Hotel. A black limousine and a Mercedes were parked in a curved driveway in front of the arched hotel doors. Valets in crisp navy uniforms scurried about assisting patrons.

Nathan took two steps when a homeless man stopped him. He groaned as he was trying to speak but could not. He choked on his words in his throat. His thick white hair was long and dirty. He was bent over from age and dressed in a tattered, loose flannel shirt and dirty black sweatpants with holes. A long and haggard white beard hung from his bony tan face. He had no shoes.

Nathan didn't understand him. The man cupped his hands and held them out. Both of his hands were missing several fingers.

Oh, the poor man. Nathan didn't have any money to give him other than the hundreds in his bag. He said, "I'm sorry. I'm in a terrible rush and I don't have any money just yet." The man made a throaty noise and hobbled away.

"That's Jeb," the snobby chauffeur said, "This is his spot to beg. I recommend not doing that again."

"Thanks for the tip," Nathan said, not agreeing. They walked into the hotel.

The large lobby was dark, with reflective sparkling black marble floors and red walls with large green plants and pools of water trickling. The hotel lobby smelled like lavender and mint, fresh and crisp. Abstract green and blue and orange paintings were hanging on the walls underneath restrained drop lighting. Grabbing a newspaper off a gold rack, Nathan followed the chauffeur up to the front desk to check in.

"Did you have a reservation with us, sir?" the man behind the counter asked without looking up from the computer.

"No, sir, I did not."

"Name?"

Nathan paused and thought for a moment. He scanned the newspaper in his hand. *I can't be tracked.*

"John Shepherd," he told him, an infinitesimal smile crept onto his face. He was pleased with how simple his new alias sounded.

"And how many nights will you be staying with us, Mr. Shepherd?"

"Just one," he said. Then he remembered the $50,000 in his bag.

"Wait," he said. "Make that a week." *That should give me enough time.*

Rushing down the red carpeted hallway on the 107th floor, Nathan opened the door to his room and threw the bags on the floor. Instantly, he smelled a citrusy sea breeze. The room was beyond anything Nathan had ever seen or imagined. He took off his boots and socks. The dark soft carpet squished between his toes. The two king beds looked like they were made of fresh white marshmallows. He surveyed the room—a huge rosewood desk stood against the wall on the left, pillows cushioned every crevice. A circular glass table for guests rested in front of an enormous floor to ceiling window that opened up a panoramic view of the city lights. Around the corner, he walked into a closet, came out and walked into a jacuzzi room with the same glass windows overlooking the city.

Heart pounding, he pulled the folders out of the bag and leaped onto the king bed. The newspaper fell and he noticed the headline *VC Firm Venture X Invests $200 Million in Healthtech Startup*. He wanted to become an investor... *Don't get ahead of yourself.* He jumped off and put the folders on the desk.

He flipped open the first folder with his name on it.

23

"He's gone," Thomas said to Tim. They stood around the island in the kitchen, under the large skylight in Tim and Tabitha's house. Bright sunlight lit the big room. A high voice softly cooed from the hallway.

"Father?" Tim's youngest daughter called to him.

"Not now, honey, Father's busy. I'll be right there. Go to your room."

Minutes ago, Thomas had stormed into their house. He was visibly worried. Tim had cleared his family from the main room to listen to Thomas.

"What do you mean, gone?" asked Tim, turning back to Thomas.

"He's not coming back. I found a note."

"What did it say?"

Tim saw the stress in his friend's face. Thomas pulled a small piece of paper from his pocket. His stomach knotted as he read it.

"'Father, I've gone to live the life I was meant to live. I hope you'll be able to forgive me someday. Nathan.'"

Tim said nothing. Thomas stared at the note in his hands. A minute went by.

"He took my safe, Tim."

"What?"

"He took my safe—the one I've always used to keep important documents... my father's safe."

"I know it," said Tim. "He stole it? What was in it?"

"Too much," said Thomas, shaking his head. "Everything."

"Tom, tell me what was in it." Thomas looked up at Tim's grave face.

"The family's financial information and personal documents."

"Not good. When did he leave?"

"I don't know," said Thomas. "I noticed he was missing yesterday at lunch. He probably took off earlier that morning."

"Where did he go?"

"He didn't say, although I'm pretty sure he went to Delorre."

"Oh, no," said Tim.

"There's more," said Thomas, battling his anger.

Under his beard, Tim looked alarmed.

"He cut the phone line..."

"You're kidding."

"I wish I was. I tried calling an old friend in the city but there was no dial tone. I went around the side of the house and found this."

He held up the snipped phone line. Tim put his hands on his head. "How is this possible? Why would he do this?"

Thomas turned away from him. He had worked for *so long* to build a stable, happy life for his family. Then Abby left him. And now Nathan. *Why? What have I done?*

Thomas's brows were in knit. "I'm going after him. Right now."

"Tom. Wait. Think about it first."

"He has the safe."

"But he doesn't know the combination."

Thomas said, more urgently, "He won't need it for that old

safe."

Tim looked at him.

Thomas continued, "He cut the phone line..."

"I don't know what you're trying to say," Tim said.

"What do you think he's going to do?"

"I'd like to think he'll just take some of the cash, until he finds a job," said Tim. "That's what I would do. He won't take anything else."

"Anything else. That's right," Thomas said harshly. "I'm going after my son. I'll have him home in less than a week."

"Thomas, stop," said Tim. But it was too late. Thomas bolted out of the house and headed for his truck.

24

THE FOLDER MARKED *Nathan* had his high school senior photo, his birth certificate, passport, social security card, acceptance letter and transcripts from Flaggert College, recommendation letters, bank account information, and six savings bonds. Nathan looked at the bank statement. $910.30. *Not much at all.*

He leafed through Paul's and found everything including the bank account balance. $59,329.10. *Probably because he didn't go to school. So it just sits in his account and rots.* He was disgusted.

In his mother's folder, he found death certificates, the obituary, funeral receipts, and four really old savings bonds. The *Farm* folder also had a bank account attached to it with a balance of $782,090.

The folder marked *Thomas* contained his father's birth certificate, social security card, passport, wealth management and retirement accounts, vehicle titles and information, insurance documents, bank account information, and a living will. $3,210,000.

Nathan peeked at the will. Thomas had Paul inheriting 65% of his assets, and Nathan 35%. *Outrageous.* Nathan's face turned crimson and he began to shred the document viciously.

I knew it. Father always favored Paul. Doesn't matter now.

An evil smile spread across his face as he set Thomas's folder to the side.

Lastly, he opened the thick *Oil* folder. There were several contracts with "Coffin Petrol Co." in slightly raised gold letterhead. He thumbed through the pages until he found the most recent bank statement. He opened it up and next to the words Account Balance, it said: $10,356,000.

Great God Almighty.

Nathan stared at the number on the paper in his hand. *Ten million dollars?*

He put it down and flipped to the actual deed of sale for the oilfield land. Just above signatures of his father and the owner of Coffin Petrol Co., Joseph A. Coffin, the sale price was written in bold Times New Roman letters: $10,000,000. The money had earned $356,000 in interest since the sale of the land twenty-eight years ago.

In the black leather chair, Nathan sat, stunned. He couldn't believe it. *How could his father not have let him go sooner? Or given him some of this money to invest after he graduated? Had this money just been sitting there for nearly thirty years? Give me a break, I studied investment management and finance!*

Everything was going according to plan, even better than expected. Now it was time to complete the act.

He picked up the room phone and dialed the number for First Bank of Delorre.

25

Thomas's white truck sped along the highway traveling at a near-dangerous revolutions per minute. Delorre was five hours away, but if he was fast enough he could make it to the bank before it closed.

He buckled his seatbelt and gripped the wheel with discolored knuckles. Inside, his anger mixed with fear and regret. *How could my son run away? Is it my fault? Is it his fault?*

Thomas knew he couldn't punish his grown son. *Will he even want to come home? Maybe I should've let him go. Why did he want to leave? Abby, I wish you were here. I wish you were sitting next to me in this truck...*

The way to Delorre was empty, several hours from the closest town. Time crawled and Thomas pounded the wheel with his palms. He needed to find a phone before the bank closed. *Just in case.*

26

Nathan stood in his hotel room with the phone in his hand and the *Thomas* folder in front of him. Tapping the desk with cold fingers, he dialed the number. It was 2:53 p.m.

A jovial, bright female voice answered. "Thank you for calling the First Bank of Delorre, this is Lauren, how may I help you today?"

Nathan lowered his voice. "Hi. This is Thomas Degland. I'd like to transfer some funds to another account."

"I'd be happy to help you with that today, Mr. Degland. What is your account number and your social?"

Nathan read the long string of numbers from the bank statement. The numbers left his dry lips methodically as he read off his father's social security card.

"Thank you. What is the address on the account?"

He kept his voice steady as best he could as he gave her the farm's address.

"Thank you. And, just for security verification, what is the maiden name of your paternal mother?"

He remember Grandma Marcy's gravestone, *Martha Livingston Walker*. "Livingston."

"Thank you. And lastly, what was the last transaction amount on the account?"

Last transaction amount? He panicked. He looked at the bank statement and didn't see any charges or withdrawals from the account. There were only interest deposits. The last deposit was for $52,991. *Was this a trap?*

"There shouldn't be any transactions on this account," he said in his father's voice. "There should only be interest deposits. The last one was for $52,991."

"Thank you, Mr. Degland. I'd be happy to go ahead and process your transfer."

Nathan moved the phone away from his mouth and sighed in relief. His heart was beating fast. *So far so good; it was working.*

"What is the amount you would like to transfer?"

"I'd like transfer the available balance, please."

The lady's voice paused. "Alright," she said, slowly. "You have an available balance of $10,356,250.20." She sounded hesitant.

Nathan assured her. "Yes, that is it."

Her voice didn't have the same friendly tone anymore. "Where would you like to transfer the balance?"

"To my son Nathan Degland's account, I have the account information here." He opened the folder.

"Okay," she said. "Mr. Degland, as an extra security measure, would you mind verifying your security phrase before we proceed?"

Nathan swallowed hard. *Security phrase?* He flipped back through his father's folder, desperately searching for some kind of clue. He racked his brain. *What would he choose for a security phrase?*

"Mr. Degland?" She asked after several moments.

He barely got it out of his mouth before he started panting. "Busy hands, bigger lands. Still feet, lost sheep."

The small handwritten note quivered in his hand. *This bet-*

ter be it. His forehead felt hot and wet.

"Thank you for that," she replied. "What is the account number of your son's account?"

Nathan held the phone away from his mouth as he tried to moderate his exhale. He gathered himself quickly and pulled out his own bank information. "It's at the same bank, so I assume you don't need the routing number..."

"What is the routing number?" She asked. She was trying to catch him. He knew it.

He rattled off the number. *Nice try.*

"And the account number?"

"223, 9800, 24, 79."

"Thank you. Just to make sure I have the correct recipient, can you verify the address for the account?"

"It's the same."

"Okay. Do you mind if I place you on hold while I process the transfer?"

He heard scratchy country music come through the phone's earpiece. *I think that went well.* He had all the information she asked for. *I don't see why it wouldn't go through.* He paced the room, his empty stomach gurgled but he had zero appetite whatsoever.

Three minutes later the music cut off. Nathan froze.

"Mr. Degland?"

"I'm here."

"The transfer went through. I have your confirmation number. Are you ready?"

Nathan's chest exploded with warm relief. He tried his best to control it. His numb hand grappled for a pen on the desk. "Go ahead." His voice trembled slightly.

She gave him the confirmation number, which he scribbled on the back of a folder.

"The funds should be available in your son's account now.

Your current account balance is zero dollars. Is there anything else I can help you with today?"

"Yes, please close the zeroed-out account. I have no need of it anymore."

"I'd be happy to do that for you, Mr. Degland." She paused. Nathan held his breath. "Is there anything else I can help you with today?"

"No. That is all. Thank you."

"Thank you for choosing the First Ba–"

He pressed the disconnector with his hand. Dazed, he turned and looked around the hotel room. The full private bar. The california king bed. The mahogany hardwood floor. The gorgeous paintings on the walls. The walk in closet. The jacuzzi room. The open window view of the city.

This was no longer a dream.

27

"You just called, Mr. Degland," the voice on the other end of the payphone said. It was 4:52 p.m.

"I assure you I did not," Thomas replied. He couldn't make it to Delorre in time. He had pulled off to an exit and found a phone booth.

"You called at 2:53 this afternoon."

"No, I did not," Thomas raised his voice.

"I'm sorry?"

"I said that wasn't me."

"It says in our system that you called two hours ago," the man's voice was growing worried. "You're saying that wasn't you?"

Thomas balled his fist and hit the plastic wall of the phone booth. *I'm too late.*

"Can you freeze the account?"

"It's showing me you zeroed out your account and closed it. There's nothing to freeze."

Thomas stood stone still as tidal waves of dark anger crashed over him. Betrayed. Stabbed. No, he would have preferred an actual knife stabbed into his back over this. Nathan not only stole from him but used him—he pretended to be him. The thought of Nathan copying his voice and lying through his teeth to the bank made Thomas feel gut sick.

"Sir?"

Thomas realized he was unresponsive, paralyzed in his rage.

"I'm going to go, thanks."

Thomas climbed back into his truck, put his head on the wheel, and swore he would stop at nothing until he found Nathan. If it was the last thing he ever did, Thomas promised himself he was going to find him.

28

WEALTH CHANGES PEOPLE. Nathan slept less than two hours that night. He read every word in every magazine, book, and brochure he could find in his room to keep his mind busy. It was only after two generous helpings of the complimentary bourbon that he calmed down enough to lay still.

At 6:30 a.m., he dressed in jeans and a t-shirt, and took a cab to the nearest computer store. He was the first customer in the door.

He spent just over $15,000 on the latest electronics equipment and paid the sales assistant to help him carry it all back to his room at The Charles. Time was critical. He had to get online.

Opened boxes and bags covered his bed. On the desk, he saw his reflection in three perfect new computer monitors. His large phone barely fit into his pocket and matched the sleek and scratchless watch on his wrist.

Time to work.

He logged into his online bank account for First Bank of Delorre. He shot to his feet and clapped his hands when he saw the account balance. $10,357,169.50. *It was all there.* He'd never had so much money before. He wished he could tell someone, but he was alone. *Stay focused.*

His dream to become an investor was literally at his fingertips. With a few clicks, he placed orders for checks, a debit card, and a credit card.

He called the court office. "Yes, I'd like to find out how I can change my legal name."

The person on the other line told him how.

"I need it to be faster than that. Is there anything I can do speed it up?"

The old voice on the other end of the line wheezed, "You can pay to expedite the process."

"Great, I'll do that."

After he hung up he found the court's website, filled out the forms, and printed them. For his new name, he wrote "John Shepherd."

29

"Do you know anything about Nathan Degland?"

Thomas was out of breath. Both of his hands were on the front desk for the City of Delorre Chamber of Commerce. The elderly lady behind desk put down the pencil and crossword puzzle in her hands and looked at Thomas, annoyed.

"Who?"

"Nathan Deglend. Have you heard anything about him?"

"Doesn't sound familiar."

"He's a young man, brown hair, blue eyes, tall and skinny…"

"Sir," she croaked. "You're aware there are hundreds of thousands of people in the City of Delorre. Sorry. Not ringing any bells."

Thomas thought for a moment. For Nathan to have made the bank transaction, he had to have gotten that safe open. Most likely, by a professional.

"Where is the closest locksmith to here?"

"Locksmith? If you go to our website—"

"No, I need a place, an actual place, with doors. Where you can actually go see a locksmith to open a safe. Do you know one?"

The lady compressed her lips at him. "There's a small shop a couple blocks away."

"What's the name?"

Another lady standing nearby, overheard the conversation and said, "Lockpoppers."

Thomas turned to her, "Where's that?"

"Go to that tall, golden building in the epicenter — the hotel called The Charles, then go down seven blocks. It'll be on your right. It's by a music store."

"You said The Charles?"

"Yep. It's a couple blocks away, just North of Alvin Park. You can't miss it."

Thomas's back was already to them. Thomas shouted thank you over his shoulder as he ran towards the door.

He moved fast. Nathan could be selling the farm at that very minute. The golden sky scraper was an acre's length away. He walked quickly. The smell of cooking sausage and warm engine exhaust filled his nostrils and brought back memories. Car horns honked and passers-by chattered on their mobile phones. He walked as fast as he could. *You're here to get Nathan.* He crossed the street and saw the ornate portico of The Charles. Just as he skipped onto the sidewalk, he stopped. Outside the large glass rotating doors, he saw a tall, well-dressed young man in a black suit lean over and hand a green dollar bill to a hairy homeless man sitting on a cardboard mat.

The young man looked like Nathan. Thomas hugged the shade of the trees as he walked closer, along the stone wall.

The debonaire man stepped towards a shiny black car as the driver opened the passenger door. Thomas bit his lip hard. *Was that Nathan?* He cursed his old eyes. His thief of a son could be right there, maybe thirty-five feet away. He watched who he thought was Nathan take a seat in the back of the car with tinted-windows. Thomas broke into a run and came out from the shadows. Ten feet away, the car shifted into gear and rolled forward. Thomas chased after it. He thought he saw the back of Nathan's head inside. He swung his fist to pound on the trunk top of the car and yelled at his rebellious son.

"Stop the car!"

He missed. The black car drove out of the pickup lane and turned right. Thomas stood in front of The Charles and watched the car disappear. His chest heaved as he clutched his arms over his head. *Was that him?*

30

Nathan quickly found he missed the people on the farm. What good was money without others to share it with? He missed chatting with Chester and discussing wine with Tim, even listening to Mary in the kitchen.

Not wasting any time, he looked up local events to find friends and make connections. Fortunately, he found The Charles was a popular venue for important events. That night, a wealthy senator was throwing a black and white party for his wife's birthday.

He showered, walked down the street, and found a barber and a tailor. The barber shaved his beard, revealing a sharp jawline, pronounced Adam's apple, and a long neck. The barber cut his hair to a cropped mop. He put product in it so that his brown hair glistened and he no longer looked like a man of the hill country. Never had he felt so dapper in his life.

He bought ten designer outfits, each between five and fifteen thousand dollars, plus the shoes and accent pieces to go with each. Three Christian Dior suits, one Dolce Gabbana, three Brooks Brothers, a Bespoke suit, and two others with European designer names.

"It's an investment," he told the man who helped him. He

had never worn clothes so soft and fitting. And expensive. The fabric felt like a smooth and flexible suit of armor. He bought red ties, blue ties, gold ties, watches, cufflinks, dress shoes, silk socks, leather belts, and more dress shirts than he could carry.

He was a new man. The farmer molted off, replaced with a sleek, professional businessman.

31

"**He never disappoints**," whispered the fancy, elderly lady with more pearls than teeth. She stood in front of Nathan with her date, waiting in line at the door of The Charles ballroom. Nathan chose to wear his new black Christian Dior suit, Vuitton shoes, and a silver Rolex. Live music poured out of the double door entrance. After a security check, he found "John Shepherd" on the seating chart and an attendant brought him to his table.

He entered the large, dark room. Flashing lights above a stage glittered hundreds of feet ahead. Round tables full of cocktail-drinking executives, politicians, and celebrities filled the room. A seafood buffet lined both sides of the ballroom. The largest white tiered cake he had ever seen towered in the corner. Well-dressed servers offered food and drinks on silver platters around the room to guests, who were all chattering above the live music. Nathan moved slowly and observantly. *I fit right in*, he repeated to himself over and over. *I fit right in*.

At his table sat a couple who looked like siblings. The man's black hair was slicked back and the skin of his thick neck spilled over his shirt collar. Also with straight black hair, the woman wore bright red lipstick and her eyes blinked red under generous layers of dark mascara. They were in their late thirties.

"Hello" Nathan greeted them. "I'm N—" he caught himself. "John. John Shepherd."

"What, did you forget your own name?" said the corpulent man in a strong New York accent. He laughed. "One of those days? I'm Tommy."

Nathan said, "Just going through big adjustments right now. Nice to meet you, Tommy. And–"

"Angeline," the woman said, also a New Yorker. When she spoke, she stretched out the syllables of her name like she was pulling bubble gum from her teeth.

"Angeline." Nathan said, taking his seat.

"So where are you both from?" he asked them. He smiled. He was thankful to be with people again.

Tommy said, "Here. We both grew up here. Been here all our lives."

"So, for what, twenty-five years?" Nathan jested.

Tommy said, "That's usually what I say before I dance naked around a pole."

"We're friends," said Angeline and winked at Tommy.

"What do you do?" asked Nathan.

"I'm a political consultant with Fortune Polls and a city commissioner," said Tommy, "I drink beer for a living." His belly jiggled as he giggled to himself.

"I'm a commercial realtor," said Angeline, "With K. M. Fern across the street."

Nathan was fascinated. "Do you like your jobs?"

"I do," said Tommy, "I deal with people, day-in-and-day-out." He chuckled. "People are like sheep. They just follow the leader as long as nobody gets hurt."

"Nobody knows what he does," said Angeline.

Tommy brayed his yellow teeth. "I don't even know. But it's important." He took two bronze-colored beers off of a waiter's platter. "I swear I make things happen."

"Everything he says is a lie," said Angeline. Her voice sounded like a well-articulated moan. "Tommy is a very good person to know. He's connected me with dozens of clients."

She slid her arm across the man's rounded back. "For which I am ever so grateful." They exchanged sultry glances.

"I've met a realtor before," said Nathan, interrupting, "Seems like it could be an interesting job."

"It's not bad, really," she said. "If anyone truly wants to be successful, they need some sort of income-generating real estate in their portfolio. I'm serious. No billionaires are made without it." She threw her hair back portentously.

"I believe you," Nathan agreed. This was no news to him. He had studied the billionaires of the world and read plenty of books about real estate investment strategies.

Angeline finished the red wine in her glass. "What about you? What's your story?"

"I just moved here from Sanctilly a few days ago."

"Isn't that the place where there are more cows than people?" Tommy said. "This must be different for you."

"There's definitely more things to do around here." Nathan joked, "I'm very excited to not watch grass grow."

"Where are you living?" asked Tommy.

Nathan pointed at the ceiling. "Right here, actually."

"At The Charles?" They both said.

"That's right." He heard the surprise in their voices. He reached for a colorful, fruity drink.

"What are you looking to do?" Angeline asked, more interested.

"I'd like to learn more about the city and the market, and eventually set up some investments."

She pulled a business card out of her purse and pressed it onto the table. "Give me a call sometime. I think I can help you. Let's chat."

Tommy grinned. "Sounds like you've got some money, bud," he said, stuffing buttered lobster meat into his mouth.

"I have a little," said Nathan.

"But do you have a plan?" Angeline questioned.

"I'm working on it," he said lightly, "I just got here. I'm not trying to rush into anything. I've done some research online. Have either of you heard of Venture X?"

They turned to each other at the same time.

"Venture X?" Their eyes were wide. Tommy stopped eating. Angeline put her wine glass down.

"Yes," he said, noticing their reaction. "Do you know of it?"

"It's the wealthiest investment group in the city. They own half of what you see on the street," said Angeline. "What is your interest in Venture X?"

She was very interested at this point.

"I don't know," said Nathan. "I just wanted to have a conversation with them and explore possibilities."

Tommy leaned over to him, "Kid, you're lucky. I happen to know a couple of 'em."

Nathan said, "Oh, really? I'd like to know."

He said, "Yeah, so would the rest of the world." He leaned back up and cracked a crab leg and drenched the meat in butter sauce.

"You don't have to tell me. I don't need to know right now," Nathan said.

Tommy's lower lip extended beyond the rest of his face as he chewed. He pointed the crab leg at Nathan.

"You're smart. I like you. Let's do a trade."

"Okay..." said Nathan.

"I'll introduce you to the Venture X members here if you tell me how much money you brought with you to the city."

"They're here?" Nathan asked eagerly. "In this room? Right now?"

"Maybe," said Tommy. Angeline nodded.

I shouldn't tell them, Nathan thought. They were nice people but he didn't know them. Money should never be talked about too specifically. *Father never talked about money.* But at that moment, the cocktail in his hand wasn't helping. He shrugged. *I'm at a party. Might as well have some fun.*

"Thirty," he said. He hadn't considered how much of his father's money he'd invest but a little bluff would hurt.

Tommy's face twisted, "Thousand?"

"Million." Nathan tried to keep his face serious.

Tommy's face smoothed out. "No, come on."

Nathan said nothing, importantly. He drank the cocktail.

Tommy and Angeline stared at him. "There it is," Tommy said. "There he is." He smiled so Nathan could see his yellow teeth again. He looked at Nathan as if he grew two feet taller.

"Come with me," he said, standing up.

"Where are you going?" Nathan asked.

He was already weaving through the crowd. Nathan followed him to the front of the room closer to the band. Tommy stopped and grabbed his arm.

"If you wanna play ball with these guys, you gotta talk so that they listen. Make every word count."

Nathan nodded and they kept moving through the chattering throng of suits and dresses. The air was stuffy with strong scents, he thought it was alcohol and something musky. He led him to a table where eight men in black suits were sitting in silence, watching the band.

Tommy crouched low and taking wide steps like a cowboy, approached one of the gentlemen from five feet away. Then he yelled, "George!"

The mature gentleman with stiff white hair and an all black suit scowled at Tommy.

"George, you ol' rascal! Let me introduce you to someone.

This here is John Shepherd. He's new to town and he has $30 million he wants to invest. I thought you two should talk."

Nathan's mouth dropped. *Are you kidding me?* He looked angrily at Tommy for spilling his secret so soon, and right in front of him. He closed his mouth and cleared his head.

"Pleasure," Nathan said and extended his right hand.

The elderly man slowly brought his arm out from under the table revealing a white-gloved hand. They shook

"George Pendleton," he said. His voice was raspy and Nathan thought he heard a subtle British accent.

He continued. "Where are you from?"

"The country. I own a large amount of real estate about five hours West."

George nodded. "Is that close to Sanctilly?"

Nathan said, "Yes, sir."

He said, "I knew a farmer out there. His name was Thomas Degland. You know him?"

This caught Nathan off guard. *How did he know Father?* Nathan thought quickly.

"No, but I know exactly where that is."

"Fine, you remind me of him, actually," George scratched his chin. "Thirty million, yes?"

"Yes."

George looked at the other men around the table who had shifted to lean forward. Receiving several short nods, he tilted his head, signaling Nathan to come closer.

He bent down to listen. He whispered in his ear, "Let's meet." Nathan felt a business card slip into his hand from another man behind him. He looked at it.

"Go to the address here on the 23rd." George nodded. "Nice to meet you, Mr. Shepherd."

Nathan gave nods goodbye to everyone at the table and received nods in return.

Returning to his table, he found Tommy and Angeline staring at him.

"So?" Angeline said.

He shrugged. "What day is it?"

"It's the 2nd."

"I've got a meeting on the 23rd."

"What! You got a meeting with Venture X?" They were incredulous.

Nathan shrugged it off. It was rather serendipitous. Tommy put his arm around Nathan's shoulders. "Cheers!"

They raised their glasses.

"Money makes the world go 'round," said Tommy. "To our new friend John, the millionaire from the country." Turning to him, he said, "You'll go far."

They drank long into the night, round after round. Surrendered to his newfound freedom, Nathan had plenty of reasons to celebrate. In less than an hour, he was on the dance floor, swirling in the sea of silk and skin.

At the end of the night, Tommy and Angeline helped him back to his room after the party. He felt dozens of business cards in his pants pocket.

"This is nothing like the farm," he mumbled to them, collapsing on the bed. "Would you like a drink?"

They laughed. "You had a good time tonight," Angeline said. "Get some rest."

Tommy patted Nathan's foot. "Welcome to the city, bub."

32

"Man, back already," said Dwayne, rubbing his eyes as a man marched down the main hall of his business. The scruffy farmer in front of him reminded him of someone but he couldn't place the memory.

Dwayne realized his error when Thomas walked into the light. "Wait, wrong guy."

Big bags hung heavily from Thomas's eyes. In his unkempt work clothes, he looked like he just walked in off the street. Thomas spoke gruffly.

"Listen, did anyone come in here with an old Sargent safe recently?"

"Yes, actually. Yesterday a fella very similar to yourself was just in here with an old Sargent."

"What did you do with it? Where did he go?"

"Hold on a minute," Dwayne held up his palm. "Sit down, will ya? Grab a chair and some coffee. You look like you could use some."

Thomas sat down, remembered his manners, and gratefully accepted a cup of coffee.

Dwayne sat back in his chair. "It appears you're interested in knowing more about the young man with the old safe."

"I don't have a lot of time," Thomas said. "Did you break

into the safe?"

"We cracked that puppy off with some liquid nitrogen," Dwayne swung his arms like a baseball bat. "Easy job."

Thomas closed his eyes and let out a focused sigh to quell the impatience rising inside him.

"I can tell you're wanting some information on this guy," said Dwayne. "What's it worth to you?"

Thomas took out a checkbook and poised a pen in his big hand. "I'll pay you $500 if you tell me where he is right now."

Dwayne grinned. "He asked which direction The Charles was in. I told him it was seven blocks up the street. Seeing his face when he saw the contents of the safe, my guess is that he's staying there."

Thomas stared at the locksmith. *The young man who drove off in the back seat of the black car in front of The Charles... That was Nathan.*

33

"BREAKFAST!"

THE NEXT day Nathan woke up to knocks on the door. He staggered out of his bed, half-asleep. He held his splintering head. *What a night.* He opened the door to a slender brown-haired girl with a hotel uniform on. She handed him a tray with an egg and bacon breakfast and a newspaper. He said thank you.

"Coffee?" She asked with a clear voice.

"Please," he said thankfully, turning to put the tray on the table of his room. She followed him in. Even with his eyes half-shut, he could tell she was looking at him a lot.

She poured the coffee. Her hand shook. He rubbed his eyes.

"Everything okay?" he asked.

"You're in the paper," she said. "And on TV."

"What?"

She said, "Forgive me, but I saw you in the paper and on the news."

Nathan grabbed the paper. In the gossip corner of the front page, there was a black and white picture of him leaning into the man from Venture X last night. The headline read *'Watch Out' Says Country Millionaire.*

His hands went cold. *Oh god.* "Was this from last night? At the party?"

"I believe it was."

He read the title. "*Watch out?* I never said that."

"Apparently, that's not all you said," she said, pointing to the paper. He flipped to the full story. Scanning the article, he found more quotes he had no recollection of saying.

The article said he was a wealthy businessman from a huge country estate and was ready to 'take the city by storm.'

"This is completely exaggerated," he said.

He picked up the stack of business cards on the clothes bureau and found Tommy's. He dialed dialed the number.

"Tommy?"

"Hey, it's the Country Millionaire!" he said too loudly for the morning.

"What happened last night?"

"You opened your big mouth and let the world know who you are. You're here to do business, brother!"

"I understand I spoke to a number of people last night but I never said anything like what this article is saying I did."

"Could've had me fooled, man. You were gabbin' away all night."

"What do you mean? How did this happen?" Nathan said, concerned.

"The press crawls those parties," Tommy explained. "Because they know it's gossip central. Everybody who's anybody is there. And stuff happens."

"A lot of this is wrong," Nathan said, looking at the newspaper in his hand.

"You were laying it on thick, my friend. Everyone wanted to buy you a drink. Not a bad plan, if you ask me."

Reading the article, he took a sip of the coffee. Four paragraphs in, the article wrote he had $120 million to invest. He choked and almost spit out the coffee.

"No!" He yelled, startling the girl who still stood in the room. She caught herself staring, and straightened up the bar.

"Tommy, I gotta go." He hung up the phone and shook his head. *What a mess. I don't have $120 million.* He sat on the edge of the bed and held his throbbing head. The girl poured him a glass of water and handed him a pill.

"I assume it's aspirin," he said. She nodded.

"What's your name?"

"Beth Jacobs. You're John Shepherd, right?"

"I'm in deep trouble, that's who I am," he said. "Yes, I'm John."

"Why are you in trouble?" she asked.

He paused. *Do I tell her the truth? Who could she tell?* He decided against it.

"I'm just not ready for this much attention yet."

She sat down on the bed across from him and said, "A little attention never hurt anyone. Besides, you seem like a nice enough guy."

In his slumber, he hadn't noticed her emerald green eyes sparkling underneath her dark eyebrows, which contrasted with her tan skin. Her long hair flowed into a bun behind her ears. Her thin frame was strong, her tight uniform accenting a well-featured body, as far as he could tell.

Noticing, she asked, "Have you been to Brew Social down the street?"

She got up and brushed passed him. "I go there on my way home after work," she smiled. "I get off at 4:30."

She left. Nathan still smelled her sweet perfume. He sensed something with the girl. *What was her name?* He had never had a girlfriend before, even less, been on a date. The farm was such a sterile place when it came to relationships. *I'm not at the farm anymore*, he reminded himself. She was pretty. *Why not have some fun?*

34

He decided to go early. At 3:00 p.m., he left The Charles with his laptop. The coffee shop was large and open, with dark colored walls, and burnished wood. The sound of smooth jazz music and the smell of roasted coffee beans filled the shop. People sat, mostly in twos, at tables and talked with chipped white mugs in their hands. Some were on computers, some read the paper. It was busy enough to sustain an energetic atmosphere but not too crowded. He ordered an americano and found a table in the corner.

One woman came up to him and sat down where Beth was going to sit. She was shaped like a former athlete, with short, spiky blonde hair and held a notepad and pen.

"Excuse me," he said. "I was saving that seat."

She said, "Sorry to bother you, Mr. Shepherd, I just read the article about you in the Times."

Nathan rolled his eyes and said, "What about it?"

"I'm a reporter for the *Delorre Daily*. I write about money, powerful people, city life, and the occasional wine review," she said. "I'm writing an article about you and I'd love for you to answer a couple questions for me."

He looked at his watch. Beth was going to be there in five minutes. He had never been interviewed before. He couldn't risk anyone at the farm finding out.

"I'll answer one question but no pictures."

She smiled and blinked rapidly. "Challenge accepted. One question it is!"

She flipped open her notepad, poised her pen, and asked, "What was it like receiving special attention from the founder of Venture X?"

The question caught him off guard. *Does everyone know?*

"You should ask him that question yourself," he said.

She smiled again, pinching her cheeks.

Begrudgingly, Nathan told her, "I was glad to have made their acquaintance and I look forward to exploring potential relationships and opportunities with the members of Venture X in the future."

She scribbled furiously.

"What's your favorite wine?"

He lowered his chin to reprimand, but answered nonetheless.

"I'll answer only because you've found my weak spot," he said. "A dry sherry from a Palomino grape, extra oxidized and paired with olives."

Mouth open, she blinked fives times rapidly and then remembered to write. Something caught his eye behind the woman. Outside, he saw her straight brown hair flow down between her bare shoulders as she walked towards the entrance.

"Alright," he interrupted the blonde writer. "You must go. My friend is here."

"Thank you, Mr. Shepherd." She got up. "Nice to meet you."

Nathan grinned politely, but it was more like a grimace.

Beth strode in the front door and spotted him in the corner. She wore gladiator sandals, tight dark jeans, a cream tank top, and sunglasses. The way her hips moved reminded him of a smooth and confident lioness. Her arms were lean and thin and her tanktop held her body tightly.

She sat down across from him by the fireplace.

"The fireplace is nice, isn't?" she said with a smile.

"It is if you're cold," he said smiling back. "Can I get you a coffee?"

"Sure," she said. "Large iced, with cream, sugar, and almond flavor."

"My pleasure," he said, getting up to place the order. He rubbed his eyes. Out of her hotel uniform, *she looked... different.* He returned to find her sitting with her legs crossed, leaning forward slightly, just enough for her tank top to swoop low in front. He swallowed, sat, and smiled.

"How do you like working at the hotel?" he asked.

"Fine," she answered. "I do it only because I have to. If I didn't have bills, I wouldn't be there at all."

"What would you do?" he asked.

"Something with art. Anything, actually. I love to paint, sculpt, draw, write... I'd probably go back to school to become a screenwriter."

"A screenwriter? That's interesting," Nathan said. *She isn't like girls out on the farm.*

"How long have you been working at The Charles?"

"Too long. Three years next month."

"We'll have to celebrate," he said, hiding a smile behind his coffee mug.

"Celebrating is for good things," she corrected him.

"It'll be a small celebration then. I'll host."

She rolled her eyes. "Did you enjoy the party? Seems like you did."

Nathan laughed and glanced uncomfortably over where the reporter was sitting. She was studying them. He shifted in his chair.

"It was a good time. I met some friends and made a few good

connections."

"I'm sure you did, Mr. Country Millionaire." She lowered her chin.

"Tell me about yourself," Nathan said, changing the subject.

"I like to cook at home. I like running and I read and write a lot, nothing special."

Nathan listened very intently.

She continued, "Especially mystery novels. You remind me of one of the characters I'm reading about right now, actually." She looked at his eyes and then at his mouth. "He arrived in a big city to look for his uncle but ends up falling in love with somebody else's wife."

"Oh, no. Are you married?" Nathan asked feigning concern.

A small smile crept onto her face. "Anyways, what brings you to the city?"

"Business," he said. She rolled her eyes.

"Boring!"

"Boring?" She was forthright and open. She spoke confidently and clearly and peppered her words with sarcasm. Nathan marveled.

She said her father was a rich businessman who divorced her mother when she was ten years old. She didn't know where either of them were. She thought her father was somewhere in the city still, and her mom remarried and moved out of the country. In order to become a screenwriter, she knew she needed formal schooling. She was four years older than him, poor, and tired of dating snobs. She said she hated money, hated politics, and hated normal people.

"Normal people are boring," she said. "Weird people are interesting because at least they're passionate about something."

They talked until the late evening, and after three cups of coffee, she gave him her number and address. He walked her out of the coffee shop and she stood on her toes to hug him.

Her hair enveloped his nose, a smell so naturally sweet and mapley his feet tingled. They said goodbye.

That night in his room, he couldn't get her out of his head. Emotions galloped like horses from his brain to his chest and back. He needed to know her more. *Was she married? What did she see in him? What did he see in her?* It was like a hunger or a craving that couldn't be satisfied until he was with her again. Perhaps it was the coffee, but he couldn't sleep. He paced his room. *Who was she?*

That night, he wrote in his journal he had met a mysterious, disarmingly beautiful woman named Beth Jacobs.

35

The front desk attendant at The Charles had no idea who "Nathan Degland" was, nor who this old countryman standing before him was. But Thomas persisted.

"I know he's staying here. I saw him with my own eyes."

"If you know he's here, then you must have his phone number," said the snooty man. "Call him."

"I don't have a phone, and I don't think he has one either," Thomas's patience wore thin. "Can you tell me what room he's staying in, please?"

"I told you. We don't have a "Nathan Degland" staying with us at this time."

Thomas's eyes burned at the whippersnapper. "Can you please try to be helpful?"

"How can I be helpful when I have no idea who you're talking about?"

Thomas gave up. "May I use your phone?"

The man directed him to the business center to the left. Thomas rang home and told Paul he'll be staying longer than he expected. Then he made a call to meet an old friend in town.

36

Every Saturday morning Beth and her friend Anna ran the river trail. Anna was an assistant physical therapist who moved to Delorre from Venezuela. At 7:00 a.m., dressed in running outfits, they met at Portside and stretched before beginning the seven-mile loop.

"I bought a new TV for my den so hopefully Brian will actually stay over now," Anna said. She had been dating her boyfriend for two years. Beth wasn't listening.

Anna chatted on, "It's a fifty-four inch screen. It's big. Do you think I should get a game system? Maybe he'll be okay without it. I'll never use it. I don't even li–"

She noticed Beth's serene and smiling face.

"Beth. Are you even listening to me?"

"No, I'm not."

Flustered, Anna said, "Why not?"

"I don't know," said Beth. She was deep in thought.

"Beth, tell me what's going on with you. Something is going on. I can't tell what it is. Did something happen to you?"

Beth pressed her arm against her chest, to stretch her shoulder. "I suppose something did," she smiled.

"Out with it," Anna demanded. "Tell me this instant."

"I met someone." Beth kicked her knees up. "Let's go."

"Met someone?!" Anna said. They began jogging.

Anna was incredulous. "I thought you were done with men after Carter. All of them." She raised the tone of her voice to mimic what Beth had once said. "Men are proof that life is pain."

Beth laughed. "I know, I know. But Anna, this one is different."

"Oh, is he now? Who is he?"

"You probably read about him. He is the new investor guy from the country—the one staying at my hotel."

"The Country Millionaire?" asked Anna.

Beth said nothing.

"John Shepherd?"

Beth still said nothing. Anna shrieked. "Are you–? He can't— You must–" She had trouble getting words out.

"Why don't you hush and I'll just tell you about him?"

"Okay," Anna said, breathless.

"He's tall," Beth began. "He smiles easily. He has broad shoulders and a thin waist. Trimmed brown hair. He has big lips."

They glanced at each other and laughed.

Beth continued, "When he looks at you, you feel like he knows you and at the same time you feel safe. He has kind eyes."

She paused. "He said his mother died and his father and brother live on the family farm out in Sanctilly. He's come to the city to be an investor. He wants to help people."

For the first time in her life, Anna listened.

Sweat beaded on her forehead as Beth continued. "He strikes up conversation and he doesn't talk about himself too much. He speaks well."

Beth struggled to keep the running pace. The words flowed out of her.

"His voice is always excited. His words are slow but each one is full with life. When he speaks, heads turn to see what is so exciting. He engages."

"It sounds like you're already living together," Anna said.

"We met at Brew Social. We talked for hours. I got more excited the more I talked to him."

"Beth!" Anna cried.

"I know I sound like I'm crazy."

"What are you going to do?"

"We're hanging out again on Tuesday night. He's coming over to my place."

37

H<small>E CHECKED THE</small> time. *6:32 p.m. Oh no, I'm late.* He threw himself into his walk-in closet, amazed at how fast the time went on the computer. He threw on a collared shirt, dark jeans, fresh socks, and leather shoes. Grabbing the cologne, he sprayed it on his neck. The scent smelled like sweet oranges. *Hopefully she'll like it.*

Beth's condo was three blocks away. He fumbled with his phone as he shot through the hotel doors, "Hey Beth, it's John. I'm on my way."

She replied, "Hello, handsome."

She opened the door and he almost fell over when he saw her. She was in a tight strapless black dress that stopped above her knees, revealing the sculpted muscles in her legs. Her neck and arms were toned. Her hair was up and she had dangling silver earrings on.

"You look... stunning," he said.

She flashed a humble smile. He had the feeling she didn't dress up very often. This was special. She gave him a hug hello. He held her for a split second too long.

She led him into the kitchen. Narrow enough for two people to stand side by side, the kitchen counters were shaped in a U, with overhanging white cupboards and plenty of dark countertop space.

Beth said, "Would you like some wine?"

"Yes, please."

She had prepared a roasted garlic lemon chicken, with rice and asparagus. He sat down at the dinner table and she lit two candles. He'd never been in such an intimate setting before. He took a hearty a gulp of wine.

"So we talked about passion last time. How do incorporate your passion into your art, Beth?"

She smiled. "That's a good question. I don't really think about it. It just comes out. If I'm in a good mood, the colors are more vibrant and bright. If I'm in a bad mood, I use a lot of grays and blacks."

"Makes sense. What's your favorite color?

"I really like red. It's a sign of life and meaning. It grabs people's attention. What's yours?"

"I don't have one. What is your–"

"My turn." Beth cut him off and bit her tongue in between her front teeth. "What do you like to do for fun?"

Her lips moved smoothly around her words. He couldn't look away from her mouth. She sipped her wine.

"I, uh, I like wine," he said.

"I couldn't tell," she said wryly, as she refilled his empty wine glass. Nathan slid the hot tender chicken off his fork into his mouth. He'd never been on a date before, not like this. He had talked with other girls when he was in school, but he was too focused on grades. No one had caught his eye.

'A good woman makes you sit straight up in your chair,' his mother had always said. Nathan never knew what that meant until now. He could feel his back muscles rigid and tight. *Relax, come on. She's just a housekeeper.*

After she had finished pouring, he picked up the wine glass by the stem. He sloshed it around the glass and put his nose over it. He said, "This wine is from 2005, it's a domestic, Napa Valley, no—Sonoma."

He smelled it. "Dark cherries, grapefruit, this is clearly a blend..." He took a sip, "It's a big wine, fruity with a dark spice, maybe some ginger, too. We shouldn't be drinking this yet. It's a dessert wine."

Beth was holding the bottle in her hand. She stared at the label. Then she roared with laughter. Nathan laughed, too. *Thank you, Tim Bjorn.*

With her head back and her neck flexed, he couldn't help notice her pronounced collar bone and the curved frame adorned by her dress. She was devilishly attractive.

After dinner, they opened another bottle of wine and sat on the couch. They flirted. Then, she offered him a cigarette.

He had never smoked before, but he agreed. They got up and went to the back patio. *Remember, you can do whatever you want now.*

He took the white tube of tobacco in his fingers and leaned into Beth's lighter. He puckered his lips like a fish.

"Is this how you do it?" he asked.

Beth giggled. "Yes, now just try a small one."

He breathed in. The hot smoke scorched his throat and he instantly coughed. Beth laughed as she blew smoke from her own lips.

He tried again, this time with a smaller cough, he managed to inhale the thick fumes. His head felt light, as if a stack of imaginary bricks were lifted off the top of his head. He exhaled the smoke and coughed.

His lungs felt dirty, and his mouth tasted like sour tar. He took a sip of wine. Beth watched him, enjoying the whole thing.

"So how long have you been smoking?" he asked. He took another draw. It burned his esophagus and the smoke tingled in his chest.

"I don't smoke often at all. Just on special nights." She bumped his hips with hers.

His insides buzzed with sensual tension. His brain felt open, more spacious. The cigarette lifted inhibitions and gave him a sense of unruly freedom.

One cigarette led to two, which led to a third. Their conversation deepened and became more intimate. She said she was married before but went through a divorce after her ex-husband Carter left her for another woman. Anger flickered up in Nathan to hear that she had already been with another man. He hated him, whoever he was. No man deserved this woman.

They finished the second bottle of wine. She said she took up art and smoking to cope with the pain.

Midnight came faster than he wanted but he couldn't leave. After two bottles of wine, they reached a vulnerable place with each other.

"I'm afraid of not doing anything significant," he said. "That's why I left the farm. I want to do something great, something big. Something that changes people's lives. Where people look up to me and listen to me and I can help them."

He was a dreamer, she thought. *So innocent. So pure.* It had been so long for her. They sat close on the same couch, speaking almost in whispers. He looked at his watch and said emptily he probably should go. He didn't want to go. Not at all.

"Don't go," She said as her hand slid across the couch and found his. His heart tripled its pace. He knew there was no place he would rather be.

"But it's getting late," he said. "I don't want to keep you up too late."

"Trust me," she said, "I'm a night owl. Plus, I'm not working tomorrow." She winked as she scooted her hips closer.

"Honestly," he said. "I wouldn't mind staying..."

"...until morning?" She cut him off and kissed him. Excitement flooded over him. He felt her body press into him through her lips. She pushed into him. Her lips were wet and large and moved his up and down. Mentally blinded, his fumbling hands found their way around her waist. He pulled her off.

"Wait," he said, gasping. *What am I doing?* She breathed heavily, her chest heaving, her face inches from his. Her long dark eyelashes blinked slowly around her beautiful emerald eyes. Her eyes didn't open all the way. Her eyelids paused halfway up, giving her a dreamy, sleepy look that said *take me.* That was it. No more holding back. He pulled her hips on top of him and kissed her neck.

38

"Never?"

"Never, I promise," Nathan said earnestly, sipping from a coffee mug at Beth's kitchen table. He wore the same clothes from the night before.

"I don't believe you," said Beth, surprised. She wore a purple nightgown while cooking eggs and bacon on the stove.

"I don't know what to tell you," he said. "It's true. I've never done anything like that before."

She brought him a plate of breakfast and kissed him. "Well, you had me fooled."

Nathan chuckled. "It wasn't that hard. I just did as I was told." He winked.

Beth sat down across from him and smiled sheepishly.

He said, "Want to go for a drive?"

"Do you have a car?"

"What kind should I get?"

Beth sipped her coffee trying not to smile.

"I don't care. You don't need a car in the city."

"Okay, I'll rent one. Let's have some fun."

In a black convertible BMW M6, Nathan and Beth drove through the streets of Delorre. On the main roads, they whizzed past highrise apartments sitting on top of retail shops, delis, and laundromats. Street vendors sold ethnic food, scarves, books, and umbrellas on the street corners in downtown. The black car drove along the Stein River which flowed through the west side of the city and pooled in a basin called Portside. The pair stopped for lunch at Portside Harbor, a scenic port with docks, yachts, and riverside restaurants.

They sat around a circular table outside a French cafe on the boardwalk. He looked around. "There is so much to do in the city."

Beth sipped a mint mimosa.

Nathan continued, "I think we passed an Ethiopian store, an Afghanistan buffet, and Greek diner—all on one block."

Beth looked across the water. She had lived there for so long, it was all the same to her. But it was interesting to hear a newcomer's point of view.

"It's nothing like the farm," finished Nathan.

"What was the farm like?" asked Beth.

"Miserable. Picture doing the same thing over and over again for your entire life. Sitting on a tractor for hours and hours everyday. The inescapable smell of manure. Milking smelly cows, feeding animals, and cleaning eternally."

"It must have been beautiful," said Beth, thinking about painting.

"Nothing like this place."

He finished his gin and tonic.

"I like it here."

Beth saw hope and innocence in his eyes, two things she wished she still had.

"Good." She put a hand on his.

After lunch, Nathan dropped her off at her condo and returned the car.

On his way home, three blocks down from The Charles, Nathan found Alvin Park, a public square with a concrete amphitheater, water fountain, and tables with chess boards around the perimeter in the shade of the trees.

He saw a table with a middle-aged African American man who wore square sunglasses and a red baseball cap.

"Up for a game?" asked Nathan.

"You bet, mate," the man smiled with shining white teeth and extended his hand as Nathan sat down.

"Murphy." He spoke with a thick South African accent.

"John. Nice to meet you."

"Likewise."

They set up to play, Murphy asked casually, "So where are you from?"

"From the country. I just moved here a month ago."

"Oh, no kidding?"

"I live right there." He pointed to the gold building that towered over its neighbors.

"The Charles? What do you think of it so far?" The game began. Nathan advanced his center pawn.

"It's a fun place. I like being right in the middle of everything. There are lots of events and parties, just about every night.

The man laughed. "Sounds about right. Have you heard of Launch Pad?

"Launch Pad," Nathan repeated. Tommy had mentioned it. "What is it?"

"It's a group for new people in town. People introduce newbies to all the different places around town. It's a sort of game—if someone can introduce newcomers to a place they've never been before, they have to buy the group drinks for the rest of the night."

Nathan flexed his chin. "Sounds expensive." He jumped his knight into his opponent's knight. The man was not very good.

Murphy smiled and his brilliant teeth lit up his dark wrinkled face. "It's a grand old time, if you can afford it."

"I don't know if I can."

Nathan beat him in twelve moves.

That weekend, he took Beth to Don Chino's, the pizzeria Franco the charter van driver recommended to Nathan. They ordered a cheese pie and sat down at a booth with fresh cola from the fountain machine.

"So what are you planning on doing," she asked him, "now that you're getting settled in?"

"I've got an important meeting coming up in a few days with a venture capital firm. I'm looking to join as an investor and get into some great businesses."

"I mean besides work. That's all everyone cares about here—work, career, goals, money. There's more to life than your career and money."

He didn't realize it at first, but she reminded him of his mother. Beth had the same mysterious determination Abby had before her sickness. They both were sharp, able to cut to the point in a second with a harsh word, but restrained by a will to be kind.

"I don't know... I know I want to keep meeting people. I can see how valuable it is, the more people you have in your network..."

Beth's plump lips were a flat line. She didn't care about his money. He liked this about her. He changed his tone.

"...maybe get into some painting?" He grinned. He knew she loved to paint. His light eyes sparkled.

"I could help you with that," she said playfully.

"I want you to teach me," he said. He slid his foot up her calf to her knee.

"I'd love to," she said, protruding her tongue out of her mouth noticeably when she pronounced the "l" in love. She clenched his foot between her legs.

The pizza arrived at their table. Nathan looked up at the server.

"Would you mind if we got a box to go? We've got to run. I'll give you a big tip." He looked at Beth through the corner of his eyes. She bit her lip.

They boxed up the untouched pizza and hurried back to The Charles. In the elevator, he put his arm around her, the pizza box in one hand, the other hand around her thin waist.

Between kisses, he asked, "Can you stay the night?"

"I can stay the week," she said, breathing heavily.

The elevator doors opened and another couple entered the elevator. Nathan pushed off of her, still holding the pizza box in his hand, and faced the interrupters.

"Pizza slice?"

Beth giggled. The elevator was quiet. On the 40th floor, they rushed down the hallway and into Nathan's room.

He lifted her onto the bed. He had never fallen in love with someone before. She unbuttoned his oxford shirt. There was something supernatural about it. He laid her gently on her back on the bed but she rolled on top of him. She taught him mind-blowing things on and off the bed. Their mouths never left each other as they fell onto the floor. They laughed. She was the only one who knew him this way, not as some Country Millionaire. But she still didn't know the truth. *No one will know. It's my secret.*

39

A week later on the day of the meeting with Venture X, he awoke up with a stress headache. He had drank too much the night before. *Again.* The hotel had had another party last night. Tommy and Angeline met him and they had a great time.

He rolled off the bed and picked up the paper from the floor in front of his door. He turned to the events page. There he was. *Country Millionaire Pledges $200k to Charity.*

He loved the attention he got from everyone he met. People looked at him with a twinge of awe in their eyes when he shook their hands. The city was getting used to his reputation. *I am getting used to his reputation.*

It all didn't feel quite right. He was a nobody from a farm who never had money or even Internet access. Now, he's a rich millionaire with expensive suits, the latest technology, drinking scotch at parties with hundreds of people and staying in the most opulent hotel in the city.

He flipped to the financial section.

Stay focused. You've got this meeting tonight. It was an important step in his plan. *So far, it's been good, right? Life is good. Come on. Right now, you've got Beth, a boatload of money, a positive reputation, and some friends. Just stay focused and get ready for tonight's meeting with Venture X.*

He walked to the bathroom to take a shower but it was locked. He tried again. Then he heard a man groan.

Whipping around, behind him, he saw a body lying on the floor on the window side of the other king bed. Blinking the sleep from his eyes, he looked closer, and recognized who it was. Face down, Tommy lay fast asleep. *What is he doing here?* Tommy groaned again when Nathan dug his heel into his back.

"Get up, Tommy," he said.

He heard the toilet flush and Angeline came out of the bathroom.

"What are you guys doing here?" Nathan said.

"Good morning to you, too, grumpy," she said in her smooth deep voice. She seemed chipper, but Nathan was confused.

He said, "Seriously, when did you get into my room?"

"We slept here, silly," she said.

"I didn't know that," he said.

"You kept buying us drinks last night during Launch Pad, how were we supposed to leave?" she asked.

"You mean you just used my tab," he shot back.

"You did!" She said. "And you bought that poor girl you were dancing with way too many drinks."

"What girl?"

"The blonde in the frilly red dress and heels."

"I don't remember."

"You don't remember? She spent the night here, too, honey. Left earlier this morning."

Nathan looked up at her and buried his eyes in his brows. "What do you mean she spent the night here?" He looked at the clock. 10:34 a.m.

"Goodness, you really don't remember anything," she said. "Yep," she let out an toothy exhale, "She slept with you. I didn't want to disturb you, especially when you were doing that one thing," she pretended to grab her neck, "and Tommy just passed out on the floor."

Nathan exploded. "Alright, get out!" He pointed at the door. "Get out, both of you," He kicked Tommy.

"What's wrong with you, John?" Angeline said.

Too much blood burst through the small dehydrated veins in his brain. Panic gripped his lungs. *Beth brings me breakfast at 9 a.m. The breakfast tray is right here.* A thought sent a shiver down his back. *Did she see the girl?*

"What time did the girl leave?" he asked, his voice elevated.

Angeline was upset. "I don't know exactly. Maybe around 9 a.m."

"God dammit!" Nathan shouted. He tried not to swear but it ripped right out of him. Adrenaline squeezed his stomach. *What if Beth saw us? What was I thinking? I don't even remember this girl. What did Beth see?* He knew he had drank too much.

Tommy finally got himself up to his feet. He croaked, "What's your deal, man? God."

"Just go," Nathan said. "I'll call you both later. I want to be alone."

They quietly gathered their things. He sat on the bed with no shirt staring at the wall. He heard the door click behind them.

Did she see the girl? He knew he shouldn't have slept with that girl. He and Beth had such a good thing going. *It can't end. Not now.* He needed to find out.

Picking up the phone, he tapped over to "Favorites" and pressed her name. She answered after two rings.

"Hey, John!"

Her voice sounded energetic and bubbly. *Maybe she didn't know.* "How are you?"

"I'm good," she said. "Busy morning, looking forward to getting off at three."

"I bet you are."

He needed to know for certain. "Did you bring me breakfast this morning?"

"I did," she said. "You and your friends were still asleep so I didn't want to wake you."

Oh, God. 'Your friends,' she said. Did that mean just Tommy and Angeline, or did she mean the girl, too? As far as he could tell through the phone, her voice was normal and showed no sign that she saw the girl. He still didn't know for sure, but he decided against pressing.

"Okay, he said. "I'll find you after work and walk you home but I can't stay long. I have the Venture X meeting tonight."

"That's right! Are you excited?"

"Very. I'll see you later."

He fell back into the bed, heart pounding. He felt somewhat relieved. She would have said something if she saw the girl, or at least she would have strongly hinted at it. He didn't detect anything. The girl must have slipped out before Beth came by. *That was a close one.*

He sat up from the bed, fuming. *You love Beth. Yes. You think she is the best thing that's happened to you. Right. You would do anything for her? Of course. Then, what in the world are you thinking bringing another girl into your room overnight? You don't even know who she is. Worse, you have no idea what you did with her. Did you cheat? It sounds like you cheated on her, and you were blind drunk when you did it? What are you thinking?*

Don't berate yourself. There's no use in that.

He had a big meeting that night and needed to research. Just get a grip on yourself and don't do it again. Drink less or something, he thought. *Beth deserves more than this.*

In less than two months, he had spent just short of $500,000. He ran some quick calculations in his head. If he continued at this rate, he'd be out of money in a few years. *Time is ticking.*

40

THAT SAME MORNING, Thomas met his old business partner, Mr. Martin, at Alvin Park. Mr. Martin suggested the park because it was new in Delorre and Thomas had never seen it. Mr. Martin parked his sports car with the roof down and spotted Thomas sitting on a bench.

"You'll sit up straight if you want to keep your back when you get to be my age," Mr. Martin said as he walked up to him.

Thomas felt the skin on his cheeks essentially crack as he smiled. It had been forever since he felt an inkling of positivity.

"Hello, old friend."

"My. Don't look so happy to see me," said Mr. Martin, immediately noticing Thomas's effort to appear glad. "What's happened to you? Obviously, nothing good, because you're back in Delorre."

Again, Thomas tried to smile. He appreciated his friend's levity, but the bitterness had consumed him night and day. His vengeful mission was a festering open wound in his heart.

The two men clasped hands and sat side by side on the bench overlooking the park.

"Mayor McDowell's sure making an effort to beautify downtown," commented Mr. Martin. "It's mostly a dog and pony show but at least the things are nice to look at."

"It's a nice park," mumbled Thomas.

"Clearly something is on your mind, Thomas," said Mr. Martin. "Tell me what's going on."

Thomas told him the story about Nathan and that he was looking for him presently but finding little success. Mr. Martin listened carefully as he watched the chess players across the park on the opposite side of the amphitheater.

"What does Abby think of all this?" asked Mr. Martin innocently.

A lump formed in Thomas's throat at the thought of his dead wife. How he wished she were there. She would know what to do. She and Nathan were so alike. Now, they both were gone. Thomas hid his watery eyes from his friend.

"Tom?"

Mr. Martin heard a vulnerable sound of a sniffle mixed with a cough come from one of the most capable professionals he'd ever known.

"How is Abby? Are you—Is she—Oh, no. God, no. Thomas?"

Without looking up, Thomas crumpled over his knees and held his nose. Mr. Martin pulled a red handkerchief from his coat pocket and handed it to his distressed friend.

The men sat in silence for ten minutes. Thomas couldn't bear to talk about her. Not now.

Mr. Martin peered at his watch and then at the chess players.

"Thomas, I know you're broken up at the moment, but hear me out for a minute. You don't have to listen to a word of it but I'm going to say it anyways because I think it will help you find your son."

Thomas blew his nose. Mr. Martin continued. "Have you ever played chess?"

It was a rhetorical opening to his monologue and Thomas didn't know much about it save that Nathan had a knack for the game.

"To win in chess," Mr. Martin went on, "You must read your opponent. You must think seven steps ahead and plan your moves carefully. You will never win recklessly or haphazardly. You must get inside the mind of your opponent and predict his moves before he makes them."

Thomas sat up and Mr. Martin turned to him.

"Nathan knew you'd come after him. Anyone who steals $10 million knows he will have pursuers. And you're probably not the only one."

41

Beth held Nathan's arm the whole way to her place. He stayed for an hour, had tea with her, and talked about the day. It sounded like she had no idea about the drunk girl in his room. She asked about who his friends were and where he met them. He told her about Tommy and Angeline, but left out the girl. Luckily, Beth didn't ask about her. They talked for a few more minutes before he kissed her goodbye and then walked back to The Charles to get ready.

Six o'clock came and Nathan gave Jeb another five dollar bill as he waited for the black cab. He got used to giving Jeb a little help every day, against the advice of the chauffeur. No one else would, and it's not like Nathan needed the $5 more than Jeb did. Jeb was always grateful and grinned through his scraggly beard before hobbling down to the corner store for a bite to eat.

Nathan rode out to Cherry Hills, a wealthy neighborhood on the north side of town. He entered the private community through a gate with a security guard. He passed through a polished downtown with a hair salon, a few bars, restaurants, and clothiers—all matching in architecture and design. He came around a lake with a fountain and saw the largest houses he'd ever seen. They towered like giant boulders in green hills and fields. The cab pulled into 1331 Cherry Main and the driver let him out.

A fountain sprayed into a the air behind him in the middle of the circular driveway. The big house stretched almost out of sight on both sides. *It must be six stories.* The door could fit four of him side by side and two of him standing on his shoulders. He knocked on the thick wood, which rejected the sound like a stone slab. *Dummy.* He rang the doorbell.

An elegant young blonde woman in a clinging light blue dress answered the door, "Good evening, Mr. Shepherd."

"Hello," he said. She knew his name.

"Right this way," she motioned to follow behind her.

The house was dark. Red carpets lined the corners, leaving a pathway of exposed wood floor. The walls were covered with huge portraits of people he didn't know. The girl's heels clopped down the wood floor. He was about to make a comment about the age of the house when a portion of the wall on the right opened automatically and smoothly slid to the right. They walked through it.

"Didn't notice a door there," he joked, trying to break the silence.

The girl said politely, "This house is full of secrets." She tilted her head to one side and flashed him a smile.

They entered an enormous room with ceilings four stories high. The carpet was red with a gold diamond pattern, and the walls were dark green with vertical lines of other shades of green. It smelled like pine and peppermint. In the middle of the room was a massive oak table that reminded him of the one in the kitchen at the farm. The walls were covered with black and white portraits of men and women all wearing the same style suit. The gold-trimmed portraits covered the entire wall in straight rows as if it were a lineage of royalty. There must have been a hundred. At the end of the table sat George and two other gentlemen he recognized from the black and white party. A huge fire burned behind their silhouettes. A snarling grizzly bear bust was frozen in mid-attack above the fireplace.

"Gentlemen, may I introduce Mr. John Shepherd," the girl said with a wave of her arm.

"Hello," Nathan said and shook their hands. George, in a purple silk shirt underneath a white suit jacket, stood to his feet and shook his hand. His hands were still in white gloves.

"Good evening, Mr. Shepherd," said George. "Nice to see you again. These are my associates, Mr. David Jefferson and Mr. Matthew Morrison."

"Pleasure to meet you both," said Nathan.

Mr. Jefferson was tall and hunched over with thin grey eyebrows above frameless glasses. He had a long nose like a banana and a sharp pointed chin, as if it was stretched from too much stroking. Mr. Morrison was a plump and balding man with flairs of red hair around his ears that matched the color of his pocked cheeks. He had a perpetual smile on his face with jagged teeth.

They both said their greetings and George motioned to sit. At the table he brought out a cigar holder from his inside suit pocket and offered each of them a custom-labeled King of Denmark. The girl appeared again carrying a silver tray of lowball whiskey glasses filled with ice and a bottle of Johnnie Walker Black.

Nathan steadied himself. It was overwhelming, but this was his dream. *Stay focused.*

"How are you liking the city?" George said as he distributed the drinks.

"It's big," Nathan said. Mr. Morrison chuckled. Mr. Jefferson didn't move.

"But I love it so far. I'm really enjoying the culture, the people, and the energy. It's great to be where big things are happening."

"Agreed," said George. "I thought it was auspicious to run into you at that awful senator's party, or should I say, you running into us. And it appears I'm not the only one glad you were at that party. The media gobbled you up like a fat boy eating candy." He over-pronounced the "f" in "fat boy." He looked at the other two men. Mr. Morrison let out another chuckle. Mr. Jefferson didn't budge. Nathan felt hot blood course through his cheekbones.

"We've read a few articles about you, Mr. Country Millionaire," Mr. Morrison's voice quavered with glee but he controlled it.

"I know your friend told us you had $30 million to invest," said George. "But the papers were quoting figures closer to, what, $120 million?" He took a puff of his cigar.

Nathan said, "I can expl— " George kept going, cutting him off.

"Which is it, Mr. Shepherd? Thirty or one-twenty?"

"I'm comfortable investing $30 million right now, I'll want to see what happens before I commit to anything else," he said. He screamed at himself. *What just came out of my mouth? Did I just say thirty million?*

"But before I even think about investing," he said. "I'd like to learn more about Venture X."

"Of course," George said. He looked at the other two men and turned back to Nathan. "We'd like to talk about what we can offer."

"Okay," Nathan said and took a sip of the whiskey. He tried to relax.

George and Mr. Morrison took turns explaining that Venture X operates one of the largest private equity funds in the nation. They said the fund is stable and generates a dependable twelve percent annual return and distributes an eleven percent quarterly dividend. Nathan's thirty million dollar investment would set him up nicely, they said, and he would have nothing to worry about for the rest of his life.

"What has been the historical performance of the fund, and who manages it?"

"The fund has never dipped below the market average, since I started it over forty-five years ago. It has always beaten any index fund. The quarterly dividend has never been skipped since the fund's instatement."

George swirled his whiskey. "The members manage the fund themselves, if they choose to. They can be as involved as they wish to be. The Venture X membership consists of eighty-nine individuals across the country and the board of twelve members manage the fund here in Delorre."

George put his glass down. "You would be the ninetieth member."

The more they talked, the better it sounded to Nathan. The fund had a time-tested management strategy and the most experienced investors in the nation.

After they had presented their opportunity, Nathan told them that he could invest $2.5 million a month over a twelve month period of time. This would allow him to get in quickly to start earning the dividend, but also allow him to ease into such a big commitment. They understood.

"We want all of our members to feel confident in their investment in Venture X," said George.

Nathan was grateful for his finance education. It was finally paying off.

By the end of the night, they were laughing and telling stories. George slapped him on the back over and over again. Morrison's face was redder than blood. Jefferson still didn't move.

Smitten with boldness, Nathan asked, "Why doesn't Mr. Jefferson ever speak?"

"Oh, he does," said George. "Doesn't he, Mr. Morrison?"

"He sure does," the red-headed balloon of a man said. "He just doesn't talk when he's watching someone."

Nathan mouth closed instantly. *Watching someone? What?*

Morrison continued, not noticing Nathan's reaction, "He saves all of his thoughts and observations for afterwards, where he'll write out a full analysis of the investment candidate we're interviewing."

Interviewing? His thoughts raced. He thought they were just talking about doing some business. His stomach lurched, punching into his lungs.

George chimed in. "Mr. Jefferson was a military psychiatrist for decades. He developed a theory where one is impermeable to influence if one does not speak nor react. It allows him to focus and observe closely and objectively."

"What exactly does that mean?" asked Nathan.

"It means he will not laugh at your jokes, or react to anything you say, he will not give you anything to go off of, nor give you the satisfaction that he is listening to you. Humans are swayed by those whom they get to know. He is getting to know you, but you are not getting to know anything about him. He is watching you, completely unaffected."

George chuckled. Nathan was starting to feel uncomfortable. "How long will he be like this?"

"Until he feels he has what he's looking for," said George. "You get used to it after awhile, I guess. It's like he's not even here to me."

His eyes connected with Mr. Morrison's and they lost it. Morrison shrugged. "Whatever. It works! It's worked for years."

They both took a sip of whiskey.

A flood of self-conscious thoughts washed over Nathan. He tried to think of a joke but all that came out was, "It's hard to get to know a stone."

Mr. Jefferson kept staring at him.

The night continued casually but Mr. Jefferson's blank stare irked him more and more. Nathan wanted to throw something at him. He couldn't wait to leave. Finally, at 11:00 p.m., George said he must resign for the night. He said if Nathan were accepted, his staff would be in touch to send him the documents for signing into Venture X. Nathan tried to warm his hand before shaking the white glove but it was ice cold. They shook and said goodbye.

As Nathan turned his back to them, his thoughts were tangled in barbed wire. *Did that go well? Did that go poorly? Even if I do pass, am I sure I want to join?*

The tall blonde led him back to the front door. She was cute. He asked her name and she said, "Rose." He asked for her number and she gave it to him. He shouldn't have but he was feeling a little buzzed. A little confidence returned as he got into the cab and drove to The Charles.

42

OVER THE WEEKEND, Nathan took Beth, Tommy, and Angeline out to a fancy dinner at Portside Harbor and told them about the meeting. They sat around a round table outside in a shady courtyard, sharing bottles of red and white wine, selected by Nathan. Beth was cautionary yet supportive, Tommy was excited for him, and Angeline was congratulatory.

Beth asked, "So are you going to do it?"

"What are you talking about?" Tommy answered for Nathan. "Of course he is. He's not stupid."

"I'm definitely thinking about it," said Nathan. I know they were a little stiff, but they're just more experienced. I'll get used to them. I'm sure I could learn a lot from them anyways. I mean, these guys are millionaires. George is probably a billionaire."

"Sounds like a great opportunity," said Angeline.

"Sure does," said Tommy. "You're a millionaire, man. You're the *Country* Millionaire. You're meant to be in Venture X."

Tommy was right. *"John Shepherd, Venture X partner" sounded too good to be true.*

Beth asked, "John, will you be putting all your money into Venture X?"

"Whattaya talkin' about, B?" Tommy attacked her. "It's his

money, let him do what he wants with it."

"Tommy, take it easy." Nathan said, "Lower your voice."

Beth raised her voice, "Why don't you let him speak for himself if it's his money?"

"He's just trying to be helpful," Angeline backed Tommy up.

"Helpful isn't the word I would use," retorted Beth.

"Trust me," said Angeline. "We know."

"Alright, guys," Nathan said. "It's fine, I'll decide. Don't worry. I'll take my time. For right now, all I can do is wait to hear from them."

Beth was furious. Nathan could tell Beth didn't like his friends at all. They were too loud and obnoxious—too thoughtless and blabbery for her.

At the end of the night, Beth and Nathan smoked cigarettes on the balcony of his room. It was a warm night. They stood side by side, looking out over the city lights.

"Apologies for my friends tonight. They can be a little ridiculous sometimes. Especially when they drink."

"No shit, Shepherd."

Nathan laughed. It was a stressed laugh.

"Who are they anyways?"

"They're my friends. We go out together. They like me."

She wanted to argue with him but she picked up on the strain in his voice.

"Is something wrong, John?"

Nathan shrugged.

She put her cigarette out and rubbed his shoulders.

"At the meeting with Venture X, we sat around a large oak table," he said. "It reminded me of the one we had at home."

He sighed. "I wish my father could see me. I think he'd be proud of me. But it's probably never going to happen."

Beth put her arms around him. "Why don't you contact him? Wouldn't he come visit?"

Nathan felt a pang of guilt. She didn't know anything about his father. Or about what happened. She didn't even know his real name. He wished he could tell her but it was still too soon.

"No, he hates the city. And honestly, I don't think he would want to see me."

Beth reached for her wine glass on the balcony. "Tell me about it. I know what that's like."

Nathan inhaled smoke. "Do you miss your father?"

"Sometimes," she said. "But I know it's probably for the best that he's not around."

"Why?"

"I don't know," she thought for a moment. "I guess when someone doesn't love you, they tend to only make your life more complicated. There's a certain freedom when things are simple."

"Reminds me of the farm," said Nathan. "There was nothing to worry about. Everything was plain, predictable, and the same. Here, my future is wide open with endless opportunities. I get restless, or feel like there's always something better I should be doing. It's almost impossible for me to feel like I'm ever doing the right thing."

Beth stood on her tiptoes and kissed him on the cheek. "Don't beat yourself up about it. You're still getting your footing here. You've got a bright future ahead of you, I know you do. You have plenty of money and you don't have a lazy bone in your body. Trust me, I know."

She winked at him and smiled. Nathan grabbed her and hugged her. "You're the best part of my life right now."

She looked at him in the eyes. She loved his eyes. Deep blue sapphire crystals full of endless transparency. She kissed him and snuggled on his shoulder.

"In other news, remember the safe I told you about?"

"The one with the diamonds and stuff?"

"Yes, the jeweler returned my call about the diamonds. She said the bag was worth somewhere between $120,000 and $320,000."

"Money, money, money," Beth poked him. Her heart skipped a beat. *Diamonds... did he keep one... for me?*

"I know, you don't like money," Nathan chided. "The antique gun collector offered me $1,500 for the flintlock pistol. I politely declined."

"Good. Wasn't it your grandfathers? You should definitely keep it."

"Was already planning on it."

43

"I don't see what you see in him, Mr. Pendleton." Mr. Morrison folded his hands over his stomach. "He's young and inexperienced. I see only problems."

George stared into the fire, his eyes glowing with the flames. Wrested in thought, he held a glass of whiskey to his thin lips. There was something precocious about the young man.

"Mr. Jefferson, what do you say?" He turned to his colleague. "What are the results of your analysis?"

Mr. Jefferson opened a folder on the table. The three men were gathering two nights after their meeting with Nathan to discuss his Venture X membership.

"Mr. Morrison is right," he began. "Mr. Shepherd is young. But is he too young? I think not. He looked each of us straight in the eyes. He was composed, for the most part. He speaks very well, and he's as sharp as a knife."

George looked at Mr. Morrison. Mr. Jefferson continued his review of his notes. "He's educated in finance from a top private school. He's ambitious, and clearly not idle. By his posture and hand control, I would venture to say he has an elevated level of confidence."

"Do you think he would do well as one of us?"

"I feel that, with much oversight and mentoring, he would

add not only his assets, but also his energy to the group—something I think we all could benefit from."

"I disagree," said Mr Morrison. "I can think of several members who will not appreciate a junior member."

"Mr. Morrison, you have no faith," said George.

"But at least I have reason."

George rolled his eyes. "Mr. Jefferson, I defer to you."

"You're concern is a valid one, Mr. Morrison, and one that we should be aware of going forward," Mr. Jefferson said. "But I do recommend a more open-minded approach to Mr. Shepherd's application. How are your children?"

"Fine," said Mr. Morrison. "What's that got to do with this?"

"Remind me of their ages and what they do?"

Discomforted by the personal shift in the conversation, Mr. Morrison said, "I have a twenty-seven year old daughter, a twenty-five year old son, and a twenty year old son. They all live with me." He stopped, not wishing to continue.

"Thank you, but what do they *do* exactly?"

"I said they live at home with me."

"We heard you say that the first time. What are their jobs?"

Mr. Morrison's face flushed red. "What exactly are you trying to say, Mr. Jefferson?"

George squinted at Mr. Jefferson. The corners of the former psychiatrist's mouth twitched.

"I mean no offense, and I apologize if this comes across harshly, but if Mr. Shepherd were as spoiled and lazy as most self-entitled young adults suckling from the ever-flowing teat of their wealthy parents, then I believe we would have picked up on this, and I would have readily agreed with you. However, with Mr. Shepherd, I detected not a hint of entitlement or laze, and while I admit it is still early, I have reason to believe he would work hard and fulfill his responsibilities."

"Do you have any children, Mr. Jefferson?" Mr. Morrison

grinned satirically, prepared to catch Mr. Jefferson in his own trap.

"I did," he said. "Regrettably, they are no longer alive."

Mr. Morrison swallowed and glumly reached a shaky hand for his whiskey and took a long and slow drink. George glared at him.

44

"**M**YSTERIOUS COUNTRY MILLIONAIRE *Joins Exclusive Venture X.*"

The headlines were everywhere. Everyone knew about it. Apparently, when the word got out that Nathan joined Venture X, the news outlets went ballistic. The people, the parties, and the press all loved it.

The night he found out, everyone celebrated his success during Launch Pad. Nathan received congratulations, drinks, and pats on the back all night.

At the third bar, Tommy and Angeline came up to Nathan surrounded by a large group of smiling admirers. He was popping a bottle of champagne and already slurring his words when they grabbed him and pulled him into a dimly lit booth in the back of the bar. Sitting in the shadowed corner was a man with pale skin and dirty gray dreadlocks.

Tommy introduced their friend Derrick. He was dressed in baggy clothes and smelled like smoke and hand sanitizer. He didn't look healthy. He greeted them in a monotone voice that sounded like it skipped his mouth and pushed straight from his stomach.

"So, what do you do, Darren?" Nathan said, ogling the shady man and not realizing he got his name wrong.

Derrick didn't answer him. He looked at Tommy and Angeline who nodded affimatively. From under the table, Derrick pulled out a syringe. Nathan gasped. Tommy and Angeline leaned forward. Nathan watched horrified but intrigued as they passed the medical instrument around, deftly shooting it into their arms.

They asked if he wanted to try it. He asked what it was.

"It's good, don't worry about it," Tommy said.

"Seriously. What is it?"

He looked at Angeline.

"You'll love it," she said cooly, "It's amazing. You'll feel perfect."

They hadn't led him wrong so far. But he didn't trust Derrick. He made him nervous. Tommy and Angeline egged him on to try it.

"It's harmless," they said.

"It's a needle, for Christ's sake!" Nathan cried. He didn't know anything about drugs or substances. The only thing he grew up with was alcohol but even that was just weak wine. They didn't have anything else on the farm. He remembered smoking with Beth. It was a new experience and he really liked it. *Could this be similar?* He wished Beth were there. She could help him, tell him what to do, or what not to do.

The club music pounded overhead. The bar felt alive. He saw bodies dancing under murky lights, glasses chinking, and bare skin showing.

"Have you all done this before?"

"All the time, Johnny," said Tommy. Nathan looked at Angeline and she nodded.

"How does it work?" he asked.

"It's simple," Tommy explained. "You pop it into your arm or whatever, push it in, it enters your bloodstream, and then your brain feels amazing. I promise you, you'll never feel anything like it. Oh, and the best part? There's no crash at the end. No hangover, no headache, no nothing. Just a pure, good-feelin' trip that lasts an hour or two. It's just like taking medicine, except it's in your arm and not through your stomach so it hits you quicker. Trust me, you'll like it."

Tommy sat back, nodded his head, and crossed his arms. Nathan shook his head.

"I don't know about this."

His conscience rang like a fire alarm. He wished he could escape.

Tommy put his arm around him. "You got nothing to worry about, my friend."

Nathan stood up to leave the booth and felt the booze in his head. He knew he couldn't walk. Downing the rest of his drink, he pounded the mug on the table, and said, "I think I'm going to have to pass, guys."

"Better watch him," Angeline said.

Nathan felt someone grip his arm and yank him back into the booth next to Derrick.

"Give him just a small dose," Tommy said, pushing Nathan's arm towards Derrick.

Nathan screamed, "What are you doing?"

"You're going to be fine, kid." Tommy quieted him down. "You're going to love it."

Like a rough physician, Derrick slapped Nathan's right arm palm-up on the table and tied a band around his bicep. Muted by the alcohol, Nathan cried out, "Stop!"

He could feel his heart rate accelerate. He felt sick to his stomach and lightheaded. *I wish I was home.*

A vein swelled up in his arm and Derrick found it with the syringe. The needle broke the skin and he plunged the substance into his arm. He felt tingles race up his arm and then a pop like a firework in his brain. Pleasure wrapped his body like a blanket, and his senses lifted in a plume of happiness. He felt light. *Am I floating?* Everything felt thousands of miles away.

"You're swimming in raw sensuality, my friend."

He couldn't help... chuckling.

After a few minutes of dazed pleasure, Angeline poked him and said they're leaving for the next bar. Nathan giggled and got up. The rest of the night blurred by. Bar after bar, drink after drink, he levitated along.

The high from the drug wore off as the night went on. Back at The Charles, when his head hit the pillow, he let out a small, "Ha."

He didn't know what to think or how to feel. He knew he had used a powerful, probably illegal, drug. If his father found out, he would be in severe trouble. *But Father doesn't know.* Though he was scared to admit it, he kind of liked it. It was wild, untamed, and thrilling. But it was dangerous and risky. *Should I really be doing this?* Whatever it was, he'd never felt anything like it. *It doesn't matter.* He didn't have time to worry about these questions. What mattered was he was feeling alive.

45

"What do you mean you can't find him?" Paul yelled into the phone. Thomas held the phone away from his ear.

"I'm close," said Thomas. "He's here. I've seen him."

"That's it? You saw him and didn't do anything about it?" Paul was upset. "He *stole* from you! You should report him to the authorities. You won't tell me how much it was, but I'm sure it was a lot. You need to have him arrested."

"That would only make it worse, Paul."

"This is so wrong," Paul said. His face was hot and he couldn't stop shaking his head. Heavy silence. Thomas knew it would help locate him, but the thought of arresting Nathan would send things spinning out of control. And Nathan would hate him all the more. *I can't arrest my own son. What would Abby say?*

"Why can't you at least find out where he is and what he's doing?" asked Paul.

"What do you think I'm trying to do?"

"What if you can't find him?"

"I will find him. You can count on it."

"What are you going to do to him when you do?"

Thomas's hand clenched around the payphone. "I will bring him home."

"What about the farm? Does he still have the power to sell it?"

"He didn't touch the other accounts. He just took the oil money and, apparently, your money."

"What?" Paul kicked a chair and it flew into the wall. His foot throbbed with pain. "He took my money?"

"I know how it feels, trust me."

"This is unbelievable. Why did he take my money and nothing else?" Paul was furious. "He will pay for this."

"Anyways, if you can hold down the responsibilities at the farm, we'll be home in no more than another week. I've notified the banks and accountants of the mistake. He won't be able to do anything else. Besides, I don't think he'll need to. Are you capable of handling things while I'm away?"

A "Yes" barely made it out of Paul's panting breaths.

46

It was a Tuesday night and Nathan was meeting George Pendleton at his house to discuss his new membership. They walked along the quarter-mile back patio, overlooking George's private lake. A butler pushed a bar cart of drinks a few steps behind them. George was dressed in a black cashmere sweater and vintage Levis. Nathan wore a dark blue suit jacket over a blue Oxford with brown loafers. Both men wore the heavy black and silver "X" pin.

"Any problem can be solved with more time," said George. "If you apply time to any conflict, the conflict will be solved. If you want to start a business and start a family, but find that they are both competing for your time, then add more time and you can do both."

"But we don't control time like that."

"Ah, but we do. Money and time are twins. They are interchangeable. You can use money to buy time. With more money, you can buy more time, allowing you to solve more problems. In our example, you can hire a team of people to manage the business so that you can focus on your family."

Nathan mulled this over. It was as if he was reading one of his books when he was younger, except now he was actually living it.

"Mr. Pendleton, I'm very grateful for the time you are spending with me. It's something I've always wanted but never had."

"We are glad to have you with us. And we are all looking forward to your contributions."

They reached the end of the patio and stopped. Ahead of them, Nathan saw a black helicopter with a silver "X" on it parked on a helipad. It was surrounded by a tall, barbed-wire fence and guards.

"Mr. Pendleton, how did you get to where you are today?"

He laughed. "Hard choices. I didn't do anything special. I began in real estate, diversified into the stock market, and invested in early stage businesses. As my portfolio grew, I bought majority stakes in growing companies. People will always say I was just lucky. But if you really want to know the truth, it's because I made harder decisions that most people would back away from. It's all about the relationships you choose to nurture."

"What do you mean?"

The crinkles in George's eyes twitched. "People think that wealth is an endless pursuit. There is no final arrival. There is only more and more. For the longest time, I thought they were right. But I worked myself to the bone, sacrificing friends, family, sleep, health, and even love, to find it."

Nathan stared at the helicopter. "Did you find it?"

George grinned. "I did. I'm alone because of it, but I have complete control of all my time."

Nathan believed him.

"Are you happy?"

"Happy?" George chuckled. "Happiness is an emotion. What does it matter?"

"I see," said Nathan. *George is not like Father at all. Opposites, really.* George was the mentor he was looking for.

Two months later, he had put five million in and received

the expected 11% dividend for the second quarter of the year. It felt great to have cash finally coming in from something he had done himself. The diamonds were completely sold and the bonds cashed out. He was full steam ahead.

47

SEVEN MONTHS IN, he was still at The Charles. In spite of the price tag of $20,000 a month, it proved to be a suitable living and office space, especially when he was making a quarterly dividend of half a million dollars.

A few surprises awaited him after joining Venture X. Some good, some bad. The perks of being a Venture X member were many, the best of which was the respect and reputation in the upper circles of the city. It fit in perfectly with his 'Country Millionaire' persona.

He wasn't expecting the fees. There was a fee for everything; a management fee, membership fee, voting fee, and an administrative fee. Plus, all the meetings and events—it cost roughly $35,000 a month. But he was learning a lot and having fun.

With only $10 million, his commitment of $30 million would have been problematic but, using his net worth and Venture X membership, he was able to secure two additional $5 million loans from two other banks. With this new revenue, he was able to keep up his Venture X contributions for about another four months.

Beth went along with Nathan and his friends one night for Launch Pad. They began the night at one of the group's favorites, Backspace Bar.

Walking into the bar, Nathan was instantly recognized by the patrons and hoots and hollers rang around the dark room. Nathan waved his hand in the air to greet them as people flooded in behind him to get their spot at the bar. The bartender called to Nathan and the crowd hushed and waited. Nathan finished kissing cheeks and then circled his pointer finger in the air above his head like a cowboy with a lasso. "Let's go!"

The crowd cheered. The bartender immediately began lining up shot glasses on the bar.

Beth pulled Nathan aside.

"Nathan, what are you doing?"

"I'm doing what I always do," he stated. "I'm buying everyone a round."

"Should you always be doing that?"

"Why not? Everyone loves it."

The bar counter was filled with full shots of liquor. Nathan held up his glass, "To friends and success!" In a organismic movement, everyone tapped their glasses and threw them to the backs of their throats. The room exhaled loudly.

Beth was concerned. "But, Nathan, what does it accomplish? It only gets people drunk."

"I have a reputation to keep. Look at the people in this room. There are lawyers, reporters, politicians, and even policemen and they all love me."

The room looked to Nathan again and waited, talking out of the corner of their mouths to each other. Once again, Nathan lifted his finger in the air and swirled it. The bar cheered even louder.

He continued, "A reputation is a person's most powerful asset, Beth. Look at them all, they are eating out of my hand."

"I'm not staying," Beth said.

"Why not?"

"I'm not okay with this."

"What? Why?"

"I don't know why," she said and turned away from him. "It's not right."

She kissed him on the cheek and turned and left. Nathan watched her go.

"What's pluggin' her up?" Tommy yelled into his ear, the pungent smell of liquor on his breath.

"I don't know," Nathan said. "She doesn't understand what it takes to manage a reputation."

"She sure don't," Tommy said. "Come on back. He's ready."

Nathan made eye contact with the bartender and motioned for one more and then to hit the music.

Nathan followed Tommy back to the closed booth where Derrick and Angeline were waiting. *Why get an awful hangover in the morning when you can trip and then wake up, feel great, and immediately get to work?*

48

A FEW WEEKS later, Nathan paid for Derrick to stay in the room next to him at The Charles. He wanted him to be nearby so he could use the drugs anytime he wanted. They spent lots of time together.

"When I first met you, you creeped me out." Nathan laughed. He laid in his jacuzzi tub with his arms spread out of the water. Derrick stood outside the pool in sweatpants and a dark hoodie.

"The way you hide your face under your hood like that," said Nathan. "It's disturbing."

Derrick was silent. He rarely spoke.

"You sure you don't want to get in the pool?" asked Nathan, not expecting Derrick would ever want to be in the same tub with another man.

Derrick turned around and took off his hoodie. He stretched his arms as he took off his baggy t-shirt. Nathan saw his bare back. Lumpy scars interlaced with tattoo ink were scrawled all over his gray skin, forming a tapestry of thorn bushes infused with words in another language.

"Oh, god," reacted Nathan. "What happened to your back?"

In a low, gravelly voice, he said, "My mother."

"I see," said Nathan. "Was she a tattoo artist?"

Derrick said nothing. He took off his sweatpants and grabbed something from the pocket. Nathan shifted nervously.

"Come on in, then."

Derrick entered the pool and sat opposite of him. His bony chest and arms were covered with dark and illegible tattoos. In his hand was a large glass pipe mechanism. He lit it and smoked. He offered it to Nathan.

"What is it?" asked Nathan.

"Weed."

"Oh," Nathan knew about marijuana. "It's harmless, right? That's what I've heard... as long as you don't have too much."

The drug he had before was much stronger. He had already sacrificed his conscience in the name of freedom. *Why look back now? What difference would it make?*

Derrick shook his head. "No, it's good for you."

Nathan laughed. "Of course it is."

He took it from him and gave it a puff.

"Where did you learn how to do all this stuff, anyways?"

"My pops."

"Did he deal drugs, too?"

"Yeah."

"Where is he now?"

"Dead."

Nathan handed back the pipe. "I'm sorry... How did he die?"

"What do you think."

"Right, my apologies."

They sat in silence in the tub, smoking and enjoying the view of the city. The room filled with smoke.

"Derrick, why do you do drugs?"

"I'm good at it."

Nathan didn't speak. He only wanted to listen.

Derrick went on, uncomfortably. He spoke in quick spurts. "I feel normal, when I'm high." He paused. "I'm not me, without something. Not worth being down."

Nathan felt bad for him. "I'm glad we're neighbors now. I want to help you. Whatever you need, I can help you with it. Finances, a job, relationships, anything. I want to help you."

Derrick nodded and blew out a thick column of white smoke.

"I'm good," he said.

"There isn't anything I can do to help?"

"No," Derek said. His face was like a brick wall.

Unfamiliar with someone who didn't need or want anything from him, Nathan shrugged. *Alright.*

Waving his hand towards the bong, he said, "My turn. Pass it over."

49

The girls at the parties were relentless. Every night, at least two of them would force their way into Nathan's arms at the bars, and make him buy drinks as they kissed him. They laughed and flirted and made it awfully hard not to play along. By the end of the night, he was able to turn most of them away. Only on occasion, for the special ones, he would take them back to his hotel room as long as they promised to be out before 9:00 a.m.

At the bar one night, he was joined by a familiar face, the athletic-bodied, pixie-blonde journalist.

"I'm not answering any questions tonight," Nathan told her. "I'm just looking to have some fun."

"I'm not asking any questions tonight," she replied with a smile. Nathan noticed her tight pants and thin top. Her jawline was cutting, and her eyes had extra layers of mascara. She was much more well-featured than he remembered.

"What kind of fun are you trying to have?"

It was an obvious advance. Accustomed to this sort of thing, Nathan recognized the ploy and decided to play along.

"Something a little more active," he said, slyly.

"I like to be active," she finished his thought for him and batted her long lashes. He took her hand and whisked her into the middle of the crowd where their bodies blended in with the undulating lake of moving flesh. It wasn't long before he took her back to his room.

She drank too much and had trouble waking up in the morning. It was 8:30 a.m. and she wasn't moving. He helped her out of the bed but she slumped to the floor, moaning. He asked her to kindly leave. He hated to be so mean but she wouldn't move. He wrapped her in a white bathrobe, gathered her clothes, and carried her to the elevator, placing her limp body on the floor. He apologized and sent the elevator down to the lobby where he had a hotel attendant waiting to assist her. He had to do it. Returning to his room, he freshened up to receive Beth in a few minutes for coffee and breakfast.

She came in.

"Good morning, John."

"Good morning, Beth," Nathan turned from his computer, stood up, and kissed her.

They laid on the bed and talked about the day, her work, her art, her running. She asked how his investments were going and he said great. She asked about his friends, about the "events", and about the people he was meeting. He told her a couple funny stories from the night before. She laughed and they kissed again.

"John, it's been over a year. I think it's time you moved in with me."

"That sounds amazing," he said quickly, although he had other thoughts. He knew she was asking for more commitment. He wasn't ready for it. He feared a ring. And even worse, a family.

"I'm not sure I'm ready to leave The Charles just yet," he said. "I still have a lot to figure out about the future."

"Why not?" she asked.

"Don't get me wrong, Beth, I absolutely enjoy you. You're

gorgeous, smart, and funny. And there isn't another woman that could even come close to you. I just want the relationship to stay how it is. Why does it have to change?"

"But if you are so set on me, then wouldn't a change be good? If your mind is so made up, then why don't you move ahead with what you are certain of?"

"I am certain." He held her close. "Let me think about it, okay? Is that alright? Let's talk about it tomorrow."

She gave him a sad face but agreed and said goodbye.

The next day, he sat back in the chair at his desk, daydreaming. Derrick sold him larger portions of drugs so he began stockpiling his own supply in the room's safe. He lived for the night. And couldn't wait to go out. It was the time to escape. He worried about the debt he was accruing to finish out the $30 million commitment to Venture X.

He shrugged. *Father would be ashamed of me if he saw how I was living.* If he knew he was smoking, drinking, partying, sleeping around, and getting high, he would be furious. *Good thing he'll never know. I bet he's caught wind of the Country Millionaire. I wonder if he knows it's me. He'll sure be surprised when he finds out.* He couldn't wait for the day when he returned to the farm with millions more than he stole. *Father's face will be priceless. No, wait, Paul's face will be priceless. Ha,* he could see Paul's jaw open wide and eyes bulge out of his head, gawking while he told their father the net worth of his assets.

Don't get ahead of yourself. There's a lot of work ahead. And that won't happen anytime soon. It's going to take years to build up to that point. You're getting into serious things, remember to be safe. Not a lot of good would come from getting sick or injured. Not even-

His thoughts were interrupted by my phone ringing. It was

Beth.

He answered, "Hey baby."

"Hi sexy, how's your day been?"

"Fine, how about yours?"

"It's been interesting," she said. "There's something I want to talk with you about." Her voice sounded as if she was about to go on stage in front of a thousand people.

"What's wrong?"

"Nothing, I just want to see you."

"Okay," he said, unsure. "I know we said we were going to talk today. I'm free for dinner. Dinner at your place tonight?"

"Yes, yes. That sounds good."

"What time shall I come over?" he asked.

She said, "How about six o'clock?"

"Perfect," he said. "See you then."

He hung up and shook his head. *What was that? I still haven't thought of an answer for her. I don't think I can do it.* He opened the freezer and poured a glass of Grey Goose. *I need to stay here.*

50

After another dead end, Thomas resolved to simply wait for Nathan outside of The Charles. If his son was staying there, he would eventually come out of those doors and when he did, Thomas would be there to catch him.

The sun shone brightly on the marble wall and sidewalk outside The Charles. He touched the ground and his fingertips withdrew quickly from the heat. Thomas looked behind him and across the way he saw a homeless man. The same one from the other day. Buried underneath his scraggly cream colored hair, his eyes watched Thomas carefully.

Alarmed and somewhat embarrassed that he would appear as this man did, Thomas continued walking into the hotel. He grabbed a newspaper, sat on one of the plush couches, and thumbed through the pages. The front page forewarned of financial misgivings. Thomas breathed a grateful sigh. Ever since moving out to Sanctilly, his business was insulated from some degree of the turbulent city markets.

A word caught his eye in one of the pages. *Palomino.* He grew those grapes out on the farm. He was drawn to the word because he had the only vineyard that grew them. No one else in Virginia could. It was a source of great pride—what was this article about?

His eyes scanned the short profile written by a Delorre reporter covering a John Shepherd, a local wealthy investor with an apparent sommelier streak. No photos were included in the piece. Thomas speculated the spoiled squirt had just gotten back from a trip to Southern Spain, the only other place in the world with Palomino grapes. He said the first thing that came to his mind, "He probably doesn't know a thing about wine."

Suddenly aware of his parched throat, Thomas continued reading the newspaper and grumbling as he found the hotel's water fountain.

51

It was 5:40 in the evening when Nathan left The Charles, gave Jeb his $5, and walked towards Beth's, smoking a cigarette.

The walk was one he had come to enjoy. He'd greet those who recognized him, wink a few times when he looked up from his phone, and walk with a confident stride. Arriving at Beth's, he looked right and left before entering, making sure no one was watching.

Beth was fixing a steak dinner, with music, wine, and candles. He snuck behind her and grabbed her hips and kissed her neck.

"Hey you," she said with a brilliant smile. Pointing to a bowl on the counter, she said, "Would you give me a hand with the potatoes?"

He smiled. *That's my Beth. Putting me right to work.* She had on a fruity, poppy perfume. Her brown hair was up, held by two red sticks, and she had on grey leggings that hugged her legs and a see-through, loose magenta button up shirt with a tan slip underneath.

"You look extra cute tonight," he said.

"Thank you, honey," she said, without looking up from the meat she was preparing.

The dinner was lovely. They ate heartily. All the while, he

was waiting for her to bring up the subject she mentioned over the phone. He thought it was about living together. She probably thought of some other option. She seemed nervous, scraping her fork and checking her hair more often than necessary. She brought out cupcakes for dessert and said, "Would you like some coffee?"

"Sure," he said, taking a cupcake.

"You remember I told you that I was taking pottery lessons, John?"

"Yes, I do," he said, his mouth full of a chocolate and caramel cupcake.

"I made you something."

"I can't wait to see it," he said, smiling.

She went into her bedroom and emerged with two coffee mugs. They both had a heart around the letters "J" and "B".

She poured coffee into the mugs and brought them over to the table.

"Aww, these are great, Beth," he took a sip. "You did really well with these." *At least they held the coffee well*, he thought.

As they ate cupcakes and drank coffee at the table, he asked her how long she had been working on them and about the process to create a mug. She still seemed nervous. He couldn't figure out why. He thought maybe he should initiate the living situation conversation. Reaching the dregs of his coffee, he took the final gulp. Inside of the mug, he noticed the coffee drain from three letters carved at the bottom. *Oh my God.*

He choked in his throat almost spitting up the coffee. He leaned over the table, and the coffee in his mouth returned to the mug as he sputtered.

"*DAD?*"

Beth was sitting straight up in her chair, wide-eyed staring at him. She nodded with her eyebrows soaring above her eyes. Her face was plain and peaceful. Serene.

His thoughts exploded. *Dad? What? How? Unbelievable!* He didn't know what to think.

"Beth!" he cried, trying to control his emotions. "Are you pregnant?"

"Yes, John," she said.

"How do you know?" he asked.

"I took three pregnancy tests today. All of them said the same thing."

His insides warred. *Damn. I'm in trouble.* He wasn't ready to be a father. *No way. But it's my baby, my child, alive and growing. Someone just like me, and Beth, the woman I love.*

Standing to his feet, he said, "This is great, Beth." He went over to her and gave her a hug. As genuinely as he could muster, he whispered into her ear, "I'm so happy."

She pulled him in close. "Me, too."

Pulling away, he said, " I guess we won't be cheering any drinks tonight, then, right?" And managed a laugh. She smiled.

"John, we have so much to talk about!" Beth said excitedly. "I've thought about this so much..."

Indeed she had. A waterfall of thoughts and visions about raising a child, living together, and being parents rushed out of Beth's mouth. He had trouble focusing. Those letters in the mug seared into his mind. Every time he closed his eyes, the letters "D" "A" "D" glared at him. And it made him cringe. *I need a drink. Or something.* He couldn't wait for later.

His fake smile was crumbling, he knew he couldn't keep it up for much longer.

"Beth, I know this is terrible timing, but I had plans for after dinner tonight." He was planning on meeting Derrick, Tommy, and Angeline at Tarantino's.

She rolled her eyes. She knew what the plans were.

"John. Please."

"I'm sorry," he said. "I didn't know. I had no idea."

She raised her voice. "Cancel your plans! This is a big deal, John. You can't just leave. I'm pregnant. Soon, you are going to have to get used to staying home. *With your family.*"

Burning, he thought, *you're not my family. I don't want to stay home.* He didn't want anything to change and *now it's all ruined because of you.* But instead, he said, "Beth, come on." He paused. "You're right, I'll change. But let me just have some fun before the baby, okay? Tonight will be one of the last nights, I promise. Come here."

He gave her a hug and she wrapped her arms around him tightly.

"I just don't want to lose you," she said softly.

"Don't worry, I'll be right here," he squeezed a little tighter. She took his hand and put it up under her shirt on her belly. "We're going to have a baby." Her eyes watered as she smiled. He smiled back.

"I'll call you tomorrow." He kissed her goodbye and left.

52

On the street in the dark, he felt like pulling his hair out. He looked back at her door to make sure she wasn't watching before he bent over and silently screamed profanity into the mug in his hand.

That night, he drank gallons of alcohol, purposely. He didn't want to think about anything.

"John, what's bothering you tonight?" Angeline wondered. Tommy, Angeline, Derrick, and Nathan sat at a bar.

He didn't feel like telling them.

"I got something for you," said Derrick. "Let's go to your room."

In Nathan's room, Derrick brought out something "special."

"It's great for weird days," he said. "Costs a little more than the usual but—"

"Just give it to me," Nathan said. "It doesn't matter."

The next morning, he woke up feeling terrible. *What's the use of heroin if you still drink and smoke? Come on.* Sitting up in bed, he saw ceramic shards scattered all over the floor of his room. In horror, he realized what had happened. The "Dad" mug shattered on the floor last night. Rushing as fast as his body allowed, he cleaned up the mess before Beth arrived at nine.

When Beth brought him breakfast, he was still out of it.

"How much did you drink last night?" She seemed worried.

"It was in celebration of the news, honey," he said, masked in perfect sarcasm.

They talked over breakfast and she went to pour him coffee in the usual hotel mug but paused with the carafe in her hand. She scanned the room looking for the "Dad" mug. He pretended not to notice. She didn't say anything and poured coffee in the hotel mug.

"Hey Beth, with the new baby on the way, it might be a good idea to get back in touch with your family, especially your dad. I know it's been years since you last saw him but with the pregnancy and all, it might be a good idea to get back in touch with him."

"We'll need the support," he added.

"I haven't heard from that asshole since I was little. He doesn't even care about me. Why would he care about our baby?"

"You never know," he said, "This could be the perfect opportunity to make things better. You don't know what he's like now. He could be a different man. It's been decades."

She thought about it and let out a sigh. "Alright, I'll try. But we don't need him."

"Good girl, that's right," he said putting his arm around her. "It would just be the right thing to do for the baby."

If I'm going to let her go, I'm going to feel a whole lot better knowing she is taken care of.

53

Tommy and Angeline were split on the subject. Tommy said to drop her because Nathan had 'a brilliant future ahead of him and it would only hold him back.' Angeline said that he would be a fool to leave Beth behind because there's not many women like her. He didn't disagree with either of them.

The next couple of nights the decision tortured him. He spent a lot of time with Derrick at The Charles.

"There's no denying it, Derrick. I love Beth. But on the other hand, the thought of being a father terrifies me. It's way too much responsibility and commitment right now. There is so much more work to be done."

He paced around the room. Derrick sat on the bed, sipping an energy drink. He was a great listener.

"Still," Nathan resumed. "It's Beth and our child—how could I leave them? How awful would I have to be to do that?"

"Did she want to have a kid with you?" asked Derrick.

"I thought we were safe whenever we were together," answered Nathan. "That was my number one rule..." Then it dawned on him. *Did Beth want to be pregnant?*

"She doesn't seem like the type to pursue it. But maybe

she did let it happen."

"I seen it all the time," said Derrick.

"Seen what?"

"It's how you keep your man around, when there's no ring."

Thinking back, Nathan didn't recall too much remorse coming from her when she told him. "You might be right, Derrick. She may have done this on purpose." The more he thought about it the more it made sense.

"Nope. I know she did. She wanted more commitment from me anyways." *How could she spring this on me without talking about it beforehand? Was she trying to force a more permanent relationship?*

"I can't imagine raising a child right now. They take time and work and split my parents apart. Look, children are great and it's something I want to get into later in life, but right now? I have too much going for me, it'd be foolish to ditch all of it to "settle down," work a regular 9-5 job, and raise a family. Forget that."

"You're the boss."

Being in the city was about freedom. Anything that took away his freedom required evaluation, assessment, and possible termination.

54

Venture X was a key that unlocked many doors, Nathan found. George had been surprisingly helpful by spreading a good word about him.

"When our members succeed, we all succeed," he said. He had introduced him to the mayor, a handful of celebrity athletes, and countless bankers.

Mr. Jefferson turned out to be much friendlier than Nathan had expected. He was part-owner of the baseball stadium in the city. He loved baseball. He took Nathan to see a game one weekend and explained how baseball is like investing.

"In the batter's box, you've got to defend the plate. Don't chase every ball. Wait for the market to send you a meatball right down the middle. When that happens, swing mightily. But once you're on base, you've got to be smart. Watch the coach, don't steal without having a good edge on the pitcher, and wait for the pop flies to land before making a run for it."

Nathan was eight months into the Venture X investment plan, with $17.5 million invested. He had received two dividends adding up to a little over a million dollars. This made up his savings. His personal expenses were sky high but he was easily covering them. Plus, he had another $5 million bank loan in the works. *A million in the bank is nothing to worry* about.

At first, $30 million seemed daunting. There were some nights where the stress was incapacitating. But now, he was over halfway there, and the banks were still agreeable. With another loan on the way, he wasn't too worried about finishing his commitment to Venture X for the full $30 million.

The only thing that did worry him were the headlines. Not so much the headlines in the gossip section that he seemed to appear in every other weekend (Tommy had become good friends with the editors), but the business and money headlines. *Market Experiencing Tremors, Investors Uncertain. Analysts Caution 'Market Correction Needed'.* His money in Venture X was not immune to the macro-economic influences of the city. He studied the headlines and index fund tickers all day.

Mr. Jefferson's chauffeur stopped his black Mercedes on the curb across from Alvin Park at Nathan's request. The game had finished up by two and Nathan couldn't refuse Mr. Jefferson's generous offer for a ride home.

"Here will be just fine," he said. "I spotted a friend of mine in the park."

With an hour left of daylight, he decided a game of chess would do him good. He clasped Mr. Jefferson's outstretched hand as the chauffeur opened the car door.

"Always a pleasure, Mr. Shepherd."

"Likewise," Nathan replied. He was caught off guard by the vice-like grip of the older man. His handshake was eerily similar to his father's.

Distracted, he sat down at a table across from Murphy as the Mercedes sped off and they began setting up the pieces. He had begun thinking about the farm and how he might not ever see his family again.

"Murphy, do you have any kids?"

"Yes, I do. Two girls and a boy."

"Do you love them?"

The South African laughed. "Of course I do."

"How old are they?"

"My sons are in their twenties. My baby girl just turned eighteen."

"Can I ask you a question?"

"Go ahead."

"I know this might come across as random but what if one of them stole from you—a lot of money—and then ran away? What would you do to them?"

Murphy looked quizzically at him. "Stole from me?"

"Yes, hypothetically. What would you do if one of your sons stole your retirement savings?"

"I'd hypothetically beat them," Murphy said, chuckling. "It's one thing to steal. It's another thing to steal from family."

Nathan pushed a pawn forward.

"So you'd punish them pretty bad?"

Murphy slid his bishop forward putting Nathan's king in check.

"Definitely. Just because I love them doesn't mean I let them get away with anything," remarked Murphy. "Well, maybe my daughter. She's a princess."

Nathan took off his sunglasses.

"But only if they came back to you. Would you chase them down?"

He moved his bishop to counter-threaten the attack.

"They'd never steal from me. I don't—"

"Would you?"

"I might," said Murphy, confused. He didn't like being put in a corner. "But they'd come back to me. They'd come to their senses."

"Would you admit it's possible you might not know what's

best for your children?"

Nathan spoke aggressively. Murphy's neck scrunched. "Of course. I make mistakes, all the time, especially with my kids, just like any parent." He smiled. "But most of the time, I'm right."

Nathan tried to grin but a hot flash of anger surged in his stomach. "But not always."

Murphy frowned. "No," he said. "I'm not always right. Is something wrong?"

"It's your turn," Nathan said quickly.

Nathan shook his head to clear his thoughts. *Get a hold of yourself.*

55

THE DAY CAME to tell Beth he was leaving her.
There was no good way to break up with a lover, especially when one is pregnant. He didn't know how it would go, except that it would be absolutely painful.

It was cold and he wore a burgundy scarf around his neck and a wool hat. He knocked on her door. The door swung open and Beth stood there in a red blouse and green apron with a grand smile on her face.

She's so happy. He swallowed the lump in his throat.

"Hi Beth," he said.

She threw her arms around his neck.

"Hey baby," she said. "Come in from the cold. Want to help me finish up a few pies?"

"Let me get settled," he said, taking off his scarf and jacket. "There's something I need to talk with you about."

"I've been wondering what this is all about ever since you asked me to talk yesterday. The last time we had a talk like this, I was giving you some news..."

She rubbed her belly. With her chin down, she looked up at him with her big green eyes and dark eyebrows.

"... but I highly doubt you're about to tell me you're pregnant right now."

He managed a dry "heh" as he went over to the coffee maker. He did not want to have this conversation right now.

"Were you ever able to get in touch with your parents?" he asked.

He brought a cup over to where she was sitting and sat down, holding the hot mug with his cold hands.

"Yes, actually," she said. "Shocking news, really. Listen to this."

She leaned forward. "My mother passed away several years ago from a brain tumor. The doctors said it was sudden and untreatable. They said they attempted to contact her daughter but were unable to find me due to the change in my last name when I married Carter."

"Oh, Beth, I'm so sorry about your mom," he said.

"It's not terrible. We weren't close, though I wish it could have been different. It would have been nice if I was there for her. But I had no idea."

"What about your father?"

"My father is alive and well. I sent that rat bastard a message and he responded positively. He said he's willing to meet."

"When are you going to meet with him?"

"We have a phone call in the next day or two."

Relief flooded over Nathan. *Good.* At least, she'll have someone to look after her and the baby.

"Good to hear," he said and took a sip of coffee. He continued, "Listen, Beth, this is not going to be an easy conversation."

She put her mug down and looked at him.

"Why? What's wrong, John?"

His mind raced about the best way to put it. He wanted to be gentle as possible and still straightforward.

"When I came to Delorre, I was an idiot farm boy without a clue about anything. You were one of the first people I met. Beautiful, kind, and funny, you showed me so much and taught me more about life than anyone else. You opened my eyes to love and the city."

The ends of her mouth curled into a small grin. His internal voice screamed. *You're being too kind! What are you doing, this is coming out too warm; it's setting her up for a greater fall.* He swallowed.

"As I got my bearings, I learned that if I'm going to succeed in this city, I've got to work hard. Really hard. And stay focused on growing the money I've come here with. My father gave it to me to build wealth and bring it back to the farm," he lied, "not to just spend and settle down..."

She caulked her head to the side. Hearing the words "settle down" alarmed her. He could feel the emotions and thoughts coursing behind her eyes. He continued his march towards the cliff of death.

"In order to stay focused on my work, I have to spend my time... economically."

Each word came out carefully. *Why am I speaking so slowly?*

"So I've been doing some thinking. I've taken a look at my life and assessed that some things need to change."

Beth shifted in her chair. She squinted her eyes and brought her coffee mug to her mouth to hide her quivering lips.

"There's no easy way to say this, so I'm just going to say it."

He inhaled, swallowed, and exhaled. The pounding in his chest caused his voice to shake.

"I think you're going to want to find someone else who can do a better job of taking care of you in the future."

He had practiced that line many times so that he could say it unfalteringly. It worked, but it sounded much harsher than he expected.

Horror swept across her face. She said, "What did you just say?"

He hadn't rehearsed any other responses. *Could I take it back?* Maybe she misheard him. It was too late. He couldn't take it back. These were the words that would separate them, and it was crushing her.

"We need to change the way our relationship works," he replied, fumbling for words and then hating what actually came out. He tried to clarify.

"It's time for us to move on."

God, that sounded so cold. Those were possibly the worst words he could have chosen.

The hurricane inside her was almost audible. Her lips tightened. Her eyes watered. She put her hand over her mouth.

"Are you serious right now?" She said. He didn't say anything. *What do I say?*

"John, no!" She stood up from the table so fast the chair toppled over. "John!"

"Beth, please," he said. "It doesn't have to be like this. Please sit down. I need you to under—"

"You think I don't know?" She exploded.

This caught him off guard. "Don't know what?"

"You don't think I don't know about the countless sluts you had in your hotel room every week? You think you were getting away with it, without me knowing?"

Nathan was taken aback. "What are you talking about, Beth?"

"You know exactly what I'm talking about, you selfish, awful cheat!"

She backed away from him and yelled across the room.

"You thought I had no idea, right? Well, I have news for you, asshole. Ever since the beginning I've known. I've seen every single tramp walk out of your goddamn room!"

Her words were like bullets ripping into his precious reputation. This was not what he expected.

He blurted out, "If you knew, why didn't you say something?"

"Because I didn't want this to happen! Exactly what's happening right now." She was hysterical. "I was scared I would lose you."

"Maybe it wouldn't be such a bad thing," he said. "You've seen what I've done, I've gone behind your back and done really stupid things. I'm not the same person anymore. I've changed. If it was hurting you, why didn't you say something?"

"Because I love you, John!" She hurled a plate at him. It missed and shattered against the wall behind him. Tears rolled down her face, "I wanted to be with you so badly that it didn't matter how many times you cheated on me. I still loved you."

Hot tears coated his eyes. He didn't want to see her in such pain, especially because of him.

"I'm just not ready to have a child," he said, trying to bring the conversation back to its initial purpose.

He continued, "Being together is great, I really enjoy it. Honestly, I've always been grateful to have you and know you. There's no one else like you in my life. But I'm just not ready to have a child at this point in my life."

Beth shook her head, "John, you're only thinking about yourself. Our child *needs* a father. You talk about your father all the time. Don't you think our child needs a father, too? Do you think I want to have this child alone?"

He didn't know what to do. The plan tonight was supposed to be to break up with her, or at least make steps towards ending it. But he couldn't get over the thought of abandoning his unborn child, even if it was barely formed. No one deserves abandonment. Yet, he couldn't bear to think about how much he'd be giving up if they did have a child together. *I'm still young. I have money. I have my life ahead of me.* He owed it to himself and his father. *What would Father say if he heard that all he did with his money is got a girl pregnant and settled down?*

"Beth, I'm sorry. We're both in over our heads. I think we need to take a break and think about what we're doing before we keep going. There's a lot I need to process."

That broke her. She slid down the kitchen counter to the floor and collapsed. She wept. He had the urge to run over to her, kneel down, and comfort her. But he just stood there and watched. Silent and frozen. There was nothing to say. Nothing he could do that would help her. He moved quietly to put on his jacket and scarf, "I'm going to leave. I'll call you later to see how you're doing."

Neither said goodbye as he closed the door and walked out into the cold with Beth's sobs harrowing in his ears.

56

Nathan canceled all of his meetings the next day and took the day off to think. Sitting in his room at his desk in a white bathrobe, he stewed in mental combat. *What a heartless animal I am. Only a brute would do something like that.* But they weren't married. They weren't even engaged. *The pregnancy isn't my problem.* He didn't want it to happen, nor was it even in his plan. They didn't talk about it. Things moved fast all of a sudden and now look where they were. *No, I made the right decision.* It's just painful to go through it. He drank a third scotch at his desk. Breakups are never supposed to be easy, Angeline told him. *She was right. They are not.*

He tried to distract himself on the computer. *I could really go for a hit with Derrick right now.* The phone rang. Nathan held the phone up to his ear.

"Hello, this is John," he said, as professionally as possible.

"Hello, Mr. Shepherd, this is George Pendleton," his voice was calm and amiable. "How are you?"

"Fine, and you?"

"Doing well," he said. "Listen, I was calling about this weekend's membership meeting. I'd like to put you on the agenda to give the city report. Things haven't been too promising lately so I'm curious to see what you come up with. Is that alright?"

"Absolutely," Nathan said bending his nervousness into a gingerly tone. "I would be happy to do it."

"Good man," George said. "Oh, and Mr. Shepherd?"

"Yes?"

"I know you're still a bit new here but I wanted to ask you something. I need a favor."

Nathan paused. *A favor? For George?*

George said slowly, "I don't mean to be so forward, but my daughter just contacted me after many years, and I need someone to look after her when I can't. I trust you and I think you'd both get along. You're both young. I don't have time for her right now. Do you think you could help?"

"Oh," Nathan let out a laugh. "That's fine. Sure, I'd be happy to help her out."

"Great," George said. "I'll text you her phone number and let her know. Thanks."

Brilliant. Another connection to a rich man. Nathan knew he had a good way with women. *What better woman than the daughter of George Pendleton?* It was a good power play.

George's text message came in with his daughter's number. It looked familiar to Nathan. Frowning, Nathan dialed it and the number disappeared, replaced with a name he already had on his phone.

My Beth.

57

"Pop, it's time to come home," Paul commanded his father over the phone. In his hotel room, Thomas stood at the window that overlooked Alvin Park and studied the base of The Charles. He shook his head.

"He's here. I know he is. I'm too close to give up now."

"Look, everyone is starting to get worried," said Paul. "Nathan disappeared and then you left suddenly—people want to know what's going on."

"Tell them I'll be back before the weekend," said Thomas.

"What about Nathan?"

"With or without Nathan."

"Promise?"

"I do," Thomas said weakly. The thought of leaving Nathan here alone with his fortune gave him the chills. It was Wednesday. He had twenty-four hours.

Hanging up the phone, Thomas grabbed his coat and left for The Charles, where he planned to wait until he found his son.

In his room, Nathan hung up and immediately wrote a text to Beth with trembling fingers. "Beth, what's your father's name?"

He sent her text after text saying to call him before she talks with her father, if it wasn't too late. Twenty minutes went by and she still didn't respond.

A cold sweat broke out on his forehead and his chest and throat felt tight. *I need fresh air.*

He grabbed a pack of cigarettes and chewed his knuckles in the elevator. He paced and fidgeted. He tried to calm down. *She probably went for a run, or just forgot about the phone while cooking or something. Yes, that's it. She went for a run.*

Nathan crossed through the lobby and went out the side exit of the hotel. He wrote her again, "What was your maiden name?"

He cursed himself for being so ignorant and not asking these questions earlier. He lit a cigarette and drew the hot, comforting heat into his chest. He breathed out slowly and headed to the park. His phone buzzed. It was a text from Beth.

"My maiden name is Pendleton. Goodbye, John."

Horrified, he froze, eyes fixated on the screen. Panic gripped his air passages. The thought was a cinder block crushing his chest. For fifteen seconds, he stood in the middle of the park staring at her message when again his phone lit up with another call. The caller's name flashed in his eyes.

George Pendleton.

At that moment, Nathan heard a man's voice yell his real name in the distance. His eyes glued to the urgent phone call in his hand. *Damn.* He should answer. He felt like throwing up.

"Nathan!"

Again, the voice said his real name. "Nathan!" He, along with other patrons, looked around the park for the shouting voice. He heard feet scuttling across the park. Then he turned and saw the bitter jaws of hell itself open before him.

58

THOMAS LOOKED RABID. Throwing his burning cigarette to the ground, Nathan put his fists up to receive his barreling father. Thomas opened his big hands and pounced, grabbing at his son's clothing. Nathan dodged him.

"I knew you'd show up at some point," he taunted his father, hiding his shock.

"I've been searching all over for you," yelled Thomas as he circled back and leaped towards him. "You're coming home now," he caught Nathan's arm but Nathan pushed him off.

"I'm not going with you," shouted Nathan.

"Yes, you are," Thomas retorted. He would not give up.

"I'm staying here and there's nothing you can do to stop me," said Nathan with confidence.

Thomas needed to get his hands on him, to stop him from running again. He bent and propelled forward, grasping for his son.

"Stop this," said Nathan, tripping his father. "Go home, old man, if you're going to be like this."

Thomas stumbled and fell to the ground. A crowd had gathered to watch the altercation. Nathan addressed the onlookers.

"Can someone call an ambulance or an officer to take this drunk back to his home?"

The crowd whispered among themselves.

"He stole from me," Thomas said loudly, gasping from his knees. He didn't want to bring it up, especially not in public, but he had no choice now. "He's my son and he stole all my money."

"He's lying," defended Nathan. "I've never seen this man before." He moved closer to his father. "Be quiet! If that's how low you are, then I will talk. Not here."

Nathan helped Thomas up and immediately Thomas grabbed his son's wrist. Nathan flinched but didn't try to escape. He pointed to a table in the corner of the park, away from the crowd. They walked to it and sat on either side of the chessboard tabletop.

59

"Lay out your terms," Nathan crossed his arms. "What do you want?"

Thomas couldn't believe his son's antipathy. He knew what he'd done and yet he's pretending to negotiate a business deal.

"I shouldn't even have to say this because I know you know it already," Thomas spoke angrily. "What you did was extremely wrong, Nathan."

Nathan shrugged. "I know. But I'm choosing not to think about it. It's time to move on. There's nothing you can say now to make me come back home with you. I'm on my own and I'm making my own way. Without you."

Thomas wanted to hit him, to knock some sense into his defiant son's head.

"Look–"

"There's nothing you can say, Father," Nathan cut him off. He didn't want him to speak. His demons didn't need any more leverage than what they already had to torment him.

Thomas sat still. His eyes blazing, his blood burning, and his mind searching for what to say. He hated words.

"Listen to me..." he began. Nathan cut him off again but Thomas slapped the table with his mighty palm. *Smack!*

"Listen, Nathan!"

Nathan's back straightened and he was silent.

"I know we don't see eye to eye on things and we probably don't have much respect for one another right now." Thomas put his hands on the table like he was holding a small box. "But you need to know that what you did was wrong. And you need to take responsibility and make it right again."

Nathan remained silent and stone-faced as his eyes bore holes through his father's skull. Surprised his son was actually still listening, Thomas continued as gently as possible, "I need you to come home, give everything back, and apologize to Paul and me—your family—and then to everyone else. Everyone has been worried sick about you."

The young man's chest rose and fell quickly and his eyes flitted elsewhere. Slowly, Thomas extended his hand to grab Nathan's wrist again. Just as it reached the hairs of his forearm, Nathan shot up to his feet.

"Said everything you wanted to say? Did you get it all out?"

Thomas got up quickly and readied himself to pursue.

"Good," said Nathan. "Now you can leave."

"I'm not leaving without you."

"What do I need to say to get it through your head? I'm not coming with you."

A thought bolted across Thomas's mind and sent a cold shiver down his spine. If he left Nathan here, he'd never come back. If they couldn't reconcile and restore what was owed, then their relationship was worth nothing. It already seemed that Nathan wanted it that way.

"You'll be dead to me if you stay," said Thomas despondent.

"Good," responded Nathan. "I thought I already was."

In that moment, the layers of anger and bitterness inside Thomas crumbled into sadness. He had failed. He failed Nathan, Paul, and his Abby.

60

STORMING BACK TO The Charles, Nathan shook off the confrontation with Thomas. He knew his father just wanted everything back to normal but that's exactly what Nathan ran from. He refused to think more about it but reluctantly decided he would mail only the documents of the safe back home. That would ameliorate at least some of Thomas's concerns, and besides, Nathan had everything he needed.

In his room, Nathan turned his attention to the conflict at hand. He didn't know if it was desperation to know the truth or perhaps a justice-seeking impulse for self-punishment, but he pressed the missed call from George Pendleton. Taking a swig of liquor, he held the phone up to his ear.

George's voice tore through the phone's earpiece like a gunshot.

"Mr. Shepherd. Do you happen to know a Beth Jacobs?"

He seethed and bit his words. His voice shook. "Answer me right now. I said, do you know a Beth Jacobs?"

"Yep, I do."

"Your insolence!" George's voice burst out of the phone like a spray of hot acid.

"I know a Beth Jacobs," repeated Nathan. He was numb. Even dauntless. Impenetrable.

"How well do you know this Beth Jacobs?"

"Pretty well," he said.

"You're goddamn right you do!" he screamed. "I heard the whole story. You slept with my daughter. You got her pregnant. And then you left her?! You're a coward! A selfish coward! What am I supposed to believe?"

"Believe what you want."

"We're through. You hear me, Mr. Shepherd? We're through!"

The phone slammed and Nathan jerked the phone away from his ear. He looked for the liquor bottle, and sat on the floor, breathing heavily through his nose.

Voices poured into his head. *You screwed up. Everything you worked hard to build means nothing. All of your hard work is about to crash down. You're alone. No one cares about you now.* Of all the people not to cross, he might have picked the absolute worst man in Delorre.

PART 3

THE LONG WAY DOWN

61

Over the next few weeks, George pulled his support from Nathan faster than a hand recoiling from a burning stove. The next day, he sent a one line email that read:

[No Subject]

Do NOT come to the meeting on Saturday.

After that, Nathan stopped receiving notes from the other Venture X members. They left him off of group correspondence. He had no way of knowing what was going on or when the next meetings were. He picked up the phone and called Mr. Jefferson. After polite greetings, Nathan asked him directly what was going on.

"Mr. Pendleton is severely upset," he said.

"Why?" asked Nathan. "Isn't he letting personal life affect professional life a little too much?"

In his typical overanalyzing way, Mr. Jefferson said, "Mr. Pendleton is making up for the decade and a half of indifference towards his daughter. It seems he's now wanting to care for his daughter, which, he feels, means protecting her from you, Mr. Shepherd. You are the enemy, in his eyes. The symbol of his failure as a father."

"Seems a little much. What should I do?"

He paused, as if thinking. "Your decisions have led you down this path," he said solemnly. "Your decisions will have to lead you out of it."

"What about my money in the Venture X fund? Should I be worried?"

"He can't touch your money without full board approval," he said. "You don't have to be concerned about that. Your money is safe in the fund."

"That's a relief to hear," said Nathan. But it didn't lift his spirits at all.

"Indeed. Mr. Pendleton is a fiery man when he is upset, but he will never cross the line into unscrupulous conduct," Mr Jefferson reassured him. "Give it some time. Perhaps it will all blow over. I wish you the best. Goodbye, Mr. Shepherd."

Beth stopped bringing him breakfast in the mornings. He had to get used to going to the restaurant to get his breakfast and coffee. Occasionally, he saw her around The Charles. She avoided him and shut down all of his attempts to communicate with her.

To fill the time he usually spent with Beth, he bought more things. Angeline insisted he go shopping with her to get a new wardrobe.

They met at The Charles and walked to the Silk District. Angeline wore a black leather skirt suit and heels which clacked along the sidewalk. Nathan hid his face behind a pair of oversized Bvlgari sunglasses.

Angeline tried to help. "You should find someone else, John. We hate seeing you down like this."

"I take a different woman out every other night, Angeline. I'm trying." He snorted. "We usually finish up at my room or theirs." His eyes fell to the ground. "It's not working."

"Beth Jacobs is not the only one out there for you," Angeline said. "Don't give up yet."

"It's only a matter of time before the word spreads about Beth, the child, and the relationship to George. When that happens, it's going to be a public relations nightmare for me. The gossip press will devour the story like wolves."

"I don't think so," Angeline disagreed. "Someone like George Pendleton does everything he can to stay under the radar. He won't want to bring this out to the public light and risk his own name."

"Hopefully not," Nathan said.

They walked into a designer store.

"At least I still have my money," he said aloud to reassure himself.

"That's right," Angeline said. "When are you going to work with me to find an investment property?"

"I just had another loan go through. And I'm working on another one. Once I finish off my investments with Venture X, I'll come knocking on your door."

His lips formed a shallow smile. It was a tricky game to play but he was managing. Once he finished the $30 million, he could live on the quarterly dividends. Then he could start investing in other assets.

"Time to get you into some new suits," said Angeline. The expensive outfits he had bought before when he still had his blue collar frame no longer fit.

"Why?" he pretended to complain.

"Look at you," she said. "You're a stick!"

He had lost a tremendous amount of weight.

"I want you to start tanning, too. You look like a ghost. You need to get back to the color you had when you first moved here."

He tried on a tailored blue knit suit jacket, a white silk oxford shirt sprinkled with red, dark slim fit jeans, and a pair of Salvatore Ferragamo Python loafers.

"Perfect," Angeline said. "We'll take it."

In front of the mirror, Nathan looked at himself. "Angeline, thank you for being here. Heaven knows I'd be a mess if you weren't here right now, my friend."

On the way back to The Charles, they noticed the homeless man outside the entrance again. Nathan held out a dollar bill. The shaggy man grabbed it out of his hand with his gnarled digits. Through the mesh of hair that covered his face, he gave them a grin.

"Why do you do that?" Angeline scolded Nathan.

"Look at him," Nathan said as they passed by. "He's helpless. Someone must do something. Why not me?"

"It's just..." She stopped in the lobby to say goodbye. "He smells."

Nathan chuckled. "Goodbye, Angeline, thank you for today. I needed it."

62

A MONTH WENT by since George's conniption, and Nathan received no phone calls. Not an ounce of newspaper ink mentioned his falling out with Beth, the child, and George Pendleton. He was beginning to think that maybe this unfortunate chapter had passed. Maybe George forgave him and didn't tell anyone outside Venture X about the mishap. Maybe the whole thing just evaporated, like Mr. Jefferson said.

Nathan found himself wanting to be alone but he had to keep partying. It was a bizarre form of self-inflicted harm. He had to keep up his reputation, but more and more he hated being around people. He found safety in books. Reading from the comfort of his own room, he could relax and be himself. But the Country Millionaire was a socialite. He was a bold and wise venture capitalist looking for opportunities to help the city. He was kind and he bought drinks for everyone. He kept his promises and followed up professionally. This was the life he had built over the years. Yet, at any moment, someone could mention the name Beth Jacobs. And then, he knew it would all be over.

But, as long as he kept buying rounds and having a good time, no one asked questions.

At Brew Social, he ordered a double-shot espresso caramel

soy latte and found his corner in the back. He studied his accounts, checked emails, and followed up with a potential real estate opportunity. His phone rang. He took a sip of coffee.

"This is John."

A deep voice on the other side said, "May I speak with Mr. Shepherd?"

"Speaking."

It was a man from the bank. After various security verifications, he said, "Mr. Shepherd, I regret to inform you that your loan application was rejected. Due to several questionable and unverifiable conditions with your income, credit, and assets, we are unable to grant you a loan at this time. I do apologize for the inconvenience."

Nathan inhaled the foam from his latte so sharply it flew into his lungs. He coughed. "What do you mean you rejected my application? What happened?"

"The bank is not granting your request for a loan from the 3rd of last month."

"I don't get it. I've never been rejected. Did something happen?"

"An investigation of your history has led to the freezing of your credit. We also noticed you opened numerous credit cards several months ago and have not made any payments."

"But I have millions of dollars in Venture X!" He shouted. "Yes, I said Venture X. I can pay anything off immediately if I wanted to. Have you ever heard of Venture X?"

"I wasn't finished, Mr. Shepherd," he said. "We were unable to confirm your membership with Venture X."

"What?"

The insolence of this man. He is completely wrong. He paid that month's membership fees and dues last week. There was no way that was true.

"You claimed on your loan application that you were a member of Venture X Investment Partners Inc.," the man said. "As a part of our screening and verification process, we contacted the organization and no one was able to confirm that you were a member."

"Look, mister, whoever told you that is a liar. I have received no such word that my membership was canceled. Don't you think I would be the first to know?"

"I'm sorry, sir, I can't help—"

"Who told you?" he interrupted him loudly. Several heads in the coffee shop turned.

"Unfortunately, I am not permitted to say," the banker said.

"Come on, tell me," he said. *Ugh, you sound so desperate.*

"I'm sorry Mr. Shepherd, but we hold the privacy of our customers at a very high level of protection."

"Alright, enough of this. I'll just take my business elsewhere."

Furious, he hung up on the bank official and immediately began calling friends who were bankers. Several of them mentioned that the entire city is going into austerity on account of the poor performance of the market. Capital was drying up, they said. He'd be lucky to find a loan that size even if his credit were in order.

There was nothing wrong with the market, he thought. He bet George was behind it all. He may not have taken it to the press, but Nathan was sure he had been spreading this lie around to the financiers.

The lukewarm latte tasted disgusting. Dejected, he picked up a newspaper from the neighboring seat. The headlines said, *Investors Brace for Market Plunge.*

The article talked about a global bank going under, a burst bubble in the technology sectors, and a two-year drought of IPOs. *Not good.* Without that loan, he couldn't complete his final contributions to Venture X. Opening his briefcase, he feathered through the folders to find the prospectus. He found the part he needed. It read:

In the event that a member is unable to fulfill the complete investment amount as agreed upon and according to the terms included in this document, the member is to be put on reconciliatory probation. A grace period of two months is given to the member to resume investment. During this time, the non-paying member is required to submit a written report of his or her financial condition as well as a plan to return to solvency and/or financial salubrity.

He needed another loan if he was going to retain his membership. He wished he had held onto the safe and other account information. He could have leveraged the farmhouse or the land.

Nathan's head throbbed. He put his head down on the table and closed his eyes. An inevitable, terrible thought struck him. *I need to think about pulling my money out of Venture X and starting over.* It would be an emblem of failure he would never live down. Not with himself. He reached for the top and got there, only to fall all the way down.

He packed up the computer and papers and headed back to the hotel. *To make ends meet until I get my money out of Venture X, I probably should restrict spending and dial down expenses.*

In a dark mood, he arrived at the hotel. He passed by the homeless man Jeb who sat to the left of the doors.

"Muhh?" He grunted as he recognized Nathan.

For the first time since he arrived at The Charles, he shook his head. "Sorry, Jeb, not today. But soon. Don't worry."

Jeb frowned and shrugged his shoulders. He looked away to

the next person. He didn't care.

Instead of dropping off his things in his room, he went straight to Derrick's. They had to talk about how he wasn't going to be able to keep paying for his room anymore. Also, he needed to bump their daily "meeting" up a few hours as he was feeling more depressed than usual.

Knocking on his door, Nathan waited outside in the hallway. Sometimes, when he was in the hallways, he wondered if he would run into Beth. He hadn't seen her in over a month now. She must've found a job elsewhere. *I mean, with George as a father, she wouldn't need to work. Ever.*

He knocked again a little louder. No answer. *What is taking him so long?* He called, "Derrick, open up. It's me, John."

Still no answer. Maybe he was out meeting with someone else. Nathan went to his own room to get the keycard to Derrick's room. He kept one as well, because it was his room after all. Putting his stuff by the desk, he grabbed the keycard and walked out into the hallway again.

He knocked a final time and said, "Derrick, I'm coming in." A picture of his torn up and tattooed back flashed in his mind and he shuddered. *Don't want to see that again.* He inserted the keycard and slowly pushed the door open.

Derrick was a slob. The fan was on, pushing around a horrid, sour smell in the air. Restaurant takeout bags and liquor bottles were all over the floor. The beds were unmade. Drug paraphernalia cluttered the desk and furniture. *Disgusting.* It didn't look like Derrick was here. Nathan tip-toed over to his desk to grab a few needles, dime bags, and a lighter.

As he stepped on the blanket in the middle of floor in between the beds, his foot landed on something squishy with ridges, and he just about rolled his ankle. It felt like a shoe. Annoyed at all the disorder, he kicked the shoe under the blanket. But the shoe was still attached to a leg.

"What the—"

He grabbed the blanket and flicked it off the messy floor. On the floor, Derrick's body lay inanimate. His skin was grayer than usual. His death metal t-shirt had bloody finger wipes all over it. A needle was half stuck in the hole in his left arm.

Oh, god. "Derrick!" He knelt down to feel the body. His fingers recoiled at the cold temperature.

"Derrick!"

He felt for a pulse in his neck. Nothing. He shook his shoulders; they were stiff and resistant.

"Derrick!"

Vomit lurched into Nathan's throat. He stood to his feet and the blood rushed out of his head. Everything went black as he fell to the ground, unconscious.

63

"Beth, would you like some hot tea?"
"Coffee, please. Decaf," Beth said to George.

She visited him in his Cherry Hill mansion. It was cold in the big red carpeted room with the dozens of faces on the walls, and the ferocious bear. She stood under the beast by the fireplace, holding her elbows.

George motioned to a maid to bring the coffee.

"I know I have a lot to make up for, Beth," he exhaled, stepping closer to her. "I want you to be assured you and the child will be taken care of."

Beth was silent. She stared into the flames. She thought about John, his friendliness, and innocence. She longed for his arm to be around her shoulders.

George continued, "First, I want you to be done with that celebrity flytrap of a hotel. You have no need to work there anymore."

She closed her eyes and nodded, gratefully. She moved closer to the fire.

George stood next to her. *Money fixes most problems, but it doesn't fix family.* He didn't know how to help her.

"You're welcome to move in with me, Beth," he offered. "You'll have plenty of room for your art and cooking. The baby will have its own room. The staff here would love your presence around the house."

She frowned. She didn't want any of it.

He kept on. "There are running trails in the back. It's been so long since I've walked them, but I'm fairly positive they lead to a lake."

The coffee and tea came. They sat down at the large oak table. George took his usual spot at the head of the table.

The fresh steam from the hot brew filled her nostrils.

Without looking at him, she said, "George."

"Yes, dear." He was slightly perturbed she called him by his first name.

"What is going to happen to John?"

George dismissed the name. "Who? Mr. Shepherd? He will probably continue to make his appearances in the newspapers, giving thousands to this charity or that charity, and going to parti—"

"I'm serious." She knew he knew more than that. She pressed him. "What do you know?"

George looked at his deranged daughter. "He won't last much longer."

Now she looked at him. He had her attention.

George said, "I had someone do a little digging into his records. There is nothing there. The IRS has been watching him closely. They are mounting an investigation."

"An investigation? For what?"

"Fraud. Laundering. Perjury. To start."

Beth's face was aghast.

"He's a ghost," he said. "No one knows anything about him. And when they do, I'm afraid it's not going to be good."

"What's going to happen to him?" she asked.

"He'll be asked to account for everything. Who he is and where his money came from."

George rolled his eyes. "I can't believe we were so blind."

Beth said, "He's a good man. I promise."

"He was a smart, ambitious professional." George lowered his brow. "But it was only skin-deep."

"No!" Beth shouted. "He was kind and generous. He was only confused."

"He knew what he was doing," George corrected her. "He did it to himself."

It was too harsh. She stood up. "I still believe in him. Even if you don't. You don't care about anyone but yourself. You've always been that way."

She walked out of the room.

George put his head down. He laughed. *Love has always been a silly thing.*

64

"John... John," Nathan awoke to Tommy nudging his chest. "John, are you okay?"

Hazy and weak, he could tell Tommy was worried. Tommy put his arm behind Nathan's back and sat him up. Apparently, he had fallen in between the two beds in Derrick's room. *Derrick.*

Derrick's body still lay partially buried by blankets and trash on the floor by Nathan's feet.

"Tommy?" he said, groggily.

"Yes, John, it's me," he said. "We've got to get you out of here. This is not good." He spoke quickly.

"Is Derrick... dead?" He could barely speak.

"He is."

He cringed. As if he were somehow responsible for his death. Maybe if he hadn't bought him his own place, he wouldn't have done this. He probably just got careless. *Why did he do this to himself?*

Tommy interrupted his thoughts. "John, let's go, buddy. You can't stay here."

Trying to get a hold of himself, he held onto Tommy as he hoisted him to his feet. His knees shook and his head felt light still. He hobbled on Tommy's shoulder out of the room and into his room.

"How did you find me?" He whispered weakly.

"I tried calling you literally twenty times. When you missed Launch Pad and didn't answer, I figured something was wrong. I came to the hotel and when I didn't find you in your room, I tried Derrick's room. When neither of you answered, I panicked. I called Beth. She came and unlocked the doors."

He put Nathan on the bed and filled up a glass of water. He did his best to sit up. He sipped the water.

"Did Beth see me?" he asked.

"No. She said she would only do it on one condition, that she didn't have to talk to you."

Nathan closed his eyes. He missed her. She still hated him. It was too much to think about. Lying back on the bed, he asked Tommy how long he was out. He said at least four hours.

"You sure you are okay? Do you need anything?"

"What are we going to do with Derrick?" he asked.

"I don't know. But I thought about it while I was taking care of you. We have two options. One, report the incident to the authorities and risk being pulled into the investigation. Or, two, take care of the body ourselves."

His face was grim.

"I wish we could just report it," Nathan groaned. "But there's no way I can risk being associated or involved with his death."

He shook his head. "I don't think we can report this, Tommy."

Tommy sat on a chair with his elbows on his knees. He looked up at Nathan and they both knew what they needed to do.

"It probably needs to happen before morning, right? Before room service comes by?" he said.

Tommy nodded.

Nathan laid an arm over his eyes. The clock ticked. It was

11:00 p.m. Finally, he said, "Tommy, you've been through enough today already. Go home. I'll take of this."

Tommy got to his feet and said, "Well, shit," and left him alone.

Nathan sat on his bed with his head against the headboard. He tried to rest but every time he closed his eyes he saw the room behind the wall. The room was still, dark, and quiet. He saw Derrick's lifeless body buried in the filth. Just laying there.

On a normal night, he'd text Derrick to turn down the music or television volume. He never replied but it would get quieter. He was an obedient kind of guy, always willing to do something or go somewhere. He was the kind of friend Nathan could count on to get food, or a drink, or a joint, or something. He listened better than anyone else he knew. He may not have been someone he looked up to or wanted to be like, but he was constant in his friendship. He didn't have to worry about him. He didn't have to think about anything he said before he said it when he was with him. He couldn't be like that with many other people. His father and Paul judged him. With Derrick, he could be totally free. Unrestrained by fear of judgment. Derrick listened to him, probably more than he realized. He would've been with him right then, if he were still alive.

He awoke still sitting up against the headboard. Bright sunlight poured into the room through the window. He rubbed his face and wiped the crusted particles from his eyes. Stumbling towards the bathroom, he flipped on the light. Then, in a moment of horror, he realized Derrick's body was still in the other room. *How long was I asleep? What time is it?* Frazzled, he stumbled towards the bed to check the time. The bed stand clock said 9:14 a.m. Room service came usually at 10:00 a.m., after Beth used to bring him breakfast, but no one had knocked on his door yet. He rushed over to Derrick's room. Pushing the door open, the pungent odor of rotting flesh mixed with soured beer and moldy food punched him in the nose nearly knocking him to the ground. Stomach acid rose into the back of his throat. He gagged but grit his teeth. *You don't have a choice, Nathan. You must do this.*

As he rolled the body up in the bedsheets, it felt as if he was bundling soft wooden logs in a blanket. The lifeless body was cold. His stinging eyes watered and tears rolled down his face. He slung the corpse of his dead friend over his shoulder. *Maybe a hundred pounds.*

He checked the hallway first, carried it to his own room's bathroom, and placed it in the bathtub. Returning to Derrick's room, he gathered the drug supplies and any indicting evidence. He threw everything into a garbage bag. Finally, he wiped down the desk and counters and sprayed the room with air refresher. He went to the lobby and checked out of the room. It was 9:51.

In his own room, he waited for the housekeepers to knock. When it came, he yelled through the door, "No thank you! I won't be needing housekeeping today."

He waited silently, listening. It took three hours for them to finish the room next door.

65

THOMAS SAT IN his office, hunched over papers, and recorded the purchases and sales of the week in a ledger. A dim lamp lit the small room. It was quarter of nine at night. The only sound was the scuffing of his pencil. Every few minutes he looked up, stretched his sore back, and stared at the family picture above his desk.

Will I ever see him again?

Thomas's back popped and he groaned. Without the backup funds of the oilfield money, he worked doubly hard to make up for it.

Tap, tap. There was a soft knock at the door.

"Come in," Thomas said.

The door creaked open and a frizzy redhead poked his head into the room.

"Good evening, Chester," Thomas greeted the boy.

"Sorry to disturb you, Mr. Degland," he said, politely. His high voice sounded like a dove compared to the rumbling voice of Thomas.

"How can I help?"

"I wanted to see if I could drive the row crop tractor tomorrow. I know it was Nathan's old job, but he isn't here anymore. And it's something I've always wanted to do."

Thomas looked at the boy's pale blue eyes and his heart sank. He saw Nathan in him. He was young, ambitious, and curious.

"You want to drive the rower, then."

"If that's alright with you, sir," said Chester.

"What if Nathan comes back, will you be fine to return to your normal cleaning duties with your mother?"

Chester's freckled forehead wrinkled. "Do you think he's coming back?" His voice sounded hopeful. He missed his friend.

Unprepared for the question, Thomas frowned. He stood, gathered the papers, and closed the ledger.

He faced the boy and put a hand on his shoulder. "You may operate the rower. Meet me by the machinery garage tomorrow morning at 7:30. Now, get some sleep."

Chester smiled, "Thank you, sir. Good night."

66

Two weeks went by. The gaping wound of Derrick's death hardened up, and his absence took some getting used to at Launch Pad parties. Instead of finding a booth in a back corner of a bar, Nathan went to the bathroom alone, found an empty stall, and sloppily shot up. He barely knew what he was doing.

One night, he didn't buy a round at one of the bars. He didn't feel like it. Tommy and Angeline gave him curious looks. He could feel the entire room sink in energy like someone had just thrown up in the middle of the floor.

He said, "Don't worry about it, I just don't feel like it. I'm still trying to get over the passing of a good friend." That was true, but he was also out of money.

He had next to nothing in his bank accounts. He needed to find out what was happening with Venture X, especially now that he was going to pull it all out. He hadn't heard anything from George, Mr. Jefferson, or any of the other members.

Smoking in his room on afternoon, he couldn't take it anymore. Recalling that he had gotten George's assistant's number, he looked through his phone for Rose Benton. Finding it, he called her, hoping to get some information out of her.

A high, feminine voice answered, "Hello?"

"Rose, I don't know if you remember me, this is John Shepherd. I'd like to take you to dinner. Would you be interested in joining me tomorrow night at Waterhouse?"

Waterhouse was the ritziest restaurant in the city. He knew she couldn't say no.

She said yes. He said to meet there tomorrow night at 6:00 p.m.

She'll know what's going on inside Venture X, he thought, hanging up the phone, and how George is doing. Plus, he put the cigarette out in the ashtray, *she's cute*.

That day he didn't go out at all. He crawled into his cold sheets, weak but somewhat hopeful. Guilt pounded at the doorway of his conscience but he didn't open the door.

He rolled over towards the bathroom wall and his nose caught a strand of the reek of human remains coming from the bathroom. A repugnant haze of Derrick's body still hung in the air; fortunately, the stench didn't leak into the hallway. But Nathan could still detect it. When he did, flashes of memories bombarded his mind of coating the body with hotel shampoo, carrying the body in a black garbage bag down the fire escape stairs in the middle of the night, and throwing it in the dumpster.

I've got to get out of here. It was time to leave The Charles.

67

Tommy and Angeline met at The Charles that night for Launch Pad. They sat next to each other at the bar, waiting for Nathan. They were both somber from Derrick's death.

"You wore black, too, I see," Tommy said, over the din of the packed room.

She shrugged. Two of their friends were missing. The money man, and the drug supplier. That night was bound to be miserable.

Tommy asked, "Is Johnny boy coming?"

She shrugged again. "I htaven't heard from him."

Tommy drank from his pint glass. "Angeline, I've been thinking."

"Wait, Tommy, please. I need a drink first."

She ordered a gin and tonic and gulped it down.

Tommy said again, "I've been thinking, John's not been his usual self lately. I know he and Derrick grew close and stuff and now that he's gone, it's seriously affecting him. I get it. But I think there's more."

"What do you mean?"

"He isn't coming out anymore. He's not buying drinks for people anymore. I haven't seen him since Derrick died."

"He's depressed, Tommy, leave him alone."

"No, I think it's worse."

A drunk banker stumbled in between them and asked where the Country Millionaire was. Angeline didn't want to listen anymore. She was slurping down her drink as fast as she could.

Tommy said he hadn't seen him and pushed the man back into the Launch Pad crowd. They were all waiting for Nathan.

Tommy leaned into Angeline and whispered in her ear. "I think he's broke."

She peered harshly into his swollen, wet eyes. He mouthed the word "broke" to her, the folds of his neck undulating under his jowls.

"No, you can't be serious," she said.

He nodded slowly, his neck pancaking onto his chest. *He might be right.*

"But how?" she asked.

"How am I supposed to know? I'm not his advisor."

"You think he could lose it this fast?"

Looking around the full room in The Charles, Tommy said, "I wouldn't be too shocked."

Angeline closed her eyes. *Poor John.*

"The reason I brought this up is I want us to be ready. If he is actually broke, we aren't sticking around. You and I both know we don't have time for poor friends."

Angeline scowled at him. She knew he would say that. "Just like always, right?"

He puffed up his chest. "Don't you love me?"

"You're ridiculous," she said. They clinked their glasses and finished off their drinks.

68

"Don't worry, ol' boy," Nathan said the next morning as he left for the Brew Social, slapping a $5 bill into Jeb's outstretched, mangled hand. It was a new day. *I'm a new me.* He stayed at Brew Social to research and analyze the infinitude of financial pathways that lay before him once he had his money back from Venture X. Currently, he had almost $24 million in Venture X. Roughly $15 million came from bank loans and slightly less than $9 million came from him. After settling the debt with the banks and credit companies, he estimated he would start over with roughly $8.25 million. *Not bad*, he thought, *it's almost as much as I started with.*

At 3:00 p.m., he lit up a cigarette and stopped by Alvin Park for a round of chess with Murphy.

In the middle of their first game, Murphy took off his shades and said, "Hey kid, can I ask you a question?"

Nathan nodded has he jumped his knight into a fork move. Murphy didn't notice—he kept his eyes on Nathan's face.

"Are you on some kind of diet? You look like you lost a ton of weight. I'm only asking because I'm your friend."

"Maybe you should stop looking at me and check out the board," Nathan quipped, pointing to the forked pieces.

"Sometimes it's not about the game anymore," said Murphy,

crossing his arms. "I'm worried about you."

"You don't have to be," said Nathan. "Your move. Go."

Murphy uncrossed his arms and sighed as he placed his queen dangerously close to Nathan's king. "I just want you to be careful. Sometimes life isn't what it always seems."

Nathan refused to look him in the eye. Disgusted, he stood up and toppled his king in surrender. "I guess so."

"Seriously, John," Murphy warned. "I'm not just talking about this game..."

Nathan turned and walked away, heading back to The Charles to get ready for his date with Rose.

In the bathroom, he shaved, combed his hair, whitened his teeth, and applied a self tanner to cover up his pale skin. He put on his charcoal grey slim fit Tom Ford "closer" suit—the one he used to make an impression on a lady. He was just getting ready to leave when he caught a view of himself in the mirror. He paused. It scared him, for a moment. He was unrecognizable. Not a single person would recognize him back at the farm. He squared up in front of the mirror and adjusted his tie. His cheekbones jutted out, his eyes sunk into his face above puffy bags of flesh, and his shoulders pinched inwards. *Murphy was right.* His hair was clipped close on the sides of his head while the top was long and combed back, gleaming with product. Even his hands were thin, sinewy, and bony. He looked ten years older. He flipped the light out.

He arrived early at the Waterhouse. The night was completely planned out in his head. He had a long list of questions he needed answered but, he knew Rose wouldn't just come and spill everything. She needed to be indulged. She needed to feel cared for before he pumped her for information. *Plus, if all goes according to plan, I may find myself back at her place before the night ends...* He scolded himself. *Be professional.*

The private table where he sat overlooked the Stein. A

stringed quartet played in the corner. The sun was setting and he had just ordered a bottle of crisp Montrachet chardonnay and a red Chateau Lafite 1865. Both bottles were several hundred dollars each.

The waiter came around the corner, leading someone behind him. Nathan could only see the long tan legs muzzled by the red high heels of the guest behind him. It was Rose.

She moved with an elegance unlike any other woman he'd seen. Her curled blonde hair flowed onto her silver dress with a low bodice, exposing just enough of her voluptuous torso. Her sculpted leg stepped out of the split in her long dress as she walked towards him. She moved with calculation and intention that exuded royalty.

Nathan stood to his feet instantly and extended a gentlemanly hand to greet her with a smile.

"Rose," he said.

"John," she said, taking his hand. Her teeth were perfect. She sat.

"Do you like your wine like you like your dress?" he said. She suppressed a giggle. "I like my wine like you like your watch." She had noticed his white watch. "Touché," he said, popping open the white wine.

He poured her a glass and said through his nose, "This wine is a supple, elegant white that boasts rich aromas of honey and tropical fruits while apples, melon and vanilla oak tantalize the palate."

She laughed with pleasure and clapped her hands.

"I'm in the presence of a sommelier!"

He poured his own. "As you can see, it's golden in hue and we'll find it slightly tart, crisp and rich in varietal character on the tongue. With aging, you get complexity and smoothness."

They clinked glasses.

The conversation was effortless. She was as smart as she

was beautiful. He spoke about wines, the art and science of agriculture, and his impressions of the city. She shared she was born in the city to two lawyers who were workaholics, and were swept away by their careers, ending in an amicable divorce. She inherited the ambition from her parents and worked her way into the position she had with Venture X by bugging George to death. She said George couldn't say no anymore and brought her on as a personal assistant. She's been working for him for fourteen years.

"I've never seen him so upset," she said, "that week when his daughter called him and said her boyfriend, her baby's father, dumped her." She put her fingers over her lips. "George boiled over."

"I heard about that," Nathan said, hoping she didn't know it was him. "How's George now?"

"He's calmed down about it, although, now, the economy is not letting him sleep. The phones have been ringing constantly from VX members wondering what's going to happen.

"Has George said anything about me?"

"I've heard your name come up in some of the meetings and over several conference calls," she said. "They are wondering what to do with you..." she lowered her voice to imitate how the members refer to each other, "...Mr. Shepherd."

He laughed. "Tell them I have more than enough money to complete my investment plan, I just haven't had the time to write them because more important matters have come up. I don't have time to hold everyone's hands. I'm only one person."

He downed the rest of his wine. He spoke with authority. "But I would like to know about my dividend, seeing that I didn't receive the last one. What the hell happened?"

"First, tell me what your plan is to finish your contributions." Rose said half-playfully.

"Don't worry about a thing—the Country Millionaire has few

tricks up his sleeve." He winked and finished pouring a fresh glass.

"What's your plan?" She said adamantly. "I need answers."

"Don't worry about it," he reassured her, dismissing her serious tone. She stared at him in silence as he took another gulp of wine.

"Rose, what are you doing? I'm trying to have a nice dinner with a beautiful woman and you're spoiling it by talking about money. Are you serious? Can't we enjoy each other's company?"

"I'm sorry," she said. "But I would appreciate it if you would inform me of your plan before the end of the night."

The smile melted from his face. He set his wineglass down on the table, and put his hands on his knees, flaring his elbows. He knew exactly what was going on. "Wait. That's why you're here, isn't it? To spy on me. George let you come to this dinner with me to find out if I had more money! Is that true, Rose?"

"No, you're wrong," she said. She looked down at her lap.

"Unbelievable," he said, casting his eyes upward. "Well, you tell George this. I have plenty of money. Mountains and mountains of it. But it's not for him or Venture X. I'm through with him and his damn fund. I'm pulling it out. All of it."

"John, you are a fool if you do that."

"It's your job to say that," he said accusingly. "It's your job to be here with me right now."

He remembered the dividend. "But I'll keep my money in for one more quarter if I can get the dividend."

Rose finished the last piece of her salmon. "It's not just you. Most members didn't receive the last dividend."

He frowned, wondering if other members were on probation. "What's the cause?" he asked. "Why so many?"

"John," she said seriously. "I'm not allowed to talk about this. Let's put business to the side and have a good time for the rest of the night." She smiled and straightened her back, bracing her shoulders. Her dress glimmered.

His thoughts screamed at him. *But this is what I need to know! Is this not the mission of this entire meal?* He needed that dividend. He had to make a decision. Press Rose for details about the multi-million dollar dividend or forget it and the night may end up lucky.

"Alright, forget it," he said. "You pressed me, it only seems fair that I pressed you back. If we're in the business of using each other..." *I'll find out another way*, he thought to himself, now was not the best time.

"I can think of other ways we can use each other," she said.

They held eye contact for a several moments to confirm the other's intentions. He said, "Your place or mine?"

He didn't trust her at all. *This could be fun.*

The waiter brought the check in a wooden bi-fold holder. The total was $774.89. He inserted his card and turned back to Rose.

A minute later, the waiter returned and said, "I do apologize, sir, your card was declined."

"Ah," Nathan said and pulled out his wallet. It was about as fat as a Rubik's cube.

"Here." He handed him another and smiled at Rose.

The waiter reappeared moments later and said, "I'm sorry, sir, that card was declined as well."

"God," he scowled at him. "Here, take three."

He handed him three cards from different banks. "Your tip is dropping five percent if you come back and say the same thing."

He grinned at Rose again and she smiled back. There was an uncomfortable silence between them as they waited for the waiter to return. His preoccupied mind couldn't think of something clever to say.

"I'm sorry, sir, none of the cards worked."

Embarrassed, Nathan yelled at him. "Do you know how to operate a damn credit card? You're saying none of my cards worked? You fool! That's not possible!"

The displeased waiter stood there, unsure of what to do.

Nathan laughed and looked at Rose. She didn't return his sheepish gaze.

Don't apologize. This is abnormal, he thought. "I don't know what's going on, Rose," he said. "This has never happened to me before."

"Let me pay for it," Rose offered.

No, no, no! Don't let her. She grabbed the wooden receipt book and put one of her cards in it and handed it back to the waiter who bowed slightly in relief.

"You shouldn't have done that," he said, "This was my treat."

"Well, it's mine now." She finished writing the tip and her signature. *Do not say thank you, maintain control.*

She stood up and gathered her things. Nathan kissed her on the cheek. "We should do this again sometime."

"Of course," she said, plastically.

They bid each other goodbye with forced smiles. When she was out of sight, the smile instantly fell off his face as he crashed back down into the chair, defeated. *Did that seriously just happen?* Disgusted with himself, he went to the bar and asked for a bottle of liquor.

"Anything," he told the bartender. "I'll get back to you with the payment another night. You know I'm good for it."

"Rough night?" The bartender overturned a shot glass and placed it on the counter in front of him.

The night faded into a drunken haze of dizziness and sloppiness. He wanted to forget about money, forget about Rose, and forget about what she'll say to George. Halfway through the bottle, he crawled into a cab and staggered back to his room.

69

The next day at the doctor's office, Nathan checked his watch. *3:00 p.m.* The nurse called him in. *Finally.* She was a short, plump woman in her early fifties with light brown hair and saggy cheeks. She wore bright pink scrub pants and a white scrub shirt with little dinosaurs patterned on it.

"Hi, honey. What's been the matter?" she asked, her voice was five times higher than it should've been.

"I've been feverish, sleepless, low energy, and weak," he said. "I'm not sure, maybe it's nothing but I thought I should see a doctor."

"Let's see if we can find out what's going on," she said. She listened to his heart and lungs, took his temperature, and took a blood sample for testing. After recording his vital signs, she said to expect the doctor shortly.

In a few minutes, a gray-haired, wrinkly-faced man in a white lab coat walked in. With a German accent, he introduced himself as Dr. Holtz. He was a fit man with a large frame, who looked as if he could effortlessly complete a triathlon in good time. He took the folder from the door and began examining the data. He asked Nathan questions about lifestyle, diet, and medical history.

"Would you roll up your sleeve? I need to get your blood

pressure."

Nathan rolled up his left sleeve. His discolored skin was dark and collapsed where he had inserted the needles into his arm. The doctor paused momentarily and squinted, and then placed the arm cuff just above Nathan's bruised inner left elbow. He recorded a few notes in the patient file.

"John, I'm going to go check your blood work. I'll be right back."

"Okay," he said.

Nathan wasn't too concerned. *It's probably just my drinking and other "recreational" activities. I've got to shape up. I'm not a superhuman.*

He had never seriously gotten sick growing up on the farm. He knew he shouldn't be surprised if he had picked something up. Plus, his daily habits were considerably different from what they were on the farm two years ago.

Dr. Holtz returned and sat down across from Nathan. He folded his hands in his lap and said, "John, I've been a doctor for twenty-four years and I've seen thousands of patients. But that doesn't make it any easier to deliver a diagnosis. What I'm about to tell you might sound frightening but I'm confident it's manageable."

Nathan's back stiffened. *Manageable* did not sound like a positive word.

"We found evidence of Hepatitis C virus in your blood."

Immediately, Nathan's imagination jumped to life-ending conclusions. He expected the next words out of the doctor's mouth to be the number of months he had left to live.

"What does it mean? Is it serious?"

"Hepatitis C is a virus carried in infected blood, often associated with liver complications. It's rare that it turned up in your blood work so soon. Normally, it takes years for the virus to show up in tests... unless–"

"Dr. Holtz, tell it to me straight. What's going to happen?"

"Before anything else, I want to confirm it is Hepatitis C, though there are substantial indications already. Your blood work will undergo more tests, and a liver biopsy may be required. It's particularly difficult to detect the disease from symptoms, so we'll be monitoring your blood on a monthly basis for the foreseeable future until we firm up the diagnosis and formulate a management plan. I'll prescribe you medications that will help with the side effects."

He stood up and went on, "In the meantime, you'll want to make sure you change some lifestyle habits: develop safe sex practices, avoid needles, especially shared needles. A reduction in alcohol and nicotine consumption would benefit you as well. While this is not an immediate life-threatening situation, it can potentially develop into chronic liver disease, cirrhosis, or liver cancer. John, you need to give your liver a break."

He put his hand on Nathan's shoulder, and looked him in the eyes. "Stop it. You know what you're doing. Stop it." He gave him a soft pat. "Get some help."

Nathan detected a flicker of anger in his voice. This direct instruction startled him. It was a chastisement. Doctors were supposed to be neutral. *They're not supposed to judge.* Perhaps what bothered Nathan more was that the doctor sounded like his father.

70

Back at The Charles, Nathan started to pack up his things. The new safe he had purchased was no longer needed. In it's near-new condition, he could perhaps sell it for a grand or two. *That strange locksmith would know.*

Nathan called Lockpoppers and Dwayne picked up.

"Lockpoppers."

Nathan told him about the safe.

"Yeah, we can take a look at it," Dwayne said. "Sounds like something we can take care of."

"I'll give you a deal if you come here to pick it up."

"I'll be over in twenty minutes."

Nathan's head, joints, and stomach kept him to a sluggish pace. Packing was going to take forever. But, at least, he had time. Now that the Venture X check was on its way there, he needed to be there to receive it. The only problem is he didn't have cash to pay for his room any longer.

He picked up the phone and dialed Tommy.

He answered on the second ring. "John?"

"Hey Tommy."

"Where ya been, big dog? I haven't seen you since... uh, since I last saw you. Everybody has been missing you. Hell, I've missed you and Angeline, too. You've not been around the past few weeks. Where ya been?

"I've not been feeling too well and I need some help."

"Sure, man. What's going on?"

"I'm pulling my money out of Venture X and they're sending the check to my room here at the hotel. The problem is, I'm out of cash until I get that check... would you be able to spot me for a few days?"

"*You* need money?" he said. "But you've always had money. Where'd it all go?"

"I put it all into Venture X. Now, I'm pulling it all out and starting over. I'm not working with Venture X anymore."

"Okay..." his voice trailed off. "What happened with Venture X?"

"Don't worry about it," Nathan said, frustrated by the questions. "I just need ten thousand dollars to get me through another week. Once the check comes in, I'll pay you back. You know I'm good for it. What do you say?"

Silence.

"Tommy, how many times have I given you money? I know it's more times than I can count. Now, I'm asking you for some money, and you're hesitating? Come on, you've got to be joking."

"No, *you've* got to be joking, John," he said. "You're the Country Millionaire, for Christ's sake! You're *supposed* to have money. If word got out that you're asking people for money, you'd be done for."

"I'm not just asking people for money," he said. "I'm asking my friends, just for a week. I'll be getting millions back when the check arrives."

Tommy asked, "How much will you be getting back?"

"I'm not sure. Pendleton didn't tell me."

"So you don't know how much you're getting back?" He asked again.

"Not exactly."

"John, you're in trouble. You're in some deep trouble—to the point where I don't know if I want to be around to see when it all goes down."

"What are you talking about?"

"I don't know a broke John Shepherd!" he cried. "I only know the rich party animal Mr. John Shepherd—the Venture X investor. Without your money, you're not the John Shepherd I know. You're someone else."

"What are you saying, Tommy?"

"Listen. We've been friends for almost two years. In the city, you've gotta choose your friends wisely because you are who you hang around with. I choose mine very carefully. They're all rich. You see what I mean?"

"No."

"You're not rich anymore, John," he said. "You're broke."

Nathan's rage burn against Tommy. *This is betrayal. This backstabbing rat used me. And I considered him my friend.*

Tommy sighed. "Ugh, this isn't fun. Listen, do you have enough to eat?"

Barely. His credit cards were shut down. His bank accounts were overdrawn. The only cash he had was in the safe, but it was drug money. He couldn't use it for food.

"I'm fine," he said. His voice was dry and scratchy.

"I'll wire you $200. It will be there in the morning. Goodbye, John."

The line went dead and he slowly lowered the phone from his ear.

Disgusted, he poured himself a drink from the decanter. It was 10:00 a.m. He debated whether he should go out that night. He knew that if he went out, he'd have to buy drinks for people and pretend like everything was okay. *I've dug myself into a hole. I need to hang back. I'm sure I could find a way to keep myself busy.* He looked over at the safe. Dwayne was probably waiting for him outside.

71

He felt the stares and whispers as he walked through the lobby of The Charles with a train of luggage carts behind him, carried by three attendants. It was his final procession. His last public appearance. His exodus. *The Country Millionaire Leaves The Charles.* He heard camera clicks and saw flashes. With head held high, he strolled across the sparkling black marble floors and bid the staff farewell. It took all his strength and focus to walk with a chest full of air and large steps.

Outside, he saw Jeb in his usual place. He handed him the mostly-empty bottle of scotch whiskey from Grandpa Walker's safe.

"You take care of yourself," he said. "This is a promise," speaking mostly to himself, "I'll be back."

Jeb took the bottle and frowned at it. It was just another bottle of whiskey to him, just like all the others. Nathan doubted the man realized its worth. He had looked it up. It was a Knappogue Castle 1951 Irish whiskey, worth $2,914. Nathan didn't care. There was something right about giving the expensive scotch to a homeless person. It felt familiar, in a freeing way, almost as if it symbolized the close of this chapter of his life. Jeb would treat the rare and precious whiskey, a relic of the Degland family, with as much diligence and care as Nathan had treated his father's money. It might last him half the night.

"I'm going to South Bennington," Nathan told him. Dwayne had given him the address of an affordable and clean extended stay hotel. "I won't be back for a while. Take care."

Through the taxi window, he watched the skyscrapers decrease in size until there were nothing but single-story stores and shops with cheap awnings and stained parking lots. The only tall buildings were multifamily apartments stacked in large red brick cubes. He passed parks full of people sleeping on benches next to abandoned shopping carts, dry dirty fountains, and poorly parked cars with rags hanging from the windows. A sinking feeling in his stomach told him he was in a very different part of town.

It was getting dark when he was dropped off at a building with light brown siding, bright blue highlights and yellow trim. It looked like a toy house reconstructed into a motel. The moving truck backed into the front parking lot and prepared to unload. Inside, the lobby smelled like burnt coffee and smoke, but it was tidy. Outdated photos of sailboats and islands covered the walls. Behind the lobby counter, a short, dark-skinned Indian woman asked him for his name.

"John Shepherd," he said. "I should have a reservation for a month."

He was planning on staying there only until the check arrived. He gave The Charles clear instructions to call him immediately if any mail came in for him. He couldn't help imagining the envelope forgotten, stolen, or lost. He bit his nails thinking about it.

As soon as he walked into his room, he saw why Dwayne called this place affordable. The bed was strangled by a decade-old maroon patterned comforter. The kitchen was made for dwarves, the dining room table was more like a nightstand, and the bathroom smelled like stale pumpernickel bread. Two entwined spiders copulated in the corner of the ceiling. He was no longer at his palace.

He dropped two suitcases on the floor, trying to imagine where his desk would go.

South Bennington was thirty-five miles away from the epicenter of the metropolis. There were not as many businesses, parks, or people. The Country Millionaire would be less seen out here, which was a good thing at this point. He could use a timeout from the public eye, to get back on his feet financially. He would miss the parties, Brew Social, the Launch Pad bars. He laughed to himself as he continued to screen the room. The small, tube television sat on a pseudo-wood wardrobe with chipped corners. The coffee maker was a pouch fed, single cup machine. He had been accustomed to espresso. He couldn't wait to see what breakfast looked like.

He plopped onto the bed. The rigid and unreceptive mattress almost sprained his back. He wondered if the room had a safe to keep drug supplies. A rusty metal box sat on the floor in the closet. He spun the lock dial and heard a disconcerting graininess, but it sounded as if it would still lock. The safe looked barely large enough to fit the syringes, powder packs, cloth, spoons, and other supplies he needed for his "operations." *Dr. Holz would be disappointed.* He didn't care.

When all his things were in the room, there was barely room to move. He stumbled over his computer equipment. *I can't stay here.* He threw a suit down on the bed and picked up the phone. He dialed Angeline and lifted the phone to his ear. It rang until it went to voicemail.

"Angeline, it's John. You probably don't recognize my new phone number. Had to get it so I could lay low for a while after Derrick... Anyways, give me a call when you get this."

He laid on the bed staring up at the yellowed smoke-stained ceiling and called her again.

Voicemail.

He waited ten minutes and called again.

Voicemail.

He had a strong urge to escape before the demons came that night. He rolled out of the bed and went to the black bag with his supplies. He locked the door. He took out the pack of brown powder, a spoon, and a syringe out of the bag and walked over to the sink. He mixed the powder with water, and a soupy yellow liquid formed in the spoon. Sticking the syringe into the mix, he pulled back the plunger and sucked up a full tube. He found the abused vein in his left arm, stuck the needle in, and pushed the plunger down.

Instantly, pure pleasure and confidence flooded his body and senses. All shame and loneliness evaporated. He sat down on the dining chair and flipped on the television and zoned out, bubbling with ecstasy. He wondered if anyone there at the hotel used. He'd like to meet them. His cache of dope was getting low. He needed to find another dealer. Tomorrow, he thought about venturing out into South Bennington to find some new friends.

72

Nathan thought moving to the Traveler's Inn would be a disappointing change, as if he were lowering himself into a sub-respectable lifestyle, but it turned out to be surprisingly stable and affordable. He especially loved his low expenses. Other than rent, he just paid for food, Internet and phone, alcohol and drugs, and the train to get around.

The train station, and the walk to and from it, was unnerving. Street people and homeless men ambled up and down the street peering at specimens as they entered and exited the train station. Nathan bought a throwing knife to carry in his pocket, just in case he was ever threatened. He still had Grandpa Walker's pistol but it was too old to function.

He found out that bad-credit lenders, such as the Cash Today around the corner, can be strung along. By taking the cash from one, he went to another and made up a convincing story about starting a business and already having sales lined up. I just need more cash to buy the inventory, he told them. He made sure to flash the cash when he pitched a business plan. The salesperson, anxious to make a deal, smiled and nodded every time.

He knew they were predatory lenders, and the interest would take the shirt off his back, but it didn't matter. A loan for a few thousand here and there would be erased in a zap when he got the check back from Venture X.

The check... While the lifestyle change was better than expected, the wait for the check was even longer. It was supposed to come in a few days. But it was turning into months without a call from The Charles.

The wait was agonizing. Every time the phone rang, he leapt towards the small device with both hands, instantly sweating. He called them every day to see if any mail had come in for a John Shepherd. The answer was always no.

Damn George Pendleton. He's probably purposely withholding my funds himself.

The people at the Traveler's Inn were not like the rich people at The Charles. They, like Nathan, lived there as a result of some poor or unfortunate circumstances. The Traveler's Inn was a home for people who had no home. A storage facility of unwanted people.

Trash laid in the parking lot around beaten up and broken down automobiles. Room doors were left open, casually allowing passers-by to view the filthy insides. People smoked and drank outside on their shared balconies and yammered on their phones or at each other.

Bobby, a skinny, dirty blonde-haired Australian girl in her twenties who lived at the hotel as a prostitute, was perpetually intoxicated. She was wildly attractive but Nathan had to remind himself that it was her job to be so, and he didn't need any further complications on top of his own disease. She lived alone, having been relegated to Traveler's Inn by a life of abusive relationships. Nathan found her to be friendly.

He knocked on her door one night to share cigarettes and beers, and was shocked when a familiar unshaven pudgy face opened it.

"Dwayne?"

"Hey," Dwayne greeted him nonchalantly. "You made it."

"What are you doing here?"

"I live here," he responded calmly. "Did I forget to mention that?"

"Where's Bobby?"

Dwayne opened the door further, revealing Bobby in the kitchen. She poked her frazzled head out from the open refrigerator door and waved. Then she looked angrily at Dwayne.

"You didn't tell him?" she slammed the door. "Idiot."

"Do you want a place to sleep tonight?" Dwayne yelled at her. She whimpered.

Turning back to Nathan, he said, "That's what I thought. Now, what's up? Like the place?"

Nathan held his tongue. "It's fine. I was coming over to see if Bobby wanted to smoke."

"She sure does," Dwayne turned back into the room and said loudly, "Doesn't she?"

"I have a meeting," he told Nathan, "I'll be back tonight. Let me know if you want more time with her."

He winked and pat Nathan on the shoulder.

An hour later, Nathan and Bobby smoked on the balcony overlooking the hotel parking lot. Two large black men who treated each other like roly-poly polar bears smoked weed and worked on their sports car in the parking lot while listening to loud music. They wore their baggy black jeans so low that when they bent over, Nathan had to look away.

Bobby was really easy to talk to and reminded him of Derrick. She spoke slowly and listened to him with no hidden objectives. She pointed out Fred the feather man, as she liked to call him, a Native American who always had a blue parrot on his shoulder and a long feather in his hat that poked out the opposite direction of his face like the back of a hammerhead.

A black leather vest covered his round belly, and he wore jeans held up by an aged belt and leather cowboy boots. What Bobby liked most about him was that he never failed to wave and grin at anybody he saw.

Nathan confessed his illness to her. To which she replied, "Aye, that's not half bad, honey, I've had the whole hepatitis alphabet. A, B, C... you name it, I've got it!" Though she struggled to carry on a cohesive conversation for over four minutes, Bobby turned out to be someone he could confide in, for which he was thankful. And she found him to be friendly and nice, unlike her partner and the majority of her clientele.

After Dwayne stumbled into the room, Nathan said goodnight and walked next door to his room. He fantasized about what he would do when the Venture X check came. He filled page after page of his journal with plans, ideas, and opportunities to pursue. He could start a wine delivery business, get his C.P.A., or open a consultancy. His suits were getting dusty. He couldn't wait for the day when he would stroll out of his room in one of his blue suits with golden inner-lining, and the rest of the hotel community would see him. He visualized Dwayne's open but speechless mouth and the cigarette dropping from Bobby's lips as they watched him walk away. He could hear the car guys quibble over who he was. Fred the feather man would just smile and wave.

73

O N HIS WAY home from the train station with groceries, Nathan felt his pocket vibrate. He dropped both the bags and whipped his phone out of his pocket, prepared to be disappointed as usual. A primal shriek came from his lips when he saw the caller. It was The Charles.

"Oh, please, oh, please," he said as he held the phone to his ears, ignoring the stares from the street watchers sitting against the stone wall.

"This is John," he said.

"Mr. Shepherd?" It was the chauffeur from The Charles.

"Yes, speaking," he said.

"We have mail for you, Mr. Shepherd," he said. "Several letters came in for you today."

A burst of joy made him want to jump in the air. *Several. He said several. One must* be the check.

"Are you looking at the letters right now?" Nathan asked.

"Yes, sir," he said.

"Turn them around and see if one has a black "X" seal on it, will you?"

He heard papers shuffling and after a pause, the chauffeur said, "Yes, sir, there appears to be one with an X on it."

"Brilliant. I'll be over this afternoon. Thank you."

On the train, he went over his plans for the money once he had it. First, he knew the market was not at its best so he was not expecting the full $25 million. *Maybe $20 million or, at least, $18 million.* It couldn't be less than that. With $18 million, he'll purchase several real estate assets and collect monthly rent, this would establish a secure cash flow from which he could grow a portfolio and start to pay off his debt. *Rounds of drinks, new suits, and cute reporters at important parties were all just around the corner.* Finally, the dice had been rolled in his favor. His heart beat steadily. *Let the next chapter begin.*

He practically sprinted from the train station to The Charles. At the entrance, Jeb still sat with his plastic bags and a cardboard sign that said in feminine lettering, "MUTE, INJURED, AND HUNGRY." *Poor guy*, Nathan extended his sympathy as he sped past him. He looked forward to helping him.

The doors of The Charles opened and the familiar smell of fresh lavender and mint rushed into his nose. He hurried across the black marble floor.

Huffing, he rushed up to the customer service desk and said, "My name is John Shepherd. I have mail."

The lady disappeared behind the wall and reemerged with a handful of letters in her hand. He grabbed the letters, dashed to a chair in the lobby and sat down. In his hands lay a crisp white envelope with black lines in the folds and a black waxed seal of an "X" on the back. The other envelopes were from the banks, and other financial institutions he had borrowed from. They were probably just promotions or statements. Or something.

Trembling, he took a deep breath and opened the Venture X envelope. He carefully opened the stiff envelope to find a thick tri-folded letter. Pulling it out, his mind raced over all the possible numbers and their associated plans he had exhaustively mapped out over the last four and half months as he unfolded it. It all depended on the amount written on the check. And now he was finally finding out. He straightened the letter and out slid the Venture X check. It said $4,366,762.12.

His jaw dropped. He felt a jackhammer go off in his chest. *Oh no. No, no, no. No! $4.3 million?! Why is it so low?* This was all wrong. *All wrong.* The amount was horribly lower than it was supposed to be. His debt more than tripled this number. *Where's all my money?* Like a lightbulb dropped on concrete, his plans shattered.

Then it hit him. *George.* He kept the money. *That god-forsaken son of a bitch!* He took all his money for his fund. *He stole it from me.* He knew it. *The thief. That goddamn thief!*

His mind scrambled for how to get it back. He could visit his house. But he'd never make it past the gate and guards. He could call Rose. She'd hang up immediately. He could call Beth. His eyes darted right and left. He looked around to see if anyone noticed him. A man was sitting on the couch across from him. He was reading a newspaper. The front page said in big black uppercase headlines *MARKET CRASH.*

Oh, no. He looked back at the check in his shaking hand. And then back at the newspaper headline. A sinking, dreadful feeling grew from his toes to his head. *Oh god.* The realization swept over him like a blanket over a corpse. *It's not George, or Venture X, or anyone.* It's not them at all, it's the market. Everyone was losing money. *The economy is going to shit.* And he was neck deep in it.

He felt his demons crawl up his spine. He knew his money had been claimed by the black hole of the market, and there was no way he could get it back. With a hot face, he got up and went to the restroom. In a stall he couldn't control it anymore. He punched the bathroom stall, and cursed anything and everything that came to mind. *Millions.* He was lost at sea with no one to help and nothing left to do but drown. He looked at the check in his hand. It still said $4.3 million. But it was barely anything compared to his monolith of debt.

Everything he had hoped for now drained from his mind. He had to restart with nothing. Worse, with mountains of debt.

Crippled with anger and fear, he sat down on the porcelain and looked through the other letters in his hand. There were three others from the banks.

He opened one. The letter was a notice that he was being sued by the bank for the five million dollars he had borrowed. His heart plummeted and beat faster. Getting sued was the last thing he needed. Still hopeful, he opened another bank letter. It was a notice of getting sued for $5 million. His stomach twisted with panic. Opening the last letter, he was fully unprepared. It was another notice of getting sued for the last $5 million loan.

He bent over and put his head in his arms. Abandoned, hated, hollow, and now sued. He didn't move, he couldn't move. He had no reason to move. His once successful life was ruined.

Slowly, he got to his feet, pushed the stall door open, and washed his face. His face was skeletal, pale, and gaunt.

Jeb, to whom Nathan was expecting to give a handsome tip on his way out, was expecting the same. His weary brown eyes enveloped by thick mangy dark gray eyebrows looked expectant as he held out a maimed hand. Nathan shook his head and said, "Sorry, Jeb, I thought it would be today, too."

Jeb recoiled his hand and shrugged with a hurt grunt. Without looking a single person in the eyes, Nathan threw his hood over his head, and walked back to the train station.

74

Mr. Martin drove his white convertible out to the Degland Farm to visit Thomas and give him a message. It was nearly noon on a Saturday. His mouth never closed as the breeze swished by his ears. He wore large sunglasses, driving gloves, and a modern madras bowtie. He pulled in front of the big house and parked.

"Well, look who it is," said Thomas who was waiting for him on the front porch.

"My stripes, you look worse than the last time I saw you," Mr. Martin grinned.

The two men shook hands and embraced.

"It's good to see you, again, old friend," said Thomas.

"Old! Who are you calling old? I'm a yogini, I'll have you know." Mr. Martin stretched is his right leg out in front of him and squatted into a deep warrior pose.

Thomas chuckled. "Still strange."

Mr. Martin, beeped his corvette locked, and the roof automatically unfolded into place.

Thomas said, "Did you enjoy the ride out?"

"It was fantastic," said the small man. "Gorgeous country hillsides, rolling pastures—I loved it."

Thomas did his best to smile, "What brings you here, friend?"

"I wanted the fresh country air, and to see my old friend again."

"Alright, then," said Thomas, "Mary, could you prepare a lunch for our guest?"

The two men walked inside and in a few minutes enjoyed sliced ham sandwiches and homemade potato crisps for lunch. The two men ate heartily and discussed business and retirement before Mr. Martin couldn't wait any longer.

"Thomas, I would very much like to see the property."

"Why, sure," said Thomas proudly. "I'll give you the tour."

Tim joined them as they walked behind the house and towards the orchards.

"You've done well for yourself, Thomas," Mr. Martin noted the view. He stopped and held Thomas's arm. All the color from Mr. Martin's face drained.

"I have some news about Nathan."

Thomas and Tim looked at him.

"Do you remember all the news and gossip about that Country Millionaire, the young fellow who came to town with millions of dollars and nobody knew anything about him?

Thomas and Tim stared blankly at the man.

"That's Nathan."

The large whites of Thomas's eyes glared at him.

"He looked a bit like you, Thomas," Mr. Martin said.

Thomas didn't move a muscle, testing the weight of Mr. Martin's statement. "How would you know? Do you know him?"

"I see his picture in the newspaper all the time. He joined a private venture capital group called Venture Q or something like that. I remember he was at the mayor's Christmas party last year when I went."

Thomas didn't speak. He remembered his failed pursuit and confrontation of Nathan in the park. He remembered Nathan's cutting words and ruthless maliciousness. It had been months now but the memory was vivid, as if painfully singed into his mind with a hot brand. Frustrated, Thomas shook his head.

"He's in trouble, Thomas," Mr. Martin said.

Both Tim and Thomas turned to the elderly man.

"I told you that I recognized him from the newspapers. Well, the last article about him said he was sued by several banks and he disappeared. He left The Charles and no one knows where he is."

What's happened to my boy? Thomas shook his head. "I tried going after him once."

"Thomas," Mr. Martin put his hand on his shoulder and looked him straight in the face. The sunshine lit the old man's hazel eyes. "What Nathan did to you was awful. But he needs you right now. If you don't save him, who will? Years ago, you tried to stop him when he was on top of the world. Of course he's going to tell you to get lost. But now, he has nothing. No one. Are you going to be there for him when he hits rock bottom?"

Thomas covered his face with his hands and sighed. Tim put his hand on his friend's back.

"It's time to let it go, Thomas," said Mr. Martin.

"I know," Thomas said, "It's just ...I can't.

"Is your grudge worth more than your love?" said Mr. Martin. "As the boy's father, only your forgiveness can redeem him now. Your bitterness only damns him further."

75

THE NEXT MORNING, Nathan barely shifted out of bed. The little money he had was more than claimed by the bank. He felt sick and depressed; he just wanted to lay still and sleep. He didn't see a way out of this. He thought about Tommy and Angeline, who were probably sinking their teeth into the next high-dollar millionaire. Venture X, he was sure, was suffering, trying to get back on its feet after so many members pulled out from not getting their dividend this last quarter. He thought about Beth. She was four months pregnant now. *She probably hates me more than her ex-husband.*

He tried to think of some way to settle with the banks, but nothing came to mind. His debt was unsecured debt. There was no collateral attached to it for the banks to seize. And the banks would only take further aggressive action if they found out about his quick-cash borrowings. A pit formed in his stomach and sucked all the energy from his limp body. He was being sued for $15 million. And he had a little over $4 million. And it was only a matter of time before the predatory lenders started coming after him.

He fell out of bed and plodded over to Bobby and Dwayne's hotel room with a pack of cigarettes in his hand. She opened the door, not wearing anything underneath her hotel bathrobe.

She groaned a greeting.

"Hey, sorry to wake you. Mind if I could talk to you for a bit?"

"Sure, honey," she welcomed him in. "Would you like some coffee?" The pot on the counter was full.

"Where's Dwayne?" He offered her a cigarette, she lit it, and sat down cross-legged on the bed.

"Working. I'll do my best to listen," she said in a raspy voice.

He took a sip of coffee. It tasted like charcoal.

"You're probably wondering why I'm here."

She yawned. "You said you wanted to talk, I thought."

"No, I mean at the Traveler's Inn. Forget it."

But he continued anyways, "I'm at the Traveler's Inn because I needed a place to stay while I waited for a lot of money. Well, yesterday, when it came, it was much lower than I expected. Not only that, three other letters came with it from my banks, each suing me."

He didn't want to tell her the amount. He was taking a break from being the Country Millionaire and found it somewhat freeing for people not to know.

Bobby fell asleep sitting up. He tapped her knee and she shook herself awake.

"The government is always looking for money," she repeated back to him. "The only money that counts is the money in your pocket."

She continued to groggily explain that she only takes money up front from her customers. In cash, and in person. If she runs into any problems, she calls Dwayne, who has a gun.

Redirecting the conversation, Nathan asked, "Have you ever been sued?"

She laughed. "No one dares to sue me." She lay back on the pillows. "I could ruin a person's reputation with a single phone call to a loved one... or the press."

She launched into a complicated story about a man she met three years ago, but it didn't last long through the yawns and stretching. She talked herself right to sleep.

Back in his room, Nathan looked in the fridge. *Empty.* The pages from his journal were still spread across the counter. Now they were worthless. He ripped every single note in half until there was a heap of paper shreds on the counter. None of it mattered. What use was it? It was only a matter of days before the banks tracked him down.

His mind was a cesspool of dark thoughts. He felt trapped in the city. Thomas would be utterly disgusted if he learned about Nathan's "investments." *I told you so*, he could hear him say. At least, the depressing reality in which he lived now seemed safer than the prison of his father's disappointment.

Food was dust. He drank cheap vodka from plastic bottles only to feel numb. Money disgusted him. Any notion of wealth gave him the chills because he knew it was all air. *Wealth, fame, success, esteem, it's all fake. It's here and it's gone.* His only comforts were a needle of heroin and a conversation with Bobby.

Bobby told him not to hate himself too much.

"The world has enough hate" she said. "If you give in to hate, you'll run out of things to love."

He deleted numbers from his phone but stopped at Beth's number and paused. *Oh, Beth.* As pitiful as he was, Beth would still be the most willing to help him out of this mess. *And she could help with George.*

"Just do it," Bobby shouted after him, smiling. He walked out out of her room with the phone is his hand. He closed the door behind him and called Beth. The fourth ring cut short.

"Hello?" Her voice was soft and tired. He couldn't believe she answered.

"Beth, this is John," he said, his voice was dry from dehydration.

"John? Is that you?" There was surprise in her voice.

"Yes," he said. "I need your help, Beth. I'm not doing well."

"Oh, John, I'm so sorry. Dad said not to t—"

"Is that what you call him now?" he interrupted her. "George is a pretty nice guy to have as a father, isn't he?"

"He has been amazing to me, you wouldn't believe it. He cares. He wants my baby to be taken care of and happy."

My baby, she said, he repeated it in his head. *It's our baby. That's my baby, too, dammit.* "Beth, if you want that baby to know its real father then you'd better do something. I'm in trouble."

"Why don't you just go home, John? Don't you come from a good place? Go home. You'd make everyone happier if you just returned to where you came from."

"Beth, I can't," he wished he could explain. "For the baby's sake, come help me. I'm at a new hotel and I have new plans. Please come hear me out and give me a chance. I literally have no one else."

She paused. He was obviously lying, but something in her head told her to not hang up. He could tell she was hesitant, probably weighing her father's instructions.

"Beth, please," he said, straining his voice.

"Alright," she said. "I'll be over tomorrow late afternoon. Briefly."

He said goodbye, and a rush of emotions swept through his body. *Do I still love her?*

Love.

Nathan laughed to himself. He needed to eat before he could love. Beth was his last connection to possible financial restoration. *Maybe she'll help me get on George's good side again.*

He looked around his hotel room. He needed to clean up. Although he had pawned off many things, there were still bottles, needles, and trashy magazines to put away. There was no need for Beth to see his current condition. She was his secret access to George's deep pockets. Her sympathy would be the key. *After all, I'm her baby's father.*

76

Thomas threw his bags into the back of his white truck. Paul had followed him out of the house, complaining.

"If Nathan's in trouble, then it's what he deserves, Father."

"Perhaps it is. But that's not going to stop me."

"What are you going to do to him when you find him, *if* you find him?"

"I'm going to make sure he's okay and bring him home."

"Like last time?" Paul rolled his eyes. "You reap what you sow. That's what you always say. Why can't you let him go?"

Paul secretly enjoyed his brother's absence. He didn't miss the competition for his father's affection. With Nathan gone, it was just him and Thomas and the farm.

Thomas walked up to Paul. "I'm afraid that's happened already. I'm not sure of what I will discover, but I expect it won't be good. Nathan is in trouble and he needs my help. I won't let him suffer alone. You'll understand one day."

"You don't even know where he is."

Thomas patted Paul on the back.

"Take care of the farm while I'm gone. I'll be back in a week."

77

The knock on the door was brief and sharp. Standing up from the bed, Nathan walked to the door and looked through the peephole. Beth stood on the other side of the door, noticeably plumper than before.

Opening the door and making his voice sound husky, he said, "Please, come in. I know it's not much, but make yourself at home."

He touched her on the arm. Her arm drew back reflexively. She walked straight in, heavy with observation, assessment, and child. He stayed by the door.

"Help yourself to a drink," he said. "There's vodka in the fridge." He realized the blunder and kicked himself. She shot him a glare and then rolled her eyes unkindly.

"So how have you been? You look—"

She cut him off, "We both know you didn't invite me over for small talk, John. What is this really about?"

He was almost relieved to get straight to the point. "I'm glad you decided to come over. I really need your help."

"I see that," she said.

Apparently, his cleaning efforts from the night before made little difference in her eyes. *God forbid she saw what it was like before.* She opened the cupboard above the sink and picked out a plastic cup from the few he had in there. She filled it with water and drank. She placed the cup on the counter.

"So?"

"Beth, things are not going too well for me," he began. "The money is all gone. In fact, it's more than all gone. I'm in trouble."

"What did you do?" she asked.

"I'm being sued for $15 million I owe the banks and I received barely a third of that back from George. I can't pay them back."

Beth listened with a stone face. She had no pity. He remembered there had been a time when she respected him. Now all traces of admiration had given way to animosity.

"Any money that I have now doesn't belong to me. The three banks I borrowed from are claiming it. And that's not including the quick loans from the past couple months."

"What do you mean, quick loans?" Beth asked.

"I had to borrow from the cash advance and payday loan shops to pay for this hotel and stay alive while I waited for your father to send me the damn check," he said. "I was expecting the check to be five to six times more but when it came, it was a fraction of that. I found myself in a tight spot. I didn't know what to do, Beth. I still don't."

She didn't pick up on his begging tone. She took a sip from the cup in her hand. She paced around the kitchen. He sat on the bed anxiously hoping she would say something like, 'Poor thing, come stay with me.' Finally, she said, "Declare bankruptcy. It's the only thing you can do."

Bankruptcy? He was stunned. *I'm not that much of a failure. Bankruptcy would be giving up. Bankruptcy would end any chance of a comeback. Bankruptcy would be the death of the Country Millionaire.*

"You're in over your head, John. It's your only option."

"How could you say that?" he said. "Don't you think I can come back from this? This is only a temporary set back."

"I don't think you realize where you are," her voice cut him with distrust. "You're buried, John, or whatever your name is."

"What are you talking about?"

"Look at this." She panned her hands across the room. "I don't even know who you are anymore. I don't think I ever knew who you really were."

She was twisting the knife in deep.

"Beth, quit this. How can you say that?"

"The only reason I'm here is because of our baby. I regret that you are the father but there's nothing I can do about that. My hands are bound."

She comes all this way to spit in my face and grind salt into my wounds. Infuriated, he said, "I never wanted the baby anyway! If you regret having it with me, then maybe you shouldn't even have it at all!"

"What are you saying, John?"

He lost control.

"I'm saying get rid of it! I'm in no place to be a father, obvi-ously, and you aren't even happy to have a child with me, so we're both better off without it. Get a doctor and erase any trace that we were together. That's what you want anyways, right?"

She slammed the cup down on the counter and screamed, absolutely livid. "You're heartless! You only care about yourself! I *am* willing, John. I am willing to make this work. It's a child's life, for Christ's sake. We're talking about a life that has nothing to do with you or me."

"Whatever," he said and threw his hands up in the air with a defeated scoff. She threw the cup at him and it smashed against the wall.

"Don't you care? It's your child. It's your son or daughter and you say 'whatever'? Do you see how selfish you are?"

"Get out," he said. He pointed to the door. He'd had enough.

"Get a hold of yourself," she said. "You're out of control."

He said nothing and glared at the floor, ashamed.

"Get out," he repeated. She needed to leave before he did something he'd regret.

"I'm not leaving until we work something out."

He shook his head, not looking at her.

"John, I'm sorry, let's work this out," she said. "Let's talk."

"Get out!" He grabbed her right arm and thrust her to the door. He used his hand to push behind her back, rushing her out of the room. He pushed more forcibly than he intended. Her body hit against the door. She cried out, "John! What are you doing?"

Grabbing her arm again, harder this time, he said, "Getting you out of here."

He opened the door and pushed her out into the rain. She fell, scraping her knee against the metal walkway, bracing herself against the wet railing.

Enraged at himself, he said, "Come back when you can be useful," and slammed the door.

He heard her sob through the door. He leaned against the closed door, his chest heaving. His face was hot and his breath was short. She was the last person that might have cared about him. Listening through the door, he heard her cry. On the counter, he saw her bag. *Dammit.* He picked it up, walked to the door, opened it, and threw her bag onto the walkway. He kept his eyes from meeting hers. The bag landed by her bloody knee. He closed the door and locked it.

If she wants to have a child, I want no part in it. I'm not ready, in any way, to be a father. She is on her own. He had to make that clear, as wrong as it felt.

Outside his door, her whimpers disappeared. *She must be heading back to the train station.* As the minutes passed, he felt increasingly regretful knowing she had to walk to the train station by herself. He could see the eyes of the thugs and homeless men eyeing her up and down. He couldn't do anything about it—*I shouldn't. But what if? What if I could be a father and maybe a husband? No. She was on her own.*

He sat on the floor for almost an hour. He abandoned her—the last person who believed in him. He left her, the woman he once loved, to walk through the dangerous street in the rain. She wouldn't make it far without some kind of unwanted attention. *What have I done?* She will not be safe. He couldn't let this happen. She needed him. *Get up, idiot.* A sudden sense of protectiveness mounted in him, and a new energy picked his head up off his knees. *Go protect her. Go say you're sorry. Go beg for forgiveness. For everything. Go hug her. Go hold her. And never let her go. Ever again.* He jumped up to his feet, unlocked the door, and yanked it open. Running down the stairs, he sprinted as fast as his strength could muster.

The sky was a dark blanket of gray clouds. Yellow lamplight illuminated the mist above the empty sidewalks. She was nowhere to be seen. He ran after her towards the train station. He ran past people sleeping in the bus stops covered in plastic bags.

The road led him into downtown South Bennington. Small groups of people smoked and chattered outside under canopies. He ran by laundromats, quick stop shops, and greasy restaurants wedged in between rundown brick buildings. He shouted Beth's name into every alleyway he passed. Walkers, patrons, and people in windows turned their heads as he yelled. He didn't want the attention, but he needed to find her.

The wind whisked rain across his face. Purpose surged in his veins. He couldn't help noticing some hope. He was pursuing her. It felt right.

Up ahead, the train station was located under several overhead highways, held up by concrete pillars. The overpassing highways sheltered the train station from rain. The pillars and supporting structures for the roads and exit ramps formed an array of nooks and crevices for homeless people to spend the night. The rain hit the asphalt causing a mist to rise from the ground. It flavored the air with stale alcohol and musty dirt. Oil stains and old gum checkered the parking lot.

"Beth?!" he called as he approached the train station. His voice reverberated off the concrete walls and structures. He noticed there were fewer street people than usual that night. *Not too many out tonight. Must be the rain.* Usually, there were scores of them. The main walkway to the train station entrance tended to be the most crowded, where they begged passers-by for money or booze. He only spotted three men this time, two were in wheelchairs and one laid down with a short-legged mutt next to him.

They watched him as he ran through the entrance gates and shouted. "Beth!"

The platform was empty. Either her train left already and he just missed her, or... *where is she?* Rummaging in his pockets, he forgot his phone back at the hotel room. He ran outside and circled the building, panting and frantic.

One of the men in a wheelchair watched him. From the corner of his eye, Nathan could tell he was a fat, hunchback man wearing a smeared yellow rain jacket and an old frayed baseball hat. The man's head tracked him as he ran about. Finally, Nathan stopped and said to him, "Have you seen a woman come by this way not too long ago?"

The man shook his head, very slowly. He didn't say a word.

"She was just here only a few minutes ago, surely you saw her." Nathan was out of breath. The man shook his head again and didn't say anything.

"Thanks for the help," Nathan said sarcastically and continued his search. *Where is she? Did I pass her in town?* He began to worry. *Did she get on the train?* He felt his empty pockets again. He really needed his phone to contact her. Soaked, he hated the thought of giving up. But, he had no choice.

He retraced his steps back to the hotel. He prayed to anyone who would listen, *let her be on the train.* He took some comfort in the fact the street riff raff was light that night.

Bursting into his room, he tore off his wet clothes and found his phone. His cold, wet fingers numbly tapped Beth's number. The phone rang but she didn't answer. His lungs burned and his skin was coated with sweat and rain. It had been so long since he exercised. He called her again. No answer. He sent her a text, "Are you okay?"

He poured a glass of water and drank it quickly. His nerves were a wreck. He opened the refrigerator to find some sort of strong drink but he was out of everything. Only a small mouthful of cheap vodka remained. He swallowed it and turned on the shower. *Why won't she respond? Can she respond?*

He sent another text, "Where are you, Beth?" The night dragged on, and he refused to sleep until he heard from her.

78

*T*hud.
A wine cask banged against the truck bed. *Thud.* Tim grunted as he and Paul heaved another barrel into the truck. The clouds above grew dark and full.

"Why," asked Paul, "Why did he go after Nathan this time? Degland men are stubborn, but we're not stupid."

Tim extracted a white cloth from his overalls pocket and wiped the perspiration from his thick brows. "You're right, it doesn't make much sense."

He took a draft of water from the bottle and offered some to Paul who accepted it gratefully.

"It's obvious Nathan doesn't want to be here," Paul said. "I think it's better that it stays that way, for everyone."

"Don't be so harsh," cautioned Tim.

"I'm not trying to be harsh, I'm just pointing out the obvious. How is Nathan going to pay back everything he stole? I know that oil field over yonder didn't sell for nothing."

Paul cast his chin in the direction of the dry land. "You think I like doing his share of the work?"

"It is for Thomas to decide," said Tim.

"And me," added Paul. "The three of us own this farm together. If Nathan lost everything he stole, then none of this is his. In fact, he probably owes more..."

Paul's thought grew quickly in his mind. "...making everything that's left..."

He circled around looking at the buildings, fields, and trees. "...mine."

Tim threw his hat at Paul, striking him in the chest and shattering his daydream. "Sorry about that," Tim said. "It just sprouted wings and flew off my head. Let's finish the rest of these barrels."

Jostled, Paul threw Tim's hat back at him. "All I'm saying is if Pop brings him back, he better not go soft on him. My little brother needs to feel as much of the pain as he's caused us."

Paul took the other side of the barrel Tim was struggling with. "He'll pay," Paul assured him. "One way or another. I'll make sure of it."

79

Nathan found a replacement for Brew Social at a gas station in South Bennington two blocks from the Traveler's Inn. It was a semi-clean establishment and the coffee machine next to the hot dog roller served a half decent dark roast. He found his regular spot at two lunch tables in the corner. He hadn't heard from Beth all morning, and would've fretted himself sick but a heroine dose fixed that.

He sipped his coffee from a styrofoam cup while he read the newspaper. *More bad news about the economy.* Once in awhile, he'd get a stare or look from someone in the gas station but he quickly buried his head in the newspaper.

That morning, he couldn't stop thinking about what Beth said. *Was she right about filing for bankruptcy? Was it the only thing he could do?* The banks would take all the money he had left but then he would be free to start again. It was almost a reset button.

A week went by since Beth's visit. After wrestling through every possible option, he finally conceded to her advice. He settled with the banks, dividing the $4.3 million between them, and declared bankruptcy. The payday and cash advance offices recognized him at the door and told him to get lost every day.

If he wanted to continue eating, he couldn't waste time being picky about a job. His drugs were running low and with no money coming in, it was only a matter of time before he'd start to go through withdrawals. He pawned off his suits for a couple hundred dollars and bought a handful of lottery tickets. The only thing he had left from Grandpa Walker's safe was the pistol.

He set out walking around the downtown retail strips of South Bennington and surveyed the businesses that were hiring. He collected a handful of employment applications, intending to fill them out that evening. He was startled by a buzz in his pocket and the sound of his ringtone. The word, "Anonymous", filled the screen. He answered.

"How did you get this number?"

"Mutual friends, you could say," a familiar feminine voice replied. Her voice sounded caramelly over the phone. "I want to see you."

"Why?"

"I want to interview you," her wet lips smacked. "Just a quickie."

He recognized who it was. And gave her the hotel's address.

80

THE ECONOMY HAD taken its toll; of the twelve stores he walked into, three were hiring: a liquor store, a mail center, and a family restaurant. One by one, the owners turned him down. His eyes were bloodshot, his skin was yellow, his last Brioni suit was tattered and wrinkled. With how terrible he looked, nobody gave him a chance.

Back at the hotel later that evening, the muscled blonde journalist stood in Nathan's room and let her coat drop to the floor revealing a tight leather dress and tall heels. He gazed at her. It wouldn't be as easy as it was before when his confidence was higher.

She circled him as he sat on the bed and asked him question after question. What happened to your money? What happened with Venture X? Why did you leave The Charles?

"I didn't know you literally wanted to interview me," he told her. She laughed it off but came right back with a question about his lifestyle change.

"Listen," he stopped her, "I guess I should have clarified on the phone... I don't want to be interviewed."

"Right."

She jumped on the bed and scooted in close to him. He smelled her soft cinnamon hair and sensed her warm skin close to his.

"Do you have any wine?" she asked batting her dark eyelashes.

"I don't," he said.

"Anything else?" She smiled mischievously.

He thought about showing her his dope cache.

"You won't like it," he smirked.

"Try me," she bit her lip and slid her hand down his chest. "I like a little bit of everything."

"Alright," he got up and walked over to the safe. It was risky but *she's obviously adventurous. Who knows, if she is into it, she might even be willing to pay for more.*

He opened it, and laid the supplies out on the counter. She came up behind him and said, "Good," and then without warning shouted at the top of her lungs.

"Hey!"

Startled, he whipped around with the bag of heroin still in his hands and then a flash of white light filled the room and blinded him.

"What the hell?" cried Nathan.

The woman put a thin camera back in her dress and grabbed her jacket and purse.

"What are you doing?"

"I got everything I needed here," she said and headed for the door. Nathan moved to obstruct her path, blocking her from leaving the hotel room.

"You're not going anywhere until you tell me what's going on," he said.

"Do you really think you can stop me?" she asked with a cold tone. Her bare neck and shoulders were larger than his. Nathan wasn't so sure but he couldn't let her get away.

"What are you going to do?" he asked.

"What I've been doing all along," she replied, chuckling.

"Write a story. I've been covering you since you came to Delorre."

Nathan remembered the *Delorre Daily* articles.

"I'm the one that came up with your nickname," she said proudly. "And now I'm the one who's going to break the story of the year. *'Country Millionaire Spirals into Debt, Drug Addiction'.*" She smiled. "The demise of the Country Millionaire."

"You betrayed me," he said. "You used me."

"We used each other," she corrected him.

"You came here to use me again tonight."

"This was the perfect end to the story," she said satisfied.

He stepped towards her and demanded she hand over the camera. He balled his fists.

She rolled her eyes. "You don't think I've done this before? Please."

She reached into her bag and pulled out a can of mace.

81

"Dude, you're broke?" said Dwayne. He was stunned, standing in the kitchen holding a beer can. "There's no way you're out of money."

Bobby's snores interrupted their conversation. Nathan stood at the door with everything he owned in a duffel bag over his shoulder.

"You don't know anything about me," accused Nathan.

Dwayne finished his beer and crushed the can. "I know that you probably shouldn't be out of money right now."

How would he know? Nathan glared at the locksmith.

"It doesn't matter anymore," said Nathan. "I'm leaving.

Cracking open another can, Dwayne eyed the thin millionaire quizzically and asked, "Where you headed?"

Nathan shrugged. He didn't know. The ability to think clearly had left him weeks ago. Only an animalistic desire to survive and avoid pain remained.

"At least give me a general idea so I know where to find you," said Dwayne. "You know, in case something happens."

"I'll probably just head into downtown South Bennington." As he pointed, a thunder clap bellowed in the distance as dark clouds began to mount in the overcast sky. The sound woke Bobby who covered herself in a blanket and walked up to the two men.

"William's leaving us, honey," Dwayne informed her.

Still dazed, Bobby kissed him on the cheek and said, "You're a good man, William,"

William. He held in a snort. He had told them a fake name as well. He didn't want them to know who he really was, though he suspected Dwayne knew him by his other name from the newspapers.

"You're always welcome to come back and stay with us if you run into any trouble, you hear?"

"Thank you, Bobby," Nathan said. "I can't thank you enough." He kissed her on the cheek, gave Dwayne a nod goodbye, and turned to go. Outside he waved farewell to Fred the feather man and slapped the car where the big men were tinkering. They grunted goodbye. With a gnawing stomach, he marched through the parking lot away from the hotel and headed in the opposite direction of the train station.

In the distance ahead, the baseball stadium loomed above the rest of the city like a huge chrome boulder piercing through a mound of gravel. Gloomy clouds rumbled and the wind scurried trash along the street. He waited for the street pedestrian light as a raindrop landed on his cheek.

Find shelter.

82

He heard muttering voices. On the other side of the bow-shaped underpass, several other people camped out under the bridge. Standing on top of cardboard mats, the group stood in a circle. They were surrounded by plastic bags, boxes, and a grocery cart. One person had a tent. It looked as if they had been there for weeks, even months.

Nathan found relief from the pouring rain under the bridge on the opposite side of the railroad tracks. He kept his eye on the chattering bunch.

There were seven of them, dressed in tattered layers of hoodies and dirty jackets, standing around a fire. Booze bottles, cans, and fast food bags littered the ground under their feet. The tall one kept looking over at him. Nathan shivered.

He unpacked a blanket and a bottle of Gatorade from his bag. He took out a cigarette and holding it to a lighter, he sat down and stared at them. As the rain poured louder, it formed a watery skirt around the bridge.

He smoked and stewed. He wished he was still at The Charles. If only he had treated Beth better. *I could have been a different person.* A stream of cold water ran down the ground and into his pants, knocking him out of his daydream.

He kicked a stone in annoyance and it rolled down the embankment and clanked against the tracks. A whistle catcalled from across the bridge and he looked up to see the bearded-gathering twisted around, looking at him. They were drinking out of brown bags and smoking. All kinds of grease and dirt stained their formerly bright colored jackets.

Trying to look preoccupied, he searched for a cardboard mat or something on which he could rest for the night. It was getting dark and with the rain, he doubted he would be moving on from this location. The group of men across the tracks gave him a sinking feeling in his stomach. The thought of closing his eyes for more than ten minutes with those loutish wretches watching sent chills down his spine.

Under a pile of trash he found an old blue tarp. He yanked it out violently like a tablecloth on a dining table so as not to disturb the mound of garbage. Catching his breath, he brushed off the tarp and after deciding it was clean enough, wrapped it around himself like a burrito. He needed sleep. The ground was hard and cold but he was exhausted and hungry enough to sleep. Against his will, his eyelids closed, and he didn't remember falling asleep.

PART 4

THE STREETS OF SOUTH BENNINGTON

83

He awoke with a start and discovered his body rolling down the stone embankment towards the train tracks. One of the men had peeled the tarp away from him and sent him plunging down the slanted ground.

"That's what you get for stealing my tarp, shitbag."

A burly man was standing right next to where Nathan landed. He bent down to get a better look.

"Yep, this is him," he growled in a deep, gruff voice. Heart racing, Nathan lay there not fully realizing where he was.

"Yeah, I knew it! I seen him in the papers," another man stood up and hollered at the others, who were preparing for bed. "This here is that Country Millionaire, boys, the one boss said we was supposed to get."

Two of them jumped down to where Nathan had fallen and joined the man in a blue jacket standing over him. They were unshaven, with black rotting teeth, their cheekbones protruding from their tan bony faces.

One of them in a yellow coat said, "Well, would you look at that, you're right, Knuckles!"

Nathan realized his hood was under his neck and his head and face were fully exposed. Shuffling his arms up, he swooped the hood over his face again.

"The Country Millionaire, you said?" The third one huffed. "I didn't get a look. Let me see."

He put his hands on Nathan's hood and shoved it open. A strong smell of liquor and smoke poured from the man's horrid mouth.

"I recognize him, too," the man said, "Barely. He looks different than the pictures."

"Ain't he the one with all the women and the parties?"

"That's every millionaire, you idiot," someone corrected him. "This one was different. No one knew anything about him. That's how he got his nickname."

The man scoffed. "Guess it wasn't too much of a fortune. He don't look so good now."

The big one named Knuckles corralled the group. "Alright, enough, we have a job to do."

That last comment jolted Nathan's eyes open. He leapt to his feet and faced the grubby vagrants with both hands up to push them away.

"Okay now," he said, keeping his voice steady. "I don't have any money. It's all gone. The Country Millionaire is no more."

Nathan saw the lot of them around him. Knuckles was a lumbering brute as wide as a door. His tattered blue raincoat draped off his heavy shoulders. A thin, red-jacketed man stood next to him, with hair sprouting in all directions from underneath his winter hat. He thought he recognized the hunched man in a smeared yellow coat. He had a shriveling face with broken spectacles resting on a long hook nose.

They looked at Nathan as if their dinner had gotten up and spoken. Knuckles walked towards him. "That's exactly what boss man told us you would say."

"I don't, I promise you, it's all gone." Those words felt like a dagger in his soul. His breathing doubled as he stepped backwards away from the man.

"We can make this as painful as you like," Knuckles smiled.

"What are you doing?" shouted Nathan. "Get away from me."

"Just trying to give you hug and a kiss," the big man joked as leaned into Nathan. Everyone laughed.

"Leave me alone," Nathan yelled at him and wished he had his knife. Over Knuckle's shoulder he noticed the yellow jacketed man hold his pointer finger in front of his lips as if to say, "Shhhh."

Nathan whipped around but it was too late. A baseball bat slammed into the side of his head. He reeled towards Knuckles and fell towards the ground. Knuckles' knee rocketed into his face, catching him in the jaw. Pain ripped into his face. His body flipped and toppled to the ground like a dead fish. Laughter filled the air. They took off his shoes while Knuckles stripped off his jacket and hoodie.

"Hey, look, he does have a suit on," Knuckles said. It was the ragged Brioni suit he wore to stay warm.

"Let me go," Nathan moaned. Though he was weak, he was not about to just lay there helpless. "I'll give you all the money I have! Just let me go!"

The four of them stopped. The hunched man was nowhere to be seen.

Nathan rolled away from them and reassured them, "I swear to you. I'll give you whatever you're looking for."

They backed off and let him stand up, which he did slowly. Knuckles, the ringleader, said, "Boss told us about you, mister money man. We know you got cash. Tell us where it is, and you can keep your teeth."

Nathan's thoughts raced for an answer as he wiped blood from his mouth.

"It's all locked away in a bank," he said. "I can give you the account number and security infor—"

"Shut him up!" The yellow jacket man shrieked from the top of the embankment by the pile of trash. "Don't believe a word he says."

He had Nathan's journal in his hand and a flashlight pointed into it.

Knuckles's big face wheeled up to the man. "Why?"

"He ain't got a dime! He's bankrupt!" squealed the man. "He says it here himself. Listen." He tried to make his old tin can of a voice sound like Nathan's.

"She was right. Declaring bankruptcy did get the banks off my back, but now I have nothing. Father can never find out."

The man squealed mockingly, "Daddy will hate me." He laughed and spit. "He's full of shit, boys."

Knuckles turned back to Nathan with his brows scrunched. "What is this?"

Nathan backed away from the man but the group circled around him.

"Is that true?" asked Knuckles. "That's not what I was told."

"Whoever told you anything was wrong," said Nathan. "I have nothing. "

"Then where's your safe?" the man in the yellow jacket asked.

"How did you know I had a safe?"

"He knows nothing," roared Knuckles, trying to cover his comrade's divulgence, and plunged a fist into Nathan belly. Nathan doubled over.

"Come on, Knuckles," said the old geezer. "What does it matter if he knows? It's not like he's going anywhere after we're through with him."

"Boss said he doesn't want his partner to know about this one," said Knuckles. He picked Nathan up off the ground and said, "Alright, out with it. Where's the money?"

"His partner? You mean *your slut*?" The driveling man cackled. "Why does Bobby care? It's not like she'll remember him."

"Shut up!" screamed Knuckles. "Shut your maggoty mouth."

Nathan eyes widened. "Wait. Did you say Bobby?"

His suspicion was cut off by a fist crashing into his eye socket. *Pop!* He fell back and sprawled to the ground.

"Check him over," barked Knuckles. The red jacket man obediently knelt and patted Nathan's body, checking his pockets.

"Cigarettes, an empty wallet, a photo... there's no money," reported the man.

"Alright," ordered Knuckles, "Give it to him good."

The men around him attacked from all sides, swinging their fists into his face. He crumpled and they drove their boots into his sides. His thin frame could not withstand the blows.

"Welcome to real life for once, you spoiled bastard."

A heel hammered into his side and he felt a snap. He gasped for air. They smacked his head against the stone ground over and over.

On the verge of blacking out, he saw the light flicker overhead and a shadow move quickly. Knuckles, who had concentrated his pummeling on Nathan's head, suddenly toppled on top of him, crushing him against the ground. Sharp pain from his rib stabbed deeper from the weight. He struggled for air. Knuckles was knocked out cold. The three other aggressors seemed to forget about Nathan. They were distracted by something else.

He tried to get a view of what was going on but he was pinned. The yellow jacket man screamed and the hairy red jacket man cried out, "What are you doing? We were just playing around."

The shadows above on the underside of the bridge flickered—merging and separating with one another quickly. The men spoke with fear in their voices, trying to address the newcomer.

"Just put it down, c'mon," the yellow jacket man said, "We

weren't doin' nothin'."

"Yeah, we were just leaving."

A bowel-curdling scream ripped through the air and a body slumped to the ground on Nathan's right. *Thud!*

"No, no!" *Crack!* The yellow jacketed man's face landed in front of Nathan with shattered lenses mushed into his eyes.

Again, Nathan tried to wrestle the big man off of him but the pain was paralyzing. His body had no strength. *What is going on?* He couldn't breathe.

The sound of running footsteps and frantic voices faded in the distance down the train tracks. It grew silent and Nathan wondered if the attacker had also left.

A large stone rolled against the ground. The sound thundered across the bridge walls. Footsteps came closer. Nathan wriggled and pushed, trying to escape. *Who is this rock-wielding bludgeoner?*

Suddenly, inches from his face, a three-fingered hand gripped Knuckles' shoulder. The hand only had a little finger, middle finger, and a thumb. The half-hand flexed and squeezed the shoulder, pulling the brute off of him. Horrified, Nathan recognized the mangled hand. He remembered placing cash in a similar digit-reduced hand.

Nathan squirmed and pulled himself out from underneath the giant and rolled onto his stomach to view his rescuer.

Jeb towered over him, looking down at him with wide eyes. His heaving breath was visible in the cold night air.

84

AFTER A QUICK stop at an equipment shed, Paul and Chester zipped along in Paul's truck along the dirt road bordering the cow field to repair a section of broken fence.

"You've done good picking up Nathan's responsibilities, I'll say that much," said Paul with a toothpick in his mouth.

"Thanks for the compliment," said Chester from the front seat. "I think I'm starting to get the hang of it."

Paul threw a sledgehammer into the bed of the truck and climbed back into the driver's seat. "I'll even say you're better at it than he ever was," remarked Paul. "It helps when you're not sitting around stuck in a book all day."

They pulled up to the splintered posts and cracked planks of the fence. The meadow of the family graveyard was directly behind the spot. Paul paused as he looked over at the gravestones.

"Chester, can I tell you a secret?"

"Sure," said the boy, eager to be confided in.

"I've already cut Nathan's gravestone."

Chester let go of the plank in his hands, shocked. "Why? Is he dead? I'm confused."

"I don't know. I figured if he was still alive, we would've heard from him by now," answered Paul. "Think about it. We haven't heard from him in years. Pop said he's in trouble and went after him. We haven't heard anything yet. So I'm just preparing for the worst."

Chester didn't want to give up so easily. "But don't you think you're assuming too much?"

"It never hurts to plan ahead," said Paul, he hurled a broken lumber shard into a pile.

Chester felt his cheeks heating up. He needed to defend Nathan. He gripped the side of the truck and raised his voice.

"Why do you hate your brother so much? Don't you wish he was still alive?"

Paul slammed the sledgehammer into a post in the ground.

"I don't appreciate your tone but I'll answer you anyway," said Paul. "Nathan's always been the 'gifted' or 'smart' one. Especially with Mom; she adored him. I was the last one to ever be given special attention from our parents. So when my little brother robs us and takes off for good, and I finally get a chance to prove myself, I think there's more justice to it than you think there is."

He swung the steel bludgeon into the wooden stake. *Crack!*

"I just don't think it's right," said Chester. "To give up on him like that. Especially your own brother. Everyone deserves a second chance."

"You don't understand," Paul said fitfully, "Hand me that other post."

He took it from Chester roughly and said, "There's a lot you don't know about, so just stay out of it."

85

Nathan froze. A million thoughts and emotions hurtled through his hurting head. Jeb stood in front of him, on two feet, with a straight back, and a full white beard and shaggy head of grimy white hair. The campfire flickered in his flared eyes as he stared at him. This was not the same Jeb he had known outside The Charles. The Jeb from The Charles was a frail, desperate, helpless, beggar. The Jeb standing before him was lean, agile, and barbaric. He wore a dirty camouflage t-shirt and black pants. He breathed heavily, his forehead and arms glistening with sweat.

Nathan wanted to scream at him. But he didn't know if it should be out of thanks or rage.

"Jeb?"

Nathan had never seen the man's skin before. Now, standing before him, he was toned and tan, with lots of body hair.

Was he *hiding* at The Charles? He wasn't a poor, crippled beggar. Standing before Nathan was conniving beast of the street. *I bet he's not even mute.* His hands were undoubtedly the same.

Jeb took two side steps toward the embankment and motioned with his arm to follow him. Nathan was still on the ground, unsure of what to do. Pain enveloped him and he thought his rib was broken. Walking was unimaginable. Jeb motioned again, more urgently. He pointed down the tracks then at the ground at his feet, indicating the men will probably return soon.

"Alright. I get it," said Nathan. "We must go. But I'm not going with you."

He tried to pull himself up but a stabbing penetration in his torso made him grapple to remain sitting up. His swollen eyes could barely blink, his bare feet were frozen, and his head throbbed.

Without warning Nathan felt the mutilated hands poking out from under his own armpits. They hoisted him up to his feet. The agony of movement forced a howl out of him and he struggled to inhale. Jeb lifted him up and put his arm around him. He did not want to lean on him but the pain gave him no choice. He couldn't breathe. There was no escaping.

Jeb made a throat clicking sound as they took two steps. He moved carefully and picked up Nathan's bag. The pain was unbearable. Nathan thought his right leg was broken. As Jeb carried him, Nathan smelled the mix of dirt, smoke, and dried sweat from his long hair.

"Where are you taking me?" Nathan groaned as they weaved in between buildings on unlit back roads under the moonlight.

Nathan had no idea where they were when Jeb laid him on the ground with his back against a metal chain link fence. The fence blocked off a construction area in the back of the baseball stadium. Jeb disappeared into the darkness underneath two glowing red exit signs.

The cold wind blew through the stadium and Nathan's swollen face felt like it was about to fall off like a mask.

"Jeb?"

Jeb reappeared holding a tall orange cone and a rope.

"Thought you left me," said Nathan.

A smile moved Jeb's beard up on both sides of his cheeks. With surprising nimbleness and deftness, he propped open a section of the fence.

"No, stop. No, Jeb."

Jeb grabbed Nathan under the arms and pulled him under the fence. His beard scratched the back of Nathan's neck.

On the other side, Jeb picked up the rope tied to the cone and gave it a strong pull. The cone buckled and jumped towards them, springing the fence back into place. It looked like nothing had ever happened.

Deep in the rear, away from the construction activity, Jeb and Nathan hobbled to a cube of scaffolding with heavy duty white tarp wrapped around it, forming walls to a one-story square room.

"Is this where you live?"

Jeb pushed through a cut flap in one of the tarps instantly cutting off the wind. Around the floor, Nathan saw cups, pots, a makeshift bed, cardboard boxes, and plastic bags. Jeb laid him down on a bed and brought him bandages and an ointment to treat the cuts and wounds.

"What are you doing?"

After a minute, Jeb brought over a gas stove and teapot, offered a mug to Nathan. Out of his pocket, he brought out a pill bottle and offered it to Nathan. *Who knows what this could be.*

Jeb put his hands together to form a pretend-pillow.

"Why, Jeb," he said quietly. He knew he couldn't answer. But he had to say it out loud. "Why are you helping me?"

Jeb pointed at Nathan's chest and then at his own chest, as if to say, "because you helped me."

Nathan stuck out an opened hand. Jeb tapped the bottle until two white pills tumbled out. Nathan popped them into his mouth and gulped down the hot tea. The hot tea warmed his empty insides.

In a matter of minutes, the pain subsided and Nathan's eyelids fattened. He took one last puzzled look at Jeb who curled up on the ground with his back towards him.

The wind howled outside against the tarp walls. He never expected to see Jeb again. Now, he slept in his bed.

86

As he sped towards the city, Thomas knew exactly where he would begin his search. He recalled his final confrontation with his son in Alvin Park in Delorre years ago.

It was late in the afternoon when he arrived outside the entrance of The Charles. In his rush, Thomas nearly tripped over the same homeless man begging on a cardboard mat twenty feet from the main doors.

"Muhhh," the hairy homeless man groaned urgently, grasping at Thomas.

"I'm sorry," said Thomas, running by him. "I must hurry."

Thomas crossed the sparkling black marble floor, ignoring the stares of wealthy guests. At the counter, the uniformed man cleared his throat at the dusty, unkempt and out-of-breath farmer in front of him.

"Can I help you?"

"I need to speak with the manager," said Thomas.

"You are," said the man. His tone was distinctly condescending.

"I'm looking for the Country Millionaire. Where is he?"

The man clicked his mouth. "Wouldn't we all like to know. He marched out of here a couple months ago. Something happened. He only left a phone number but I'm af–"

"What is that phone number?" Thomas interrupted him.

The man finished his sentence. "...I'm afraid I can't give out that information."

"He's my son," Thomas said sternly.

"Better be careful saying that," the man laughed. "The papers would be all over you if they caught wind of the Country Millionaire's father being in town."

Thomas's dark eyes flashed. "I'm serious, can you help me?"

"I've been asked that same question thousands of times."

"Please, I just need to contact him."

"Sorry, I can't help you."

Thomas's face was stone. "I'll give you money."

"Look around you," the man said with contempt. "Does it look like I need any money?"

"One thousand dollars." Thomas took out his checkbook, wrote the check, and held it out in front of the haughty manager.

The man paused, checked over his shoulders, and grabbed the check.

"Come this way," he walked passed Thomas, took the check, and motioned to follow him.

In a private office, Thomas dialed the number on the piece of paper the manager gave him. He put the phone to his ear. It immediately went to a voice recording that said the number had been disconnected. Thomas realized he had been holding his breath. He redialed the number but got the same result. He slammed the receiver down, got up from the chair and opened the door.

"What was the name of that investment group he was involved with?" Thomas called to the manager who excused himself from another customer.

"Venture X. Why?"

"How do I get in touch with them?"

"I'm sorry, I can't give out that information."

Thomas took out his checkbook again, scribbled on it, and tore out the check.

"Here's another thousand dollars."

The manager rolled his eyes. "How do I know these will even work," he inhaled and shook his head. He wrote a number on the notepad and gave it to Thomas.

"This is the number of the chairman's assistant," he said. "Good luck."

87

Nathan woke up from a nightmare with his heart beating quickly. Panic-stricken, he had no idea where he was. His memories of the previous day were helter-skelter. His right leg barely responded to any commands from his brain. It didn't move below his knee.

Seeing the tea mug, he remembered having tea the night before with Jeb.

Jeb.

He spun around too quickly to look at the opposite corner of the room. He was gone. *My back.*

The sun shone through the tarp coverings illuminating what looked to be Jeb's home. He heard the faint sound of engines and machinery in the distance from the construction site. Dust specks floated in the air. Clothes were folded neatly, the cooking and eating supplies were stacked in order, and several photo frames were set up on top of an old wooden chest.

Cardboard boxes lined the walls on the floors. In one corner of the room, a hose threaded through the tarp wall and snaked up the beam and hooked down towards the ground forming a sort of chest-high shower head. A segment of the hose had been spliced where a shut off switch had been installed. Nathan's cold fingers stubbornly obeyed as he turned the switch.

Water gushed out of the spigot and into a bucket. Next to the bucket was a soap station, sponge, and a washboard.

He splashed the water into his face with his hands. The brisk water soothed his aching face and stinging hands. He picked up the soap jar. A strong, clean lavender aroma cleared his nasal passages.

He studied the five framed photographs on the wooden chest and set them down on the ground. Unlatching the chest, he opened it. Books filled the chest from side to side.

He winced as a small laugh escaped his tender chest. He was surprised to find books. He knew Jeb couldn't speak but wrongly assumed he couldn't read. This collection looked like the treasure chest of an avid reader.

Moving down the wall, he inspected the other boxes, opening the cardboard flaps. He found books. *More books.* He shook his head in disbelief. He opened the next box, labeled *Science*. It contained a dozen books. He was shocked. He looked around—they all were labeled. *War. Space. Agriculture. Psychology. Fiction.*

Jeb's humble home was a library consisting of over one hundred books. *Does he collect books?* He almost had more books than Nathan had back at the farm. *Did he read all of these?*

If Jeb has read all of these books he must be smart. His living habits suggested he was. This place was clean, functional, and—Nathan couldn't believe he was saying this—relatively comfortable, in an austere way. Like a soldier's quarters.

His thoughts were interrupted by the flap rolling up. Jeb entered with a plastic bag in his half-hand. His wooly hair spilled over an old lime green spring jacket. Nathan looked at him with new eyes. First he was a negligible, decrepit old crippled beggar. Then he was a swift, violent protector. Now, he was a well-read bookworm bringing him breakfast. Compared to Nathan's own pathetic homelessness, before him stood a resourceful, albeit handicapped, survivalist.

Jeb noticed Nathan had been exploring. The look on Nathan's bewildered face said *who the hell are you?*

Jeb took out a plate and placed biscuits on it from the bag. He turned on the stove and heated water for tea. Taking a carpeted mat, he motioned to sit. They sat across from one another, eating biscuits, and waiting for the water to boil.

"Jeb," Nathan broke the silence.

Jeb nodded and with his hand made a circle in the air, alluding to the room, and raised his eyebrows with a nod.

"Yes, I'm very impressed. You've made a nice place for yourself."

He gave a crooked thumbs up.

"You're a lot smarter than people think you are, aren't you?" he said. " I saw the books."

Jeb's eyes strained and he crossed his arms.

"I'm sorry, I should have asked," Nathan said.

Jeb held up his finger to silence him. He got up and retrieved a pen, paper, and dictionary, which he handed to Nathan. He flipped in the dictionary and pointed to the word *write*. He flipped a few pages and pointed to *words*. He tapped on the piece of paper with his finger.

"You want me to write words down on this piece of paper."

He gave him a thumbs up. He held up one finger. Flipping the dictionary pages, he pointed to the word *what*. Nathan wrote it down. He flipped to the word *who*. Nathan wrote it down. He flipped to the word *how* and then *why*, *where*, and *when*. And then he gave a thumbs up and a nod.

"Why did you have me do this?" Nathan asked.

Jeb opened the dictionary to *system* and then to *questions*.

Amused, Nathan said, "Not sure if I get it, but okay."

Jeb nodded, reassuring him. Nathan could tell he was trying to hide a glint of enthusiasm.

They sat across from each other in the middle of the room as Nathan told his story. Jeb listened carefully. At the part when Nathan mentioned his deceased mother, Jeb tapped Nathan's leg and held up a finger. He flipped in the dictionary and found a word. He pointed to *how* on the piece of paper and then to the word *died* in the dictionary. He was asking how his mother died. Nathan stared without blinking at him for a few seconds in a gawk.

When Nathan was in his sophomore year at Flaggert, Abby became ill. She coughed a great deal and her energy expired quickly. She grew weaker until she could barely stand from a chair. Thomas had called the doctor out to the farm. Dr. Smick stayed with them for several days. When he had finished his examination of Abby, he said it was unclear what was causing her ailment. He encouraged Thomas to bring her to Delorre to be seen by a specialist with proper equipment. But Thomas refused. He denied that it could be worse than anything but a fever. "It will pass," he said.

This angered Nathan. His poor mother could barely walk or eat. Yet Thomas didn't think it was anything serious. Nathan could only assume it was because his father didn't want to take the time off from his work.

Nathan's heart broke to see his mother, so strong and kind, bound to a bed, feeble and unable to serve others. She dismissed any sort of inquiry about how she was feeling, and her stubborn pride stopped her from asking for too much. He tried to help but nothing he did took away the pain, though she denied any sort of discomfort. She would just say, "I'm fine, Nathan. Go get us some tea."

Almost a year later, the "fever" didn't leave and Thomas took her to the hospital. But she refused to stay and wanted to be home. Her sickness worsened and she slept more. At home in bed, she spoke deliriously about a deli, horses, and Thomas. Her appetite for food dropped and she refused everything except broth and tea. Her voice diminished to a weak whisper, and her skin matched the white bed sheets in which she slept.

One morning, Nathan woke up to find Abby's hand cold. Jerking awake, he whispered, "Mother?" She didn't stir. He put his ear above her open mouth. Nothing.

"Mother!" he shrieked, hoping to jar her awake.

"Please," he said, propping up her shoulders and holding up her head. Her body was light and bony.

"Please, Mother," he said again. He kissed her on the cheek. Her skin felt cold and dry against his lips. Falling to his knees at the side of the bed, he held her, tears rolling off his chin. *Wake up, Mother.* But she didn't move. He laid his head on her shoulder. She was his best friend, his biggest fan, his closest companion; a beautiful person.

Jeb's face was serious. Slowly, he pointed to the paper. *When.*

Nathan said, "About eight years ago." It seemed so far away now.

With a hand over his heart, Jeb offered his condolences and motioned to continue.

Nathan took a big breath and told him about his frustration at the farm, how he didn't get along with brother and father, and how he ran away with millions of dollars.

Jeb's eyebrows rose. He had seen Nathan at The Charles so it wasn't a complete surprise.

"Anyways, I fell in love with the brown-haired girl named Beth who works at the hotel. But when she got pregnant, I had to break up with her."

When Nathan told Jeb the story of when he kicked her out of the Traveler's Inn room and how she walked in the night rain to the South Bennington train station, Jeb's face turned white.

Aghast, he stood up, went to the wooden chest and returned with the coral scarf she wore that night. Nathan recognized it immediately.

"Where did you get that?"

Nathan's eyes narrowed as a sinking feeling overcame him.

"Jeb, where did you get this?" He screamed and tried to get to his feet. "What did you do?"

A flood of anger exploded in Nathan. Jeb shook his head vigorously, his beard sweeping right and left. Nathan sniffled as he yelled, "Why do you have that?"

Without getting within Nathan's reach, Jeb pointed to a word in the dictionary.

Protect.

"What do you mean, protect?"

Jeb nodded. His face was stone, his warrior eyes resolute.

88

Thomas sat in the corner of Brew Social holding a cup of hot coffee in his hands. His work boots tapped anxiously. Every time the door opened, his eyes jumped to see who it was. He had no idea who this Rose Benton was, except that she was the assistant to the chairman of Venture X.

A professional blonde woman in her early thirties wearing a red top and black skirt sat down in the chair across from him.

"You must be Thomas," she said.

"Thanks for meeting with me, Rose," Thomas greeted her.

"You said on the phone you were John's father," she began. "You certainly look similar, but I still need some convincing.

"I'm flattered you think we look alike but Nathan got his good looks from his mother," said Thomas. "Not me."

Her brilliant smile matched the pearl necklace around her neck.

"Did you say Nathan?"

"That's his name."

"The Country Millionaire I know is named John Shepherd," corrected Rose.

"My son's name is Nathan Degland."

She pulled up a picture of John Shepherd on her phone. "This is who I'm talking about."

"That's Nathan," said Thomas, searching for the right words, "That's him. He must have changed his name."

Rose sat back in her chair and squinted her eyes. "So you're saying John Shepherd is a fake name?"

"Yes."

"How do I know you didn't do a deal with him and it went sour because he lost all his money, and you want to find him to get your money back?"

Lost all of his money? Thomas hid his distress. "He's tall and skinny. He has dark hair and blue eyes."

"Am I supposed to be impressed? You're not the only one who's seen a picture of him."

"He knows wine like a preacher knows the Bible," said Thomas. "His mother taught him that."

Rose chuckled emptily with a frown on her face. She remembered the embarrassing night with John at the Waterhouse restaurant. *He did know a lot about wine.*

"Alright," she licked her lips. "I'm listening."

"His real name is Nathan Degland, his older brother's name is Paul. His mother, Abigail, passed away when he was nineteen. He went to Flaggert College and studied business and finance, he loves to read, play chess, and drink sherry secretly," a sad smile spritzed across Thomas's face. "He thinks I don't know, but Tim, our winepress manager, tells me all the time when he sneaks it out to the barn."

Rose sipped from her coffee and looked at her gold watch. The man sounded sincere.

"Even if I wanted to help you, I can't," she said. "Nobody knows where he is. He was let go from Venture X several months ago, on some pretty bad terms, unfortunately."

"What do you mean?"

Rose sighed. "His relationship with the chairman took a turn for the worst. Personal problems."

"I see," said Thomas, "I'd like to meet with the chairman."

"He is a very busy man..."

Thomas took out his checkbook and began to write a handsome check. But Rose reached across the table and plucked the pen from his hand and started to write on a napkin. Thomas was taken aback.

"I don't care about money," she said. "If you are who you say you are..."

She handed him the napkin.

"Come to this address tomorrow at 11:00 a.m.," she said. "Ring the doorbell when you arrive."

89

Just as Nathan had expected, the withdrawal symptoms slaughtered him. Pain in his bones, nausea and vomiting, and diarrhea plagued him all day.

He tried to nap and nurse his wounds but his body craved heroin. He had expected it would be bad, but this was worse. Booze, cigarettes, and pain-killers were not enough.

Jeb always left him with crackers, cheese, and water when he departed to do his usual begging at The Charles. He'd come home in the evening with twenty to fifty dollars in his pockets.

One day when Jeb got home Nathan pulled something out from behind the boxes. He threw a stack of cardboard signs in front of Jeb.

"I made these for you."

Jeb picked one up. In big black capital letters, it read, "ARMY VET, HOMELESS & HUNGRY".

The second one said, "ANYTHING HELPS. GOD BLESS YOU."

He looked up at Nathan. His eyes studied him and then he pointed to the word *why*.

"So you can test which one works best," explained Nathan.

Jeb put the signs next to his original "MUTE, INJURED, AND HUNGRY."

He got up and retrieved the gas stove and teapot. He sat down next to Nathan.

"You know, I never heard your story."

It was just before dusk when Jeb decided to share his story. He was hesitant at first, but the more they talked the more he got into it. Jeb scribbled down a few more keywords to point to and he referenced the photographs on the wooden chest. Over the next two weeks, they pieced together his story:

His father was an alcoholic power tool salesman in Delorre who wouldn't bother to change out of his work clothes before he started to drink every day. His mother was an unambitious seamstress. Their family ate only one meal a day, washed their clothes once every two weeks, and bathed in cold water. So when his mother became pregnant, after a manic interrogation from his father to confirm that, first, she was actually pregnant, and that, second, she was actually pregnant with *his* child, they dreaded the thought of supporting a newborn.

Joshua "Jeb" Bure was born mute. The doctor said it was caused by a genetic deformity of the voice box. His parents didn't know where it came from. When they saw him, his mother's heart melted while his father's heart hardened. Jeb grew up loved by his mother and tolerated by his father. The photo of the boy on a playground with a woman watching was Jeb and his mother. His mother was slender with black hair, tan skin, blue eyes, and a winsome smile. His father, depicted by the photo of the professional in a suit, had a mustache, combed hair, and dimples.

His father hated him. One wintry night when his mother was snowed-in while visiting a client in the country, his father, in a drunken oblivion, locked six-year-old Jeb outside in his pajamas. When Jeb pounded on the door and his father realized his mistake, he instead bolted the door and backed away from the window pretending not to hear or see him.

Tears welled up in Nathan's eyes when Jeb pointed to the next word in the dictionary. *Frostbite*. Frostbite claimed the fingers missing from Jeb's hands that night. When his mother returned home late the next morning, dropped off by the client, she found little Jeb laying in the snow, frozen stiff.

After that, Jeb's parents couldn't afford to keep him so they sent him to live with his grandparents in the country. They lived in a small town called Feddington, north of the city. They were the embracing elderly couple in one of the photos. His grandparents loved him and encouraged him to read and run, two things he could do just as well as anyone else. Bullied, he could not play sports, or act in plays, or prove himself. He struggled to write and sign. But he read ferociously. He loved books. The authors provided a safe life for him to live. He trusted them.

When his grandparents passed away, he returned to the city but had trouble finding a job. He thought about returning to his parents but feared his father. Instead, he lived on the streets. For thirty-seven years, he lived on the streets, begging, scrounging, fighting, exploring, building. He had one goal: to save his money to go to Dr. Hans Schrodinger, a laryngologist who has written books about a breakthrough surgical procedure that can reverse muteness. Jeb showed Nathan all the books. He believed Dr. Schrodinger could fix him so that one day he might approach his father and speak to him.

"What would you say to him?" asked Nathan.

Jeb took a deep breath. He turned the pages and pointed a shaking finger to *forgive*. Then he put a hand over his heart. *Me*.

Nathan gasped, "Jeb, no."

Jeb thought it was his own fault. He thought that if he could speak his father wouldn't be angry. Jeb blamed his father's anger on himself. That's why he wanted the surgery—for his father to be happy with him.

Nathan asked, "Where is Dr. Schrodinger, now?"

Jeb retrieved a map of the city and opening it, pointed to the large medical complex building next to The Charles. No wonder he sat outside The Charles every day.

"How much money do you need?" Nathan asked.

With his finger, Jeb held up a one, another one, a zero, and three more zeros. *Poor fellow.* At his current rate of saving, he will be dead before he reached that number. Nathan tried not to show any hopelessness on his face.

"Where are your parents now?"

He shrugged and pointed to the East side of the city. He thought they were in the same condominium he grew up in, although he wasn't sure.

As they climbed into bed, Nathan told himself *I need to get better, and soon.* His uselessness burdened Jeb and he was drawing from his delicate savings. He would not see his parents any sooner with Nathan staying any longer. It was time to move on.

90

Thomas drove his truck through the opulent Cherry Hills neighborhood. He remembered a conversation from years ago with Mr. Martin about purchasing a home here. He'd never driven out here before, but now that he saw it, he shook his head. The bastions of wealth were unnecessarily enormous. He expected to see as much on his way to meet with the founder and chairman of Venture X.

Thomas saw the entrance gates to the Pendleton Estate in the distance. The mansion loomed above the wet green trees. The large pale villa seemed dark in front of the white clouds; all the window curtains were drawn. Thomas drove up the driveway, wrapped around a fountain, and parked in front of the entrance.

He walked up to the thick door and ran two fingers down the side of a panel. *Lignum vitae.* The door was made of the densest trade wood in the world. The door was a solid rock. He rang the doorbell.

The wooden wall swung away from him, revealing Rose Benton in a short golden dress.

"Mr. Degland," she greeted him. "Please follow me."

He followed her inside down the dark hall. The smell of her sweet perfume mixed with a strong piney wood polish wafted in his face. Thomas breathed through his mouth. The sound of her heels echoed down the hall as they passed painting after painting. Just when he thought they were going to turn left, the side wall panel opened on the right. They both watched it slide open smoothly.

Thomas asked, "Why isn't there a door here?"

"It's a very important room."

"Of course."

They stepped into the large four story ballroom with red carpet and portraits lining the walls. Shadows flickered across the portraits from the roaring fireplace. Thomas's eyes found a man sitting underneath the taxidermy of a giant bear at the end of a long oak table. The white bearded man was dressed in a white cashmere sweater with a plaid collar. He looked up from the paper in his hands.

"Ah, Mr. Thomas Degland, the true Country Millionaire from Sanctilly," George said, standing to his feet.

Thomas walk towards him and his worn coarse hand wrapped around George's soft gloved hand.

"I'm from Sanctilly, yes," said Thomas, "But I'm no Country Millionaire."

"That's right. Not anymore, that is." An evil smile twitched in the corners of George's mouth.

"Please, sit," George motioned to a chair. "Would you like a drink?"

"Water is fine, thank you."

Both men sat, Rose left to fetch the beverages.

"I'm not sure what you mean," said Thomas.

"You know exactly what I mean," George laughed. "A young boy doesn't come to the city with millions of his *own* money."

George's gray eyes flashed with a spit of anger. Thomas stared at the man, lips parted.

"What do you know about my Nathan?"

"Rose mentioned you called him by a different name," George continued, "You didn't send him here, did you."

"No, he ran away," admitted Thomas.

George clucked his tongue and shook his head. "Your son runs away with all your hard-earned money. You must be furious."

"I was, especially when I came after him and he refused to return home."

"Why would he, when he has millions of dollars?" prodded George.

Thomas put his water on the table and leaned over his knees in George's direction. "Listen, if you know anything about my son, I'm willing to pay a large sum of money to find him."

"Aww," George said. "Isn't that nice."

Thomas was perplexed by this sinister man. "He was involved with your firm, was he not?"

"You really have no idea about your son."

"I know he's in trouble. That's why I'm here."

"I'm sure you'd like to know, wouldn't you?"

"Wouldn't any father want to know about his missing child?"

His words reminded George of his neglect of Beth for so many years and instantly, George's face twisted. "Your son is a failure, Mr. Degland," he bit into his words rabidly. "He failed at everything he touched. He's a disgrace and you should be ashamed of the boy you raised."

The sudden anger caught Thomas off guard and he rose to his feet insulted. Rose stopped at the door, frozen.

"Look, I don't know what happened between you," rebutted Thomas, "But you best not talk about my boy in that way."

"No, you need to hear the truth," George stood, raising his voice and pointing at Thomas, "As if losing your millions wasn't enough, he lied about having more, lost everything, slept with my daughter, got her pregnant, and abused her!"

The two men glared at each other. George was gasping for air, his wrinkled veiny neck filled with hot blood. He hadn't expected to explode but he couldn't stop himself. Thomas clenched his teeth and balled his fists. The men held each other's eyes until Thomas blinked, realizing what he just heard.

"What did you say?" Thomas's heart was still beating fast.

George's face burned. His shoulders moved with his breaths. "You heard me," he muttered. It was all he could get out.

Thomas swallowed hard. He clenched his molars so tightly they began to grind. He tried not to imagine the news. *Nathan, no. What have you done? Who is this woman? Do I have a grandchild? How is this possible?* He looked to George.

"Did they marry?"

"No. He left her shortly after he found out."

George watched Thomas process the news. Thomas's face was solemn.

"Sit," invited George, regaining his composure. "I know it's a lot to hear all at once."

The blacks of Thomas's eyes were large and moist, reflecting the flames of the fire. The room was quiet, filled only with the sound of the crackling logs and the silent turmoil of Thomas's thoughts.

Finally, Thomas looked up at George. "What's your daughter's name?"

"Beth, Beth Jacobs."

"Where is she?"

"She's living here with me."

"May I speak with her?"

George shifted uncomfortably in his chair, displeased by the request.

"Why?"

"I want to meet her."

"After what's been done to her, she doesn't need any more...

torture than what she's already been through. Trust me."

"Please," Thomas said. "She's carrying my grandchild, too."

George narrowed his eyes. He leaned forward and pressed a button underneath the oak table. In a few moments, Rose appeared.

"Rose, would you call Beth?"

Rose turned and disappeared. Both men took large gulps of their drinks, trying to calm down. In a few minutes, the most beautiful woman Thomas had ever seen entered the room.

Thomas's back straightened when he saw Beth. Her deep set emerald eyes were sad and her forehead wrinkled with hurt underneath her brown hair. Her dark eyebrows furrowed above pronounced cheekbones. One of her thin bare shoulders was red with scratches and her round belly protruded from underneath a simple white tank top. Immediately, Thomas's heart broke.

She took small steps towards him, unable to place all of her weight on her right leg. She was hesitant and afraid, not knowing what to expect from her ex-lover's father.

"I've heard a lot about you, Mr. Shepherd," she said in a soft voice.

The small smile that broke across Thomas's trembling face quickly disappeared.

"I'm Thomas Deg—"

He stopped. He didn't know what to say. He just wanted to put his arms around her gently and hold her. He didn't even know this woman but he knew she needed care and compassion.

"...I'm sorry."

"You don't even know the half of it," George snarled.

Thomas stood still for five minutes, letting the waves of anger and disappointment in Nathan crash over him. He held his head with his hands and focused on breathing.

When he gathered himself enough to speak, he said, "Where is he?"

Smack!

George slapped the latest issue of the Daily Delorre onto the table. "See for yourself."

The headline read *Bankruptcy, Drug Addiction: The Demise of the Country Millionaire.*

91

The next morning, the cravings were stronger. Jeb had left for the day. Nathan laid in bed, staring at the ceiling, surging with desires and aches.

Flexing the muscles in his legs, they felt flimsy from weeks of immobility. His ankle was swollen and his foot was blue. His knees were thin and bony.

Disregarding the pain, he rolled over and up to his knees. Grimacing, he planted a foot down in front and pressed up to a standing position. It was a little too quickly. His vision turned completely dark. His head filled with air like a balloon and he lost awareness. He stumbled forward and fell over boxes of books. His outstretched hands looked for a way to stabilize his timbering body but they only found the tops of closed empty boxes. Falling through them, his hands became fitted with cardboard boxing gloves while his toothpick legs flew into the air and he landed in a heap of blankets, boxes, and books.

He half-laughed, half-gasped for air. His side felt like a hatchet was lodged in it. Nevertheless, he didn't let it stop him. He was leaving and that was final. He picked himself up and got dressed. Packing up the bagel and apple juice box Jeb had left for him, he readied himself to leave. Just before leaving, an idea presented itself with convincing logic.

Poor Jeb. Deep down, Nathan knew he would never reach the $110,000 that he needed. *A few hundred dollars wouldn't make a big difference.* He turned and walked to the corner of the ceiling where the key was. He found it instantly. Moving to the wooden chest, he shuffled the books around until he found the bank bag. The key inserted snugly into the lock and with a *click-click* it opened. He stuffed his hand into the cold, tender cash. His skin tingled. *Just a couple hundred.* He counted out $300, zipped up the bag, locked it, put it back in the chest, and returned the key to its normal spot.

The plan was to purchase clean clothes, a sleeping bag, find a dealer, purchase a bag or two of brown grade heroin and a handle of vodka and some cigarettes, just enough to get him back on his feet and reduce the withdrawal symptoms. Then he could go job prospecting again. A handful of lottery tickets couldn't hurt as well.

Lifting the tarp flap, he took one last grateful look around Jeb's place. Jeb saved him. Without him, his life may have ended. Nathan wished him happiness and left.

A rush of fresh, cold air filled his nostrils. The raw sunlight hurt his eyes. Blinking, the construction area was dead. His legs were sore as he walked, and his ribs throbbed. Jeb's oversized boots clomped along like large paper weights attached to the ends of his stringy legs.

He entered the public stadium grounds and saw several workers buzzing about cleaning, setting up signs, and stocking concessions. There was a home game the following night. Judging by their displeased looks, he didn't think he was supposed to be there.

He stopped a young man, several years younger than him, who immediately appeared uncomfortable. "Hey— "

His voice cracked. It was the first time he had spoken that

day. As soon as he spoke he knew he should have cleared his throat first. It sounded as if someone had just stepped on the tail of an old, dying cat.

"...I'm looking for a job here. Where should I go?"

The young man frowned as if Nathan had just intentionally sneezed in his face. He pointed above the bleacher stands to an office and said, "Fill out an application and give it to the manager up there."

"Thanks, buddy," he said, more normally.

For the rest of the day, he busied himself filling out the application. In the squalls of withdrawal, his shaky handwriting looked like a seismograph recording an earthquake. He needed to find a drug dealer. Fast.

92

About a half mile from the stadium, he exited the supermarket with a plastic bag in each hand. In the back of the parking lot sat a black SUV with white smoke pouring out of the exhaust pipe. This triggered an array of memories about Derrick. He said dealers tend to drive large black SUVs with tinted windows. He practically lived out of his black Escalade before living in The Charles with Nathan. This SUV in the parking lot fit the picture.

Walking across the parking lot, he saw a white Tahoe pull up to the SUV, driver to driver. It paused for about fifty seconds before pulling away. He kept walking. *That was all the time that was needed for a deal to go down, right?* His suspicions were confirmed when he saw another vehicle, a black Buick pull up to the SUV moments later. It stayed for no more than a minute and half. This time, he was in front of the SUV so he saw the items exchanged between the drivers windows.

It had to be true. A dealer sat in the black SUV, he was sure of it. He veered across the parking lot and walked towards the SUV.

Sweat broke out of every pore in his skin. There was a chance he was wrong. But he was willing to take the chance if it meant he would be rid of the shakes. Thoughts raced through his dehydrated brain. *What if the dealer was unfriendly or paranoid? What if the dealer was aggressive, or not even a dealer—an undercover cop?*

Fifteen feet away, it was too late now. The glare of the sunlight in the windshield hid the driver as Nathan approached, though he was sure he was being watched. It was a good sign the SUV did not drive away. *They must be willing to talk.*

Nathan limped up to the driver's tinted window, he saw his own reflection. *God, you look like a druggie.* The window lowered slowly to allow a two inch opening. Smoke seeped from the cracked window.

Nathan cleared his throat. "Got any cigarettes?" he asked, even though he had just paid someone to buy a pack for him in the supermarket.

An unseen hand held a pack of Camel's through the crack, with one poking out from the rest. He took it and put it his mouth.

"Got a light?"

A dark-skinned, thin hand holding a lighter slithered out of the window. He exchanged the pack of cigarettes for the lighter. The hand disappeared into the smoke. He lit the cigarette in his mouth.

"What do you need?" It was a woman's voice — hard, piercing, and twangy.

His eyebrows flickered.

"Got any H?"

"How much?"

"How much is a gram?"

"$150."

"I'll take one and a third."

From inside the vehicle he heard the woman shout through her teeth to wake up.

"Get the smack," she said. Moments later, a baggie hung out

of the window.

"$200," she said.

Another car pulled up in front of the SUV and parked. Nervously, Nathan tried to count out $200.

"Hurry up," she said. He fumbled with the money. *Screw it.* He handed her all the money he had left. She asked, "What's your name?"

"No name." He took the baggie. "Cheers."

As soon as he walked away, the other vehicle crept toward the SUV. He scanned the parking lot for any onlookers but didn't see any. He walked back to the stadium and looked for a place to stay for the night.

The parking garage next to the stadium turned out to be promising. He found a spot in the staircase in between the second and third floor. It was roped off where three steps were broken. After surveying the area, he determined the stairs should be private enough. He sat down against the cement wall in the corner, out of breath.

He fished the vodka out of his bag and took two swigs. With shaking fingers, he put a rubber band around his bicep. The freedom was just seconds away. *Almost there.* He could barely handle it; he was giddy. He filled the needle and inserted it into the bruise in his arm and squeezed it in.

The sun had gone down hours ago. He curled up into a ball in the corner while flashbacks of parties with Derrick, Angeline, and Tommy zipped around his mind. He held a girl's hips, twirled another, and flirted at the bar. A room full of people tapped the shots of tequila on the bar counter in unison, *thud-ud-ud*, and threw them back. Such laughter, as Tommy called out, *Another!* A girl laid on top of him in his room. Derrick handed him a custom bong. He kissed a girl in a cab. Beth's candle-lit bedroom. Her smooth skin. Her loud, piercing voice.

He got up and hid his supplies in an old fire extinguisher case in the stairwell and walked around the garage. The faded orange lights lit the floors in large spots. He walked, led and followed by his hooded shadows, towards a woman in heels and a professional suit. She doubled her pace to her car when she saw him coming. He laughed at her. She threw herself into her car, locked the door, and sped away.

Nothing mattered because he felt good, safe and warm. In less than ten minutes, drowsiness overtook him and he returned to the staircase. He collapsed and slept until morning.

93

Thomas's white truck pulled into the parking spot next to the decrepit black sports car at Traveler's Inn in South Bennington. It looked just like the one in the newspaper. Beth had told him Nathan was staying here. Thomas wiped a bead of sweat from his temple as he looked up at the clouds. *Rain.* His eyes followed the line of motel room doors down the corridor on the third floor. *He's in room 303.*

Leaping up the stairs, he walked passed a thin blonde woman in torn jeans and a loose shirt smoking a cigarette on the balcony.

"Howdy, stranger," she called to him, smiling.

With a serious look on his face, Thomas didn't answer. He strode down the metal walkway, imagining the scene of Beth's fall on that rainy night. His mind spun with the stories she and George had told him about his son. About the parties. About Tommy and Angeline. About Derrick. He didn't know what to believe. What he did know was Nathan truly was in trouble and needed his help. *I need to find him and make sense of all this.*

He saw the number 303 hanging sideways on the door. He knocked on the door with his fist. *Thud thud thud.* No answer. Something caught his eye to his right. It was a man with a feather in his hat waving kindly. *Thud thud thud*, he pounded against the door again.

He yelled, "Nathan!"

No answer.

"Nathan!" He shouted again. "It's your father! Let me in."

He put his ear to the door. No sound came from inside.

"He's not there anymore," the blonde woman said.

Thomas whipped around to face the woman. Her legs were crossed and she looked like she was about to fall over. She went on, "And why are you calling him Nathan? That's not his name."

Flustered and embarassed for shouting, Thomas squared his shoulders to the woman.

"I'm sorry," he said. "Who are you?"

"I'm Bobby," she said and held out her limp hand professionally. "William and I were good friends."

"Who is William?" His large hand closed over hers.

"William was my neighbor in 303. I'm in 302, see?"

She opened the door to her room and invited him in. Thomas felt uncomfortable.

"Come in," she beckoned.

"Bobby," a man's voice yelled from inside her room. "We're not open right now."

"But Dwayne," she called back. "You'll want to see this."

"I'm sorry…" Thomas began but was interrupted by a loud crack of thunder and it began to downpour. Dwayne poked his head from the bathroom door. "Who is it?"

He looked Thomas up and down. "I'll be damned."

The locksmith? Bobby grabbed Thomas's arm, "Come out of the rain and have some tea."

"Wait," Thomas hesitated, "What's going on here?"

"Bobby," Dwayne said. "Don't bring him in here."

"William kinda looked like you, actually," said Bobby. "One of the nicer fellas."

"Bobby, stop," Dwayne spoke seriously. "I said don't bring that man in here."

Bobby lifted the boiling water kettle off the stove and poured the steaming water onto a tea bag in a brown mug. Thomas sat at the counter in the kitchen. Dwayne smoked nervously in the corner of the room.

"You knew Nathan?"

"You keep saying his name is Nathan," said Bobby, crossing her arms and squinting like a detective. "Are you sure you know who you're lookin' for, mister?"

"William, John Shepherd, the Country Millionaire—whoever he is—"

Thomas turned to Dwayne. "You know who I'm looking for."

"Nope," Dwayne said quickly. "We don't know anything about him." He glared at Bobby.

Frustrated, Thomas said, "Who lived next door?"

Bobby sipped her hot tea and winced, sticking out her pink tongue. "William did."

She tested the sensitivity in her tongue.

"William?" Thomas repeated. "And he looked like me?"

"Yep. We talked a lot."

"Bobby, shut up," interjected Dwayne. He walked over to the fridge, pinched her side, and grabbed a beer.

"I think Bobby has him confused with someone else," said Dwayne. "We don't know your son."

"Yes, we did," said Bobby, oblivious to Dwayne's attempts to get rid of Thomas as fast as possible. Dwayne pushed her out of the kitchen. "Honey, can you go somewhere else so the men can talk in private?"

She stumbled into the bathroom and Dwayne closed the door behind her. He turned to Thomas. "Look. I can tell you what happened to your son, but it'll cost you."

"Name it," said Thomas. He pulled the checkbook from his pocket and put in on the counter. "What happened?"

"Alright," Dwayne slurped from the can in his hand, "But I can't promise it's good news."

94

Revving car engines awoke him. The empty parking garage turned into a busy ant hill of cars. *What day was it?* Nathan rubbed his eyes. He needed water. Checking his bags and pockets, everything was still there. He found a bathroom. In the mirror, he straightened his scruffy hair and splashed water on his face. *Time to put on my best.* Today was the day he would get a job.

After cleaning up, he took one last look in the mirror, and a voice in his head cursed him for the drug-ridden night before. *Stop it. Get going. It's a new day.* With the application papers in his bag over his shoulder, he strolled out to the stadium grounds, not ungrateful for the refreshing light rain. He felt hopeful. Things were about turn around. He was going to get his life back together. Maybe even see Beth, and hear about his child.

At the stadium, he crossed the open asphalt towards the bleachers of the manager's booth when he saw Mr. Jefferson walking straight towards him. He walked with a cohort of professionals dressed in dark jackets and holding umbrellas. He looked older with less hair and more wrinkles, but his stride led the pack, each yuppie grappling over the other to hold an umbrella over his bald head.

Nathan had forgotten he owned a majority interest in this stadium. He stepped into their path twenty feet ahead of them, directly in line with Mr. Jefferson. Two men noticed him and stepped ahead, ready to usher him away. He called out.

"Mr. Jefferson!"

He looked up from the paper his assistant was showing him. "John Shepherd?"

"Yes," he said and stepped towards him a little too gingerly, knees shaking.

"Mr. Shepherd?" he repeated in disbelief. The eyes of those around him looked back and forth from their boss to the street ghoul standing in front of him, trying to make sense of the encounter.

Nathan said in typical Venture X fashion, "Good to see you, Mr. Jefferson."

Turning to the group, Mr. Jefferson said, "Give us a minute," and brushed the air with his hand. They dispersed, grumbling. He turned back around to Nathan.

"What on God's green earth happened to you? You disappeared."

"I, uh, I'm going through a little bit of a personal recession, I guess."

"You look like hell," he said.

"I know," Nathan said, and instantly changed the subject, "How's business? How's Venture X?"

Mr. Jefferson didn't respond. Instead, he slunk into an episode of intense analysis, assessing Nathan's wrinkled clothes, oversized boots, and gossamer complexion.

He shook his head and lowered his voice, "How much do you need?"

His words were a slap in the face. The word *nothing* stopped just short of the tip of Nathan's tongue. It was habit to not need anything from anyone. He swallowed. "I just need a job."

He felt ashamed for asking a former investment partner for an hourly job. Mr. Jefferson thought for a few moments.

"I'll do anything," added Nathan.

"Mr. Shepherd, if I may speak frankly to you, you do not look well enough to perform the duties of any customer-facing position in any company I own. Have you seen yourself? Are you aware of your condition? God, you look like a starving prisoner of war."

His comments stung. "But, Mr. Jefferson, surely you don't mean that," he said. "You know what I can do."

"I'm afraid I don't. Something terrible has happened to you. I can see it."

"Don't worry about me. I'm just trying to get a job, and I'm asking a friend for help. If you don't want to help, fine."

He took a step back and pretended to turn his back. Mr. Jefferson put a large, gloved hand on his wet shoulder.

"We are looking for..." An inhale straightened Mr. Jefferson's back and he exhaled sharply. "...a facilities attendant. It's a housekeeping job that cleans the grounds, common areas, and restroo—"

"I'll take it." Nathan cut him off. *Any job. I will take any job. Even if it means cleaning toilets.*

Mr. Jefferson's hawkish eyes searched Nathan's face for some trace of humor or lying. Finding none, he said, "Done."

He waved over one of his reports and said, "Take this man up to the office and tell Kyle that he starts tomorrow as a facilities attendant."

The suited young man nodded and motioned to follow him. Nathan extended his hand to Mr. Jefferson.

"Thank you."

"Don't mention it. Good luck, Mr. Shepherd." They shook and Nathan felt a paper bill crinkle into his hand. The gentleman turned and walked away under the umbrellas of his associates, leaving Nathan under the umbrella of a tall young man in a suit, as the rain pattered around them.

95

In victory, Nathan strolled to the supermarket and then to the bookstore in downtown South Bennington to get a book for Jeb. The clock hands pointed to 3 p.m. when he left the bookstore. The history book under his arm was about Ludwig Van Beethoven's struggle with bipolar disorder. He thought Jeb would enjoy it.

After forty-five minutes of walking at a brisk pace, he recognized the way to Jeb's hidden outpost in the back of the stadium construction. Coming up to the metal fence, he found where Jeb had dragged his half-conscious body underneath. He glanced right and left before lifting up the bottom of the cut fence. He crouched down and as he climbed underneath, he realized his mistake. The fence scraped the back of his leg, the steel points digging into his right calf. Cursing, he remembered how Jeb propped the fence open with the cone and pulled it with the rope to get under the fence.

With an even greater limp, he walked through the projects and into the scaffolding storage area. Seeing Jeb's tarp-wrapped home, he called out.

"Jeb, it's Nathan. I'm back!"

More excited to see him than he expected, he hurried. At the tarp corner, he felt a smile sneak onto his face, thinking he might be able to surprise him, but knowing it would be impossible because of Jeb's augmented hearing.

Opening up the tarp flap, he said, "Jeb, ol' boy!"

A horrid smell clawed at his nose. The tarp walls were slashed and shredded. Books were strewn on the floor everywhere. Broken glass and ceramic shards smashed on the ground. Clothing and cookware scattered across the floor.

Then, he saw him.

96

"Jeb!" he cried.

He was laying on his bed, face down with both arms by his sides. His right hand still gripped Nathan's broken flintlock pistol. Dark red blood soaked the blankets around him. He didn't stir. Nathan panicked.

He knelt down and put his arm on the Jeb's back. He was breathing. Frantic, Nathan tapped him and said, "Jeb, Jeb. Wake up, Jeb. Where are you hurt?"

Lifting his shoulder, Nathan turned him around to see what was wrong, he gasped. Jeb's chest was full of holes. Blood gushed from multiple openings in his clothing. *Knife wounds.* Jeb's eyes were open but unfocused. Blood filled his mouth, spilling onto his beard. His breath was weak and sputtery.

Shaking with adrenaline, Nathan looked around. *What happened?* On the ground, a path of blood trailed to where Jeb lay in his bed. *Should I move him?* The holes in his torso bled whenever he tried to move him. But the bleeding needed to stop. He remembered when his mother mended one of the workers at the farm when he was gored by a bull. She cleaned the wound, sewed the opening closed, and applied sterile gauze and bandages. The thought of sewing Jeb's gaping flesh brought vomit to Nathan's mouth. He swallowed hard. He had to get him on his back.

"Jeb, if you can hear me, I'm going to turn you over."

On his knees, Nathan put two arms underneath Jeb's chest and waist. The blood was hot and wet up to his elbows. As gently as he could, he turned him over. Jeb groaned and coughed up dark blood. He struggled to breath on his back and Nathan lifted his chin.

He counted seven punctures in Jeb's jacket, each letting out blood. He didn't have much time left. Nathan felt helpless and powerless; *what do I do?* He needed an ambulance. Nathan rummaged through his bag to find his phone. But it was dead. He threw it against the wall.

He could try to carry him. But after scanning his shredded belly, Nathan was afraid he would just come apart. *It's too late.* His attackers had fatally wounded him and left him to die, knowing that he would.

Nathan burned with anger. *They didn't have the honor to take his life. They stabbed and left him alive to die slowly.* Furious, he cursed them. *What evil violent demons would do this?* Jeb didn't deserve this. *I deserved this.* He wished he could switch places with him. *I should be the one to die.* Jeb's eyes didn't blink.

Knowing the end was near, Nathan held Jeb's broken hands.

"Jeb, can you hear me?"

A faint, weak squeeze twitched in his hands. He looked at Jeb's eyes and thought he saw an infinitesimal blink.

"I'm so sorry, Jeb."

He had so many questions. *Who did this? What happened? What can I do?* But he knew it would do no good.

"Jeb, when I was near dead, you saved my life. You rescued me and took care of me. There is so much more to you than people know."

Hot tears welled up in Nathan's eyes but he didn't want to let go of Jeb's hands to wipe them away. For a moment, Jeb stopped breathing.

"Hold on, Jeb," Nathan's voice was high and shrill. "You're okay. I'm right here."

Nathan rushed to put his arm under his head and lifted. Jeb coughed up more blood and gasped for air.

"You're not like others," said Nathan. "You're kind. You are a true friend."

Jeb's right hand twitched and then his body went limp. His breathing slowed to nothing. His heartbeat stopped. He was gone.

With his arm around him, Nathan held him until dusk. He couldn't bear to move. He sat in silence. *I deserved this. I should've been stabbed and left for dead. It would have been a better ending. Jeb was actually kind. He was an unknown gift to the world. He certainly was to me.*

He looked at Jeb's still body. *How did it come to this?* His arms were numb. His tears fell onto Jeb's lifeless face.

That night, Nathan questioned why he was living. What good had come from his life? No person was glad he was alive in the city. He failed his father. *Mother would turn in her grave if she knew what I've done.* Jeb lay dead in front of him. Paul, Beth, and George hated him. Everyone else didn't care. There was no one. *What reason do I have to keep going?*

Finally, he rested Jeb down next to him and crawled over to an old half-empty liquor bottle. He finished the remains and cast the bottle away. He fell, a bloody mess, to the side and felt the alcohol relieve the watchmen of his mind. In the spinning darkness, he slept and did not wish to wake.

97

With her hands in cotton oven mitts, Mary placed hot pots of mashed potatoes, peas, and chicken legs on the large oak table in the Degland house. Paul and his now wife Marissa, Tim and his wife Tabitha, Thomas's sister, Lydia, and her husband, and Thomas all held hands together around the table.

"Our Father," Thomas prayed, and everyone bowed their heads.

"We give you thanks for this day, and for this food, and for the family and friends you have blessed us with. We pray that you would remember Nathan at this time, protect him and keep him safe, whereever he may be."

Thomas paused, his face crumpled. Paul looked up at him with accusing eyes. Thomas inhaled and cleared his throat and finished his prayer. "Bless this food and the hands that have prepared it. In your son's name. Amen."

The group passed plates around the table and served each other great dollops of steaming food as the dinner discussions began.

Paul leaned over to his father and covertly whispered, "When will you tell us what happened in the city?"

Instantly, the dinner table became silent. Everyone was on edge ever since Thomas had returned the night before. He had been quiet all day, and not as productive as usual. Everyone had been waiting for the question to be asked and Paul's clandestine attempt became the focal point of the dinner table. Mary's hands paused for the first time in her life in order to hear the news about Nathan.

Thomas's plate was empty.

After a long pause, he said, "I couldn't find him."

"You couldn't find him?" Paul repeated. "You were gone for a week."

Tabitha asked, "Did you hear anything more about what happened to him?"

Faces flashed in Thomas's mind, Rose, Beth with the baby, George in front of the fireplace in his mansion, Bobby and Dwayne at the Traveler's Inn.

"He..." Thomas hesitated, "...got in over his head."

"Is he okay?" Mary asked from the sink with concern in her voice.

"I don't know," Thomas replied.

Tim said, "You're obviously stressed about this, Tom, maybe we better not talk about this at the dinner table."

Thomas agreed gratefully with Tim.

"But, Dad," Paul wasn't satisfied. "You were gone for a week. Surely, you found out something about him."

"He was doing well for a time, but ended up making a number of poor decisions, and things fell apart."

Thomas winced recalling the news about Nathan's parasitic friends and drug habits, "Mr. Martin was right. Nathan was the Country Millionaire. But he isn't anymore. He went missing about a month ago."

"What happened to the money?" asked Paul.

Money was the last thing Thomas wanted to talk about. He mumbled, "It's gone."

"Where did it go?"

"I don't know."

Paul noticed the pain in his father's face but he wanted to know what happened to his brother.

Paul pressed more, "What kind of trouble is he in?"

"I don't know."

"Do you even know if he's alive?"

"I don't know!" exploded Thomas. He stood violently to his feet, jolting the table. That was the one answer he did know but he was too afraid to believe it. He feared putting it into words, even though Dwayne had made it unmistakably clear Nathan was gone.

Thomas tried to scold Paul but his throat was too tight. He faltered and hurried out of the room.

Tim shook his head. "Too far, Paul, too far."

"What?" Paul was defensive. "I just want to be realistic. It's been years. Am I the only one who wants to face the facts?"

98

THE SUN ROSE the next day and Nathan awoke with it. Dried blood covered his arms and stained his clothes. Jeb's body lay in his crusted, stiff bed. A ball-and-chain slammed into the sides of Nathan's head like a clock pendulum every time he moved.

The odor of Jeb's dead body baked in a tarp-insulated room overwhelmed his nose. He wretched the alcohol.

Dismal thoughts from the night before inundated his mind. He had no defenses—no way to combat the onslaught of hopelessness.

A bleak thought entered his mind—his job. He remembered he started at 10:00 a.m. at the concessions behind section 14. For a reason he could not identify—perhaps the thrashing, dying creature of ambition still inside him, or the physical pain of staying here—he knew he had to move. He covered Jeb with clothes and blankets. It was not the burial he deserved but it was the only one he could give him. Memories of Derrick's dead body jutted into mind as he covered Jeb. Emotionally, he was a stone. Nothing mattered now.

He tried to clean himself up under the freezing water gushing out of the water hose. He found decent jeans and a long sleeve shirt in a bag and changed into them. With one last look at the mound of blankets and cardboard above Jeb, he left the rancid room and dragged himself to the stadium.

Staff scuttled to and fro, again abuzz with pre-game preparations. The schedule showed a game at six that night.

The large, planet of a man from the manager's office stood in a draping red t-shirt outside the supply shack. He held a mop and stood by a cleaning cart with a mop bucket under the handles. Cleaners, solutions, scrub brushes, and sponges filled the cleaning cart. Nathan walked up to him.

"You're late, Joey," he said.

"Whatever. I'm here," Nathan said. He was too tired to care about anything.

The man said, "Take these, fill up the bucket and take the cart to the bathrooms on the ground level. Get them clean. We'll get your paperwork taken care of tomorrow. Time's ticking. The pre-game starts in a couple hours and the bathrooms need to be cleaned."

Nathan filled the bucket and squirted soap into the warm water. He pushed the cart to the first bathroom. With a knock on the door, he checked to see if anyone was in the restroom. No reply; he entered.

The smells of the bathroom and the strength of the cleaners pounded against his head. After the twelfth sink and eighth toilet, his motivation waned. The small prick of energy that came from fulfilling a responsibility rapidly evaporated with every scrub of the toilet. His body wasn't ready for the manual labor and he dreaded it. He felt sick. On a stadium map, he counted twenty-eight restrooms on the ground floor. His dread turned to despair.

The monotony of the tasks let his mind reflect on his fallen life. There was nothing else to think about. He was cleaning excrement and urine from the floor and walls, unclogging toilets, and mopping dirty floors. He had failed and the wreckage of his life was unsalvageable. Numbness, isolation, and the inescapable cloud of despair darkened everything. He had not one positive, hopeful thought; he was alone with nothing but shame and guilt.

I should have never been born. From the cart, he took the most potent drainage cleaner and left the cart in an open stall. He stepped into the next stall and locked the door behind him. *This is what I deserve.* This is justice. He sat down on a toilet, unscrewed the cap of the cleaner, and held it up to his lips. *This is the only way out.* He tipped it up, poured it into his mouth, and guzzled it. The lukewarm chemicals stung his tongue and ran down his esophagus. A severe burning erupted in his stomach, ever sharper and more painful than hard liquor. Immediately, his throat swelled and closed. Circular saw blades in his stomach whirred and thrashed and spread up to his chest. His breathing stopped, and his heart raced faster and faster. He tried to steady himself on the wall, but he fell. He lost sight, taste, and all feeling in his skin. Hot magma scalded his lungs and vomit blocked his throat.

PART 5

BACK FROM THE DEAD

99

"Son! Look, son!" Crouched by a campfire, Nathan held an iron frying pan with butter in it and a fork in his other hand. He dropped them and ran as fast as he could to Thomas who was hunkered down, pointing into the distance ahead. Nathan knelt down next to him.

Early morning mist filled the dense, green forest. Behind them, their smoldering campfire gave off wisps of smoke from the night before. Next to their orange tent, the limpid stream where they had caught crawfish the day before flowed by. Thomas had gone to fetch firewood and Nathan had been preparing for breakfast.

They were up in the mountains—just the two of them—exploring, camping, and hiking. Every year, Thomas took his son up to Wishbone Pass one weekend for a father-son adventure.

He put his big hand on Nathan's upper back and said, "Look, Nathan, do you see?"

He peered ahead. Fifty feet away, a sizable bear stood on its hind legs with its back against a tree. Wagging its snout in the air, the bear jiggered around, pressing its back against the thin trunk. The small tree shook as the brown giant snorted and waved its paws in the air, enjoying its scratch.

Then, the bear rubbed a little too vigorously to one side and missed the tree. It toppled backwards, swinging its stubby legs in the air and crashed to the ground in a fluffy jumble.

They both snickered at the sight. Hearing his father laugh, made him laugh. When Thomas heard Nathan laugh, he laughed even harder. Soon, they both laughed so loud they were weak. The bear quickly regained its feet on all fours, its nose combing the air, aimed right at them.

They composed themselves but it was too late. The bear saw them. They looked at each other and then back at the bear. Nathan didn't know what was going to happen.

"Do you see any cubs?" whispered Thomas.

Nathan looked around and for a moment, he was scared. The bear could charge any second. But the fear left as soon as the bear turned and sauntered off into the dense woods.

He turned to his father and noticed his face was red from the restrained laughter. With a pronounced exhale, they both realized they had been holding their breath. The simultaneity of their exhales sparked another round of levity.

"Son! Look, son!"

Suddenly, he was crouching by the campfire again with the frying pan and fork in his hands. Thomas was pointing to the bear again. Nathan dropped the cookware and ran up to him. The memory replayed again. Then, again. And again.

Then, a different voice shouted, "Son! Look, son!" It was not his father's voice.

"Son! Stop! Look what you're doing!" The other voice continued.

Nathan's eyes cracked open. The cement floor. The bottom of a urinal. Two pairs of feet. He blinked. Tiny droplets splashed close to his face. He blinked again.

The left side of his face was smashed against the cold dirty slab floor. He didn't know how long he had been there. *Where am I?* More details slowly came into view. He laid at the base of a toilet. Vomit covered the floor. Two pairs of feet—one larger standing behind one smaller—were pointed towards a urinal a yard away.

A tiny stream sprayed into the urinal. The father continued to correct the son for his wayward aim.

Steel axes flew into the sides of his brain. He remembered where he was. He was in the stadium bathroom stall. He turned over and saw the cleaning cart wheels in the adjacent stall. His mouth tasted horrible.

Then he remembered his unsuccessful attempt at taking his own life. He wondered if he should try again, maybe it would actually work.

The memory of his father in the woods with the bear still remained vivid in his mind. *It felt so real.* He could still hear his voice calling him, and feel his arm on his back, and sense the uncanny mix of fear and hilarity they shared in that moment.

There were times when Father did enjoy being with me. When they spent time together like that, he felt like he could do no wrong. As a small boy, he always looked forward to it. Time alone with his father up in the mountains was always an adventure. *He taught me how-*

A cold wave of darkness swept over his crumpled, aching body. Voices broke in: *he will hate you now. Look what you've done with his money. He will beat the living hell out of you, as you deserve. Just wait until he finds out what you've done.*

Another voice inside his head cried out, *You're not his son anymore. You don't deserve to be his son.*

Yes, he thought. *That's it! I won't be his son. I'll tell him to treat me as somebody else. Don't even consider me to be a son, I'll say. View me as a stranger — forgettable and unimportant. That's what he could tell him. Look at me like an ex-convict or as an employee to work on the farm. I'll do all the worst tasks. You don't even have to talk to me. Just feed me and keep me safe. That's all I need.* At least he'd be able to get away from who he had become in this god-forsaken city.

The more he thought about it, the better it seemed. The risk of rejection or punishment outweighed the death he sought here. For some reason the giving up of his sonship felt like it might be a proper exchange for the millions of dollars he stole from him. He would work his way out of the guilt he had built up. It sounded like slavery but if it was a different life than the one he was currently living, it was worth a try.

He sat up and leaned against the porcelain. *Who knows how long I've been here.* He held his stomach; his eyes bleared. Standing to his feet, he stepped in the vomit on the ground. *I should be dead.* Then it came. His stomach unloaded more of the poisonous drainage fluid. All of it. It felt like a blow torch coming out of his stomach. The son and father, who were washing their hands stopped their chattering and were quiet. Nathan checked to make sure his teeth were still there. The father said, "Hurry. Let's go."

He sat on the toilet, shaking, sweating, and miserable. He stuck a hand into his pocket. The hundred dollar bill from Mr. Jefferson was still there.

It may just be enough to pay for a ride home.

100

Only the sixth taxi pulled up to Nathan's pitiful, doubled-over appearance. He desperately clung to the large water bottle in his hand. The window rolled down and Nathan heard a familiar voice.

"Kid?"

Franco's tiny bald Italian face looked in wonder at his old passenger. "Where ya headed?"

"Home," said Nathan.

"Get in."

Nathan climbed into the cab with no belongings, only the squalid clothes on his body. Franco agreed to drive him for the one hundred dollar bill.

As they departed the city of Delorre, the buildings began to fade into the distance. Nathan felt like a released prisoner, escaping the walls of damnation for so many years.

In the back seat of the car, he rehearsed over and over again—as much as his throbbing head would allow—the story he would tell Thomas.

Chewing gum loudly, Franco piped up. "I can't take it any longer—I gotta ask. What in the *woild* happened to you? You look like you got run over by a truck."

Nathan tried to laugh. "Where do I begin?"

"We do have five hours."

Nathan fought sleep and carsickness as he told him the story.

"What're you going to tell your father when you see him?"

Nathan had been thinking about it all day.

"If he doesn't kill me the second he sees me, I'll tell him not to consider me to be his son anymore. I don't deserve it. Just give me a job and I'll work."

"Right."

Nathan's eyes closed and exhaustion consumed him. The car stopped and Nathan woke up to see the Degland Farm road.

Franco opened the door for him. "You said you were a father?"

Nathan got out of the car and struggled to his feet. "Yes," Nathan replied. "But I never met my child."

"Well, when you do, you'll see."

"What do you mean?" he asked. "What are you talking about?"

Franco checked his watch. "Sorry, it's late. Gotta get back."

He got in his car and drove off. Nathan stood at the mailbox at the end of the driveway, the same place where he had met the van in the middle of the night almost four years ago.

He took a couple steps down the driveway, listening to the familiar crunch of the dirt and gravel. It was a long walk to the house. He looked over his shoulder to the road to see if the taxi driver was still within earshot. He was gone. There was no turning back.

Uneasiness grew inside him with each step. The only motivation that kept him going was that he could tell Thomas he was not his son anymore and then, maybe, he could eat something. *When he hears that, hopefully he'll be sensible.* He knew the consequences would be severe. But maybe he would be reasonable. He wasn't sure.

He tried not to think of the times when Thomas got upset. His anger was fierce and quiet. Grandpa Walker was loud. Thomas never raised his voice, except for a few times. The time he was upset at an accountant for misreporting money; the time he yelled at Paul when he disrespected their mother; the time he chased after Nathan when he slapped the horse with a broken foot.

Normally, he says nothing when he's angry and just ignores people. Nathan hated it growing up, especially towards the end of Abby's life. His father would just sit there and do nothing or leave and work outside. But this time, maybe it will be good. He could deal with being ignored. He wanted to be ignored.

Just don't tell him, a voice in his head said. *He doesn't need to know everything. Make something up. Tell him a believable story. Tell him the money is gaining interest in banks, and that you are living in a nice place in the city, and you are just stopping in for a visit.*

Right, he thought, his tongue still wrapped in the residual taste of putrid stomach acid. With his filthy clothes, broken shoes, dirty pale skin, and hollow sickly body, he knew he would never believe him.

No, I'm done lying. He'll see me as I am and I can only hope he will accept my terms.

The cool breeze licked his sweat-coated palms. His head pounded. He reached the turn of the driveway just before the view of the house. The road widened around the bend and the dark forest opened up like drawn curtains. The landscape opened wide before him, full of familiar sights. He saw the windmill, the barn to the left of the house, and the acres of crops, streams, and dirt to the right of the house. The wind carried the ruddy smell of freshly overturned soil into his nostrils, rekindling years of memories in his mind.

The vineyards and orchards covering the hill looked bigger. Corn and wheat fields extended out of view to his immediate right and left. The dirt road extended hundreds of feet to the family house in front of the setting sun. It looked the same. Despite the shade, he saw someone moving on the front porch. He squinted but couldn't see who it was.

As he walked closer, his stomach wrung with fear. He didn't want to keep going. The person on the porch wore a dress and stopped moving; she stood up straight facing him.

Then she disappeared inside. *Who was that?* He felt like running but didn't know in which direction.

Moments later, he saw a man burst out of the front door. He ran right up to the edge of the porch and put his hand above his eyes like a sailor scanning the seascape. Nathan couldn't tell who it was, though his frame seemed familiar.

With a shout, the man bounded down the steps skipping several at a time and nearly tripped over his feet in his hurry. He took off running straight towards Nathan. He was two hundred feet away.

He ran fast. Nathan couldn't tell who it was. *Why is he running? Is this good or bad?* His heightened levels of fear amplified even more as he balled up his fists, ready to fight. He took two steps back. The running man shouted again and Nathan recognized his voice.

101

"Thomas, sir!" Mary scrambled into the kitchen, looking for him. She found him sitting in the family room with his reading glasses on and a book in his lap. He looked up at her bewildered, "What's wrong, Mary, did a runaway chicken outpace you again?"

Panting, she cried, "Come quickly! I think he's come home!"

The smile from his face turned into raw calculation. "What do you mean?"

"Get up and come see," Mary pushed him out of the chair. "He's walking down the drive right now!"

Thomas couldn't believe his ears. "Mary?"

She nodded enthusiastically with wide eyes. He stumbled for the door, forgetting his boots, and turned the doorknob.

The setting sun shone into his eyes as he stood on the edge of the porch, blinding him from seeing into the distance. A dark figure stood several hundred feet away. The figure was tall but hunched. *Nathan? Could it be?*

Thomas sprinted down the steps and took off running. He ran as fast as his old legs would carry him towards the shadowed person standing in the driveway. He slowed his steps to a trot and blocked the sun with his hand so he could get a better look.

He shouted, "Nathan?!"

The figure didn't move. The shoulders looked like him.

Could it be my boy?

A growing realization of the possibility of his son alive and standing in his driveway threw Thomas forward and he tore into a sprint heading straight towards the visitor.

102

Thomas was a hundred feet away when he slowed down to get a better look. Nathan held his breath. Thomas was seventy-five feet away when he burst into an even faster run. *What is he doing?* Nathan took two more steps back. *Why is he running?*

Nathan wanted to run away. He looked behind him.

Less than fifty feet away, Nathan turned back to see the man even closer. *Father.* This was it.

Eyes blazing, Thomas recognized the face of his son. *He's alive. Oh, God. He's alive!*

"Nathan!"

Nathan shook in terror.

"It is you!" cried Thomas.

Head spinning, the sight of his actual father sprinting towards him was too much. His knees gave out and he fell to the ground. His hands fell forward and the rocks and dirt stuck to his wet palms. He picked his head up, just in time to see Thomas only ten feet away. It broke Thomas's heart to see how pale and gaunt his son's frame had become underneath the filthy rags. Thomas wanted to wrap his arms around him and never let him go again.

"My boy!"

He bent down to put his arms around him but Nathan held his hand up and shouted loud enough to make sure he heard him.

"No! Stop," his voice was unnaturally deeper. "Don't come near me."

It did nothing. Thomas stepped towards him and dropped to a knee, Nathan saw Thomas's socks and crawled away from him.

"No!" he shouted.

Thomas watched him scurry away. Seeing his son act like a scared animal in front of him was like a strange, cold knife digging into his heart.

"Oh, son—" Thomas said with a shaky voice.

Nathan struggled to his feet and limped backwards.

"You're alive, Nathan," Thomas said from his knee.

Nathan backed further away.

"Don't say my name. You don't know who I am anymore."

Thomas's forehead knotted in confusion. He stood to his feet and opened his arms to embrace Nathan. Terrified, Nathan kept backing away.

"What's wrong?" Thomas asked, noticing his son's fear. "What happened?" he said. "Nathan, what's happened to you?"

Suddenly, Nathan turned and ran for the road. Thomas took off after him, tearing his socks open on the gravel.

Nathan's heart thumped in his chest. *Here it comes.* In his present condition, he knew he couldn't outrun his father. He dreaded this moment. It was time to face the consequences, regardless of what they were. The fear and anxiety crushed his chest.

Thomas yelled, "Stop, Nathan," as he watched his son run from him.

"You can't go back now," Thomas said. Nathan slowed his hobble back to a limp but he couldn't bring himself to turn and face his father. His chest burned with oxygen and his head felt light.

Thomas caught up to him. He saw Nathan's thin shoulders heaving, as he gasped for air. Thomas put his hand on his shoulder. Nathan squirmed away from it.

"Don't touch me," his voice was ragged. Thomas's shoeless feet silently stepped closer to Nathan. He stood there, waiting.

Finally, Nathan spoke. His voice still hoarse.

"I'm not your son anymore."

Thomas's face twisted. It was worse than he thought. He stepped around Nathan and stood between him and the road. "I'm not letting you go again." He opened his arms as wide as they would reach to form a wall with his body. Nathan recoiled away from him, as he did his foot stepped on his own bootlace and he stumbled to the ground.

He fell straight backwards and landed on his back. Pain shot through his rib cage and everything blurred around him. The sky turned black and Nathan's broken body began to shut down.

Then he felt an arm reach under his back and another under his legs. "Leave me alone!" He screamed.

He felt his body lift into the air, carried by two strong arms. He swung his fists, striking at his father's chest and face and kicking wildly.

"Put me down!" He demanded. Put it was no use. Thomas carried his delirious son in his arms, staggering towards home. He held him tight and would not let him go. Nathan fought for as long as his strength enabled him, but soon gave up his futile struggle. His body went limp, his head rested against Thomas's arm, and sleep overcame him.

On the front porch, Paul, Tim, Mary, Chester, and the whole farm watched Thomas, his fierce eyes stained red with sweat and tears, limp slowly down the driveway and back to the house with his long lost son asleep in his arms.

103

The day Nathan came home was a week before the 37th Degland Farm anniversary. He remained asleep in his room most of the week to beat the withdrawal symptoms and showed no sign of recovery anytime soon.

Thomas said the party should continue as planned and assigned someone to check on him every hour.

Paul had been especially looking forward to the anniversary party because he knew he was going to receive the praise and accolades he was due. Over the last few years, he had stepped up and taken on more responsibility from Thomas, who was getting older. He essentially saved the farm in the wake of Nathan's damaging actions. The fact that Nathan returned just before Paul's special day cast a shadow on his leadership efforts and he took it personally.

One day, Paul volunteered to watch Nathan for a few hours. Thomas was elated as it seemed his older son was beginning to accept his younger son's return.

Paul, however, had a different, more insidious, plan in mind. Waiting for everyone to be out of the house, he walked up the stairs with a glass of lemonade for Nathan to drink. The beverage was heavily laced with lime sulphur, a highly toxic pesticide. He brought the glass into Nathan's bedroom and placed it on the nightstand.

He sat in the chair for a few minutes to share his final thoughts.

"Why did you come back? Everything was getting back to normal and then you turned up again and now Pop can't think about anything else."

He nudged the glass closer so Nathan could reach it.

"It's a shame you never got better from whatever you picked up in the city." He stood up and looked at his sleeping brother. "You're a smart guy, Nathan, and there's something to be said for that, but you're no Degland Man."

His last words before he shut the door were: "You know you'll just do it again so trust me, it's better this way, for everyone's sakes."

As he shut the door, he heard footsteps on the stairs. Tim rounded the corner with a wine bottle in his hands.

"How is he?"

"Still asleep, not much better, I'm afraid," reported Paul. "You better let him sleep."

"Alright," said Tim, "I'm just going to drop this off."

Paul watched as Tim slipped into the room quietly.

"Tim," he said. "You don't need to do that. I'm watching him right now."

Ignoring him, Tim found Nathan sleeping. "Brought you something, my friend."

He uncorked the bottle and looked for a glass. He picked up the glass of lemonade Paul had brought him and gave it a quick sniff.

"Blech," he scraped his tongue on his moustache to clean it from the smell. "We can do better than that." He took the lemonade to the bathroom, dumped it, and washed the glass. He replaced it with a generous portion of Nathan's favorite strong Palomino grape sherry and put it back on the bedside nightstand.

104

For the first time since he arrived home, Nathan had enough strength to go for a walk. He didn't want to talk to anyone except Thomas. On the afternoon of the anniversary party, he and Thomas walked to the family graveyard, just like they used to.

Without getting too close, Nathan let him come within four feet and they walked side by side along the cow field. It took several minutes for Nathan to work up the courage to speak.

Eventually, he told Thomas the whole story, from why he left, to The Charles and the partying, the drinking, sleeping around, and drugs. He told him about Beth and George, Venture X and the Traveler's Inn, and losing everything.

When Nathan finished, he wiped his glistening eyes and searched his father's calm face.

"Why aren't you angry with me? Why aren't you yelling and beating me like I deserve?"

"Because I know all of this already."

Thomas explained that he had come after him a second time and how he had met Rose, Beth and George, and Bobby and Dwayne.

"Those backstabbers," said Nathan. "They betrayed me." He told Thomas about what happened under the bridge and how

Jeb saved him.

Nathan spoke quickly, "I stole from him to buy drugs, and returned to find him with dozens of knife wounds in his chest and stomach. He died right there in my arms."

His voice broke, "Do you know what it's like to have someone care for you, then you slap that person in the face, and watch him get murdered?"

Thomas looked away, hiding his face. *Was that not what he did to me?*

Nathan reeled and squeezed his eyes, pushing a tear onto his cheeks. "I could go on and on." Images attacked his mind. Derrick's dead corpse, Beth's crying eyes, George's scalding voice, Dr. Holz's diagnosis.

They stopped in front of the gravestones.

"Father, don't you see!" cried Nathan. "I am evil. I don't deserve to be alive. I should be dead."

His father was too calm. Nathan hoped to hear crushing words, the words he deserved. He needed justice to be free.

"I wish your mother was still here," said Thomas, looking at her name. "She would have much better words to say to you than me."

Thomas turned to face his son.

"I haven't been the best father to you, Nathan. I've made mistakes I'm not proud of and I'm afraid I drove you away."

He turned away from Nathan and looked towards the house. "Not a day goes by that I don't regret it."

A volcano of fury well up inside Nathan. *What is going on? Stop apologizing to me. It isn't supposed to be this way. This isn't justice.*

Thomas went on, "You turned out to be smarter and more ambitious than the typical Degland, but I wanted you to love the farm. Instead of forcing you to stay, I should have listened to you, like your mother, and worked with you to go after your dreams. I'm sorry."

Nathan couldn't stand another minute of his father droning on.

"I tried to kill myself!" He exploded. "Did you know *that*? I poisoned myself because that's what I deserved."

He jumped away from his father and circled back to face him, speaking venomously. "I needed to end the circus of lies and depression. I didn't want to live anymore. In a dirty bathroom stall, I drank the drainage cleaner. All of it. Hoping to die."

Thomas's eyes welled up with tears. He pressed his lips together to control it, but he couldn't hide it. Finally, the dormant storm inside Thomas broke loose.

"How could you do that? He spoke severely, "What were you thinking? I thought you were dead but now you're standing right before me and now you're telling me you tried to kill yourself? Your life is worth nothing to me dead! Do you not know how much your life means? Don't you dare rob me of my son."

The fierceness in his voice scared Nathan. The fortification of his demons budged. Nathan looked up from ground. Thomas's face was firm.

Nathan protested. "But I'm too dirty. I've done things you can't imagine."

"It doesn't matter."

"Father, you're not listening. You know I've done too much."

"It doesn't matter. You're still my son."

"No, I'm not," Nathan yelled. Inside, his soul warred against itself. "Stop pretending to be kind and just give me what I deserve!"

Thomas put his hand on Nathan's neck and looked him in the eyes. "You tried to take your own life. Promise me you will never do that again. You can run away as many times as you want and I will always come after you but I can't get you if your dead."

Thomas and Nathan glared at each other. The dark voices in Nathan's head were out in the open. Nathan's blood-shot eyes locked into his father's fiery eyes.

"I refuse your request," said Thomas.

"What do you mean, you refuse?" Nathan peeled off his father's hand.

"I refuse to treat you like a worker, like you asked, to give you 'justice' by not considering you to be my son anymore."

"There's no other way," said Nathan, unwilling to give up.

"That's not true," said Thomas, "Did your actions take away your sonship? Does your past prevent you from being my son now? As long as you are alive—"

Thomas put both hands on Nathan's cheeks and looked him straight in the eyes. "You will always be my son. And I am always proud of my son."

Nathan's shoulders trembled under the weight of his father's hands. His voice was a desperate whisper. "But I'm evil..."

"I refuse to see you that way," said Thomas. "Regardless of anything you've done, I love you."

Nathan looked into his father's eyes. They glowed like the morning sun rising above the horizon, emanating pure light.

In that moment, the talons of his tormenters lost their grip and he broke free. His arms under hooked his father's and he pulled him in tight. Thomas folded his arms around his son.

"I'm sorry, Father," Nathan sobbed, burying his eyes in the crevice of his shoulder.

Thomas held him and could feel his son's stomach twitching. They were in the middle of the meadow standing by Abby's grave surrounded by woods under the maroon clouds of the late sunset night. He patted his son on the back and head.

"Let's go home."

105

Around the fire, Thomas welcomed the gathering and addressed the matter on everyone's minds. "We all thought Nathan was dead," he said gravely. "But now that he is alive and safely home, we have much to be grateful for this year."

His eyes twinkled. "Due to Nathan's arrival last week, and his recovery this week, I think we should do something special tonight. Let's break out the special wine! Cue the music, it's time to celebrate!"

The musicians and drummers resounded into a lively tune. Thomas leaped towards Nathan and grabbed his son's feeble hands. Nathan's side stung and his leg dragged with pain, but he didn't care. They spun, jiggering around unspectacularly, smiling and laughing. Others joined. Much to Nathan's embarrassment, his feet would not obey any sort of coordinated command; he only hoped his tripping would be misconstrued to be some semblance of dance. He did everything he could to hold onto the contents in his stomach.

"Stop this!"

Paul's voice blasted above the music. "Stop all of this."

"Paul, what are you doing?" Thomas still held Nathan's hands in his. The music died down.

"Look at you," Paul cried. He stomped into the middle of the circle and kicked a hay bale into the fire. It burst into flames. The crowd hushed.

"Paul, what are you doing?" Thomas let go of Nathan's hands and approached Paul with open hands. "What's wrong?"

"You know what's wrong." Paul stabbed his father with his eyes.

"Today was supposed to be about me, remember?" He circled around the roaring fire. "Who's been managing the farm these past few years? Who's been keeping our livelihood—your legacy—alive? Maybe *I* should run away with the family's money, too. Maybe then you'll finally recognize everything I've done!"

Paul went up to Nathan and pointed his finger in his face.

"Then he comes home and nobody cares how much he cost us." He pushed his finger into Nathan's forehead and knocked him off balance.

"Well, I care and I'm not going to forget what he's done."

Thomas stepped in between his sons. "Paul, listen."

"I'm tired of this," yelled Paul.

"Paul, let me ask you something," said Thomas. "You don't care about success, do you? You don't need money, right? A career? You don't want it. You love the farm and you have everything you need. And you've always been grateful. A hard worker. A true Degland man."

Paul backed away from his father, eyes lit by the firelight.

"Why are you saying this?"

"I know you don't think this is fair, but—"

"Don't try to fix this, Pop," Paul held up his thick palm and shook his head. "We both know it's not fair."

Thomas spoke louder. "Why? Do you think you're better than Nathan? Do you think you're a better person than he?"

"I know I am."

"Then why aren't you putting your arms around and congratulating him? If you're so above him, and such a good person, then wouldn't you be happy for your brother's life?"

"Because that's not what he deserves."

"What does he deserve, then?" Thomas grabbed a flaming stick from the blaze. "Do you want me to beat him with this stick? Would you like to see that? Do you want me to turn him around and send him back to Delorre? Do you think I should disown him as my son?"

All eyes turned to Paul. He smoldered. "Yes. Would that not be fair?"

"I suppose it would be," Thomas threw the stick back into the fire. "But I would never do that."

"I know you wouldn't. Which is why I'm the one who has to suffer for it."

"Paul, listen. Whether you've done all the right things or all the wrong things, it doesn't change the fact that you are both my sons. Paul, you've served me well for years and years and most of what I have left is yours. Nathan wronged me and ran away. But I don't love him any less than I love you and I don't love you any less than I love him."

Paul shook his head. "I can't believe this..."

Thomas cut him off and pointed to Nathan. "He has to face the consequences of his actions, many of which you will never know, and your life may be better off than his, but I would be careful. The rock that you would throw at your brother may be tied to a rope around your own neck. Your judgment only tightens the noose."

"Paul," Nathan's weak voice sounded from behind his father. All eyes turned him. He trembled as he stood to his feet. Paul sweating face watched his younger brother stand. Thomas stepped away.

"I'm not proud of what I've done," Nathan's voice shook. "I've hurt a lot of people, especially the ones I love most." He blinked and saw images of Jeb's hairy face and Beth's beautiful eyes. "But one of the people I've hurt most is you, my brother."

Paul stood still, his angry eyes piercing Nathan.

Nathan pushed the air out of his lungs and into his voice. "I'm sorry."

It was barely a whisper. He could hardly speak and his eyes were swollen and wet. He held out an open shaking hand to Paul.

His older brother's face relaxed. He looked away, turned swiftly, and his boots crunched on the ground as he ran from the fire through the crowd and into the darkness towards the old barn.

106

Six months later, after a long road of withdrawals, Nathan's health finally recovered. Though his body would never fully regain its original vigor, he reworked the strength back into his arms and legs and the color returned to his face. He enjoyed working the land, grateful for a hard day's worth of work and seeing the results of his hands. At Thomas's prompting, Paul begrudgingly agreed to let Nathan manage the books. In less than a year, operations were streamlined and output doubled.

At 10:30 one night, Thomas was reading in bed. A knock came from his door.

"Come in," he said. *What could possibly be going on at this hour?*

Nathan peeped his head in and said, "I can't sleep."

Thomas put his book down on his lap. "Come sit, tell me what's bothering you."

Nathan sounded as if he'd just finished running a race. He paused and caught his breath.

"I need to go back. I want to get Beth and my child. And I want you to come with me."

Thomas smiled and responded, "How soon can we go?"

THE END

AUTHOR'S NOTE

WHEN WRITING A novel, many will say that there comes a point when the book starts to write itself. The characters, the events, the dialogue—it all begins to shape itself and as the author, my job is simply to record what I see and hear.

I wanted to write this story because I couldn't wait to see what the father would say to his sons at the end, especially the younger. The original parable in Scripture is one of the most powerful stories of unconditional love and forgiveness in history. I wanted readers to see that there is nothing we can do, no type nor number of wrongs, that can stop the Father from loving us. To depict this, I sought to immerse myself in the parable and attempt to experience depth of the two sided Gospel: first, in the extreme darkness of arrogant, selfish living—the outcome of which is addiction, depression, and death—and second, through Jesus Christ's saving grace, our rock bottom depravity is undone and we are freed when we return to the healing and redeeming words, emotions, and actions of our loving Father.

While Scripture remains the original and more beautiful narrative, I hope that through this modern retelling of one of the greatest stories Jesus ever told, you were able to experience the unconditional love and forgiveness of our faithful and good Father in Heaven.

AFTERWORD

Based on The Parable of the Prodigal Son
Luke 15:11-32

Jesus said, "There was a man who had two sons. And the younger of them said to his father, 'Father, give me the share of property that is coming to me.' And he divided his property between them. Not many days later, the younger son gathered all he had and took a journey into a far country, and there he squandered his property in reckless living. And when he had spent everything, a severe famine arose in that country, and he began to be in need. So he went and hired himself out to one of the citizens of that country, who sent him into his fields to feed pigs. And he was longing to be fed with the pods that the pigs ate, and no one gave him anything.

"But when he came to himself, he said, 'How many of my father's hired servants have more than enough bread, but I perish here with hunger! I will arise and go to my father, and I will say to him, "Father, I have sinned against heaven and before you. I am no longer worthy to be called your son. Treat me as one of your hired servants."' And he arose and came to his father. But while he was still a long way off, his father saw him and felt compassion, and ran and embraced him and kissed him. And the son said to him, 'Father, I have sinned against heaven and before you. I am no longer worthy to be called your son.' But the father said to his servants, 'Bring quickly the best robe, and put it on him, and put a ring on his hand, and shoes on his feet. And bring the fattened calf and kill it, and let us eat and celebrate. For this my son was dead, and is alive again; he was lost, and is found.' And they began to celebrate.

"Now his older son was in the field, and as he came and drew near to the house, he heard music and dancing. And he called one of the servants and asked what these things meant. And he said to him, 'Your brother has come, and your father has killed the fattened calf, because he has received him back safe and sound.' But he was angry and refused to go in. His father came out and entreated him, but he answered his father, 'Look, these many years I have served you, and I never disobeyed your command, yet you never gave me a young goat, that I might celebrate with my friends. But when this son of yours came, who has devoured your property with prostitutes, you killed the fattened calf for him!' And he said to him, 'Son, you are always with me, and all that is mine is yours. It was fitting to celebrate and be glad, for this your brother was dead, and is alive; he was lost, and is found.'"

ACKNOWLEDGEMENTS

This book would not have been possible without the support, feedback, and encouragement from numerous individuals.

First, I'd like to thank Jesus Christ for saving me and telling this story in the first place back when he walked the earth.

I'd like to thank my beautiful wife Steph for her patience and love (and editing prowess) throughout this journey.

I'd like to thank all the beta readers and editors who offered feedback and advice on each version of the book. My grandparents, Rod and Sandra Schools, my sister, Annie Schools, my friends, Bill Jolley, Andy and MaryLou Dovan, and my editor David Sorenson.

Finally, it's worth mentioning my gratitude to the /r/writing subreddit, the members of which offered helpful insights into the making of this novel.

ABOUT THE AUTHOR

Dave Schools is a columnist for Inc. Magazine, the founder and editor of Entrepreneur's Handbook, a publication dedicated to helping entrepreneur's succeed on Medium, and the co-creator of Party Qs, an app for conversation starters. He holds a bachelor's degree in entrepreneurship from Grove City College and his writing has appeared in Smashing Magazine, The Next Web, Business Insider, Fortune, and Quartz. In 2015, he won first place in Dictionary.com's poetry contest. He wrote *Runaway Millionaire* while living in Johnson City, Tennessee, Washington, D.C., and Phoenix, Arizona. He travels around the country with his wife and two cats, moving to a new city every three months. He enjoys cold-brewed coffee, ambitious hikes, and interesting people. Connect with Dave on Twitter at @DaveSchoools or contact him through his website www.daveschools.com.

Made in the USA
Middletown, DE
29 August 2018